Rowdy in Paris

ALSO BY TIM SANDLIN

Sex and Sunsets

Western Swing

Skipped Parts

Sorrow Floats

Social Blunders

The Pyms: Unauthorized Tales of Jackson Hole

Honey Don't

Jimi Hendrix Turns Eighty

TIM SANDLIN

Rowdy in Paris

Riverhead Books

A MEMBER OF PENGUIN GROUP (USA) INC.

NEW YORK

2008

RIVERHEAD BOOKS
Published by the Penguin Group
Penguin Group (USA) Inc., 375 Hudson Street, New York, New York
10014, USA • Penguin Group (Canada), 90 Eglinton Avenue East,
Suite 700, Toronto, Ontario M4P 2Y3, Canada (a division of Pearson
Penguin Canada Inc.) • Penguin Books Ltd, 80 Strand, London WC2R 0RL,
England • Penguin Ireland, 25 St Stephen's Green, Dublin 2, Ireland
(a division of Penguin Books Ltd) • Penguin Group (Australia),
250 Camberwell Road, Camberwell, Victoria 3124, Australia (a division
of Pearson Australia Group Pty Ltd) • Penguin Books India Pvt Ltd,
11 Community Centre, Panchsheel Park, New Delhi–110 017, India •
Penguin Group (NZ), 67 Apollo Drive, Rosedale, North Shore 0632,
New Zealand (a division of Pearson New Zealand Ltd) •
Penguin Books (South Africa) (Pty) Ltd, 24 Sturdee Avenue,
Rosebank, Johannesburg 2196, South Africa

Penguin Books Ltd, Registered Offices:
80 Strand, London WC2R 0RL, England

Library of Congress Cataloging-in-Publication Data

Sandlin, Tim.
Rowdy in Paris / Tim Sandlin.
p.   cm.
ISBN 978-1-59448-974-7
1. Cowboys—United States—Fiction.   2. Americans—France—Paris—Fiction.
I. Title.
PS3569.A517R68   2008   2007035972
813'.54—dc22

Printed in the United States of America
1   3   5   7   9   10   8   6   4   2

Book design by Amanda Dewey

This is a work of fiction. Names, characters, places, and incidents either are the
product of the author's imagination or are used fictitiously, and any resemblance to
actual persons, living or dead, businesses, companies, events, or locales is entirely
coincidental.

While the author has made every effort to provide accurate telephone numbers
and Internet addresses at the time of publication, neither the publisher nor the
author assumes any responsibility for errors, or for changes that occur after publication. Further, the publisher does not have any control over and does not assume
any responsibility for author or third-party websites or their content.

ACKNOWLEDGMENTS

Thanks to Kate McCreery, who was with me at the Coffee Bean on Sunset when Rowdy came into my life.

Aude-Noëlle Nevius translated my weird BabelFish French into the real thing. Stephanie Cardon—the same Stephanie who took the photo on the cover—lives in Paris but doesn't have a French accent. She added her insights and language skills.

I'd like to thank the Paris American Academy for providing me and my family with an apartment on the rue St. Jacques. Kevin McKenna and Lucy Butler lined me up with these fine folks and explained the proper way to order coffee in Paris—one double café au lait with two shots of espresso to throw into the mix.

Alice Richter did everything humanly possible to get me thrown into a Paris jail. Erin Buell and Dan Mortensen gave advice and aid on rodeo lore.

For Carol

Colorado

1.

Self-evident Truth #1: *The world over, cowboys are the envy of honest men and heart's desire of adventuresome women.* Real cowboys are the top link in the food chain and bull riders are to cowboys what cowboys are to the rest of the male population. A man can dream of no higher aspiration than to survive eight seconds astride a rough-stock bull.

Out loud, people who can't climb on 1,200 pounds of pissed-off beef say those who can are crazy, that we have needs normal life cannot fulfill. But deep inside their guts and nuts I've never met a man yet who doesn't wish he had what it takes.

The bull was a rank Brahma name of Ripple. It was second go of a two-go rodeo in Crockett County, Colorado, on a Labor Day weekend Sunday so crackling hot the stock pens shimmered from rising stink. I'd rode my first bull to a 66, which may not sound like setting the West afire, except only three others stayed on a full eight seconds and all three of them had been bucked off in the second go. Or, to be faithful to reality—which I promised myself I would be because when you're telling a story you ought to either tell the true way it was or shut up—two bucked off and Neb Parks was so keyed up he drank a pint of 151 and got shook off in the chute.

Neb leaned forward to heave, fell over the bull's right shoulder, and pinned himself against the back of the chute. Neb's bull, who was named Loose Stool, kicked him in the face on the way down, then stomped his ribs into kindling before the gate men could turn him out. Neb lay against the bottom slat, on his smashed head, his feet and boots curled up over his belt buckle. I was up on the chute over, preparing to mount, and from my view, Neb looked like one of those boneless straw men the clowns build so as to give the bulls something to stomp.

The EMTs took a half hour strapping on neck braces and stabilization devices and all that guff they do while Neb's little East Coast bride was throwing a hissy like she married him not knowing his occupation. The crowd drifted off to their trucks to drink and feel up one another's spouses, and I'm on the fence, set to mount Ripple, who like I said was so rank if Neb had taken the chute dive under him there'd be nothing left but a reconstruction challenge for the mortician.

There's not much worse than timing your adrenaline for a ride only to have it put off. You can't just relax and write a poem because you don't know how long it will be. Besides, Neb's bride is losing her composure and from where I sit I can see down her blouse onto a set of breasts so evenly colored you'd think they never saw sunlight. She was unblemished as a new sink. So I rewound my left-hand rig, then unwound it again, then wound it, all the while looking appropriately long in the face for Neb and his bride, when mainly what I'm doing is trying to come up with a rhyme for purple. Every kid over eighth grade knows there's nothing rhymes with orange, but they don't tell you about purple. Girdle? Hurdle? The poem was about a Virgin Mary I once saw in a thunderhead cloud east of Raton Pass. Cars were pulled off all over the highway, looking at this thing, and everyone who saw it agreed it was the Virgin Mary, although anytime you see a woman's face in a cloud or a tortilla or even an oil stain in a puddle in that part of the world somebody's going to call it the Virgin. They don't know. One thing I've learned in life—Self-evident Truth #2—*You can't tell a virgin by her face.*

This Mother-Mary-in-the-clouds stuff is outside the norms of cowboy poetry subject matter, I grant you, but I don't aspire to normal cowboy poetry. My goal is Andy Devine dates Walt Whitman. Or Emily Dickinson finds bliss with Brad Pitt and they both write an ode to the afterglow. Forget the cloud—purple is as rhyme-proof as orange. I'll describe the silver head.

What rhymes with silver? Squat, that's what.

The EMTs finally scraped Neb up and carted him off. As the ambulance wailed into the night the announcer said, "Let's give a big hand for Neb Parks." He got a smattering but not what I'd call a big hand. It wasn't like Neb got busted up in the arena in front of the crowd. Most people didn't even know what happened until the ambulance came through, so it's not like they were emotionally involved.

"Next up we have Rowdy Talbot from GroVont, Wyoming. Rowdy here hasn't finished in the money in a month of Sundays, but today is his big chance, so let's all put our hands together for the cowboy who rarely wins."

No applause at all.

Yancy Hollister said, "What the hell you doing?"

I pulled folds of loose hide up forward under the bullrope. Ripple had about twice as much skin on him as was needed. "Secret to riding this bastard is you got to knee up on his shoulders. Ride the hump instead of the bull."

"Secret to riding this bastard is to get off without getting killed."

"That, too."

Yancy Hollister was my flank man in charge of drawing the back-end rope up from under Ripple and making it secure. Yancy comes from Texarkana. He has this cold tar accent I swear is fake but I've never caught him out of it. He's six-three and a steer wrestler and pretty much my only friend on the circuit, if it's possible for a short man to have a tall friend. I'm not certain. Yancy thinks bull riders have a death wish, which isn't true, but his belief in my insanity tends to balance out his extra eight inches of height, so we get along. Most of the time, anyway.

The gate puller was an old-timer called Chicken Jim, who'd lost his tongue to cancer on account of Beechnut. He couldn't swallow his own spit so he stuffed his mouth with Kleenex to absorb the saliva. Chicken Jim was the same puller who'd taken his sweet time turning Loose Stool out while Neb's face was undergoing the change, and Neb's wife had been rude to him. She called Chicken Jim a "fool." The Bible — Matthew — says you'll go to hell if you call anyone a fool. Doesn't say a word about *bastard, asshole,* or *son of a bitch,* but it's real specific on *fool.*

Chicken Jim couldn't say anything back to the woman because of no tongue and a mouth full of Kleenex, and he was feeling put upon.

He looked up at me and grunted the question.

I said, "Not quite," and he pulled.

Ripple hooked the half-open gate and slammed it into Chicken Jim, knocking him over the fence onto his back, which served the tongueless wonder right for going when I wasn't ready. The bull blew into the arena, fifteen feet in a single bound. He whipped a horizontal with my spurs at his ears before heaving forward onto his front hooves. His big head plunged between his legs and I saw nothing but dirt and horns. I threw my riding arm away right before the forward slamming thrust, which almost caught me.

Same damn move the bastard used to break my cheekbone in Calgary — popped me with a horn and threw me off the front end, that time — as opposed to the counterclockwise spin he'd made to separate my shoulder out in Cheyenne. Every rider has a deep personal relationship with one bull, the sort of love-to-hate deal you develop with a woman you marry and lose three times, which is something else I've pulled. Hard to say which has been harder on my body, drawing Ripple more often than is statistically probable, or marrying Mica over and over. They've both led to extensive rehabilitation.

The bull stretched out, jackknifed, kicked his rear quarters way over my head, like he was trying to kill me from the backside. He went into a right-hand spin where the snot string whipped around us like a trick rope, or a halo. I'm a person who can see an eight-foot snot string and think *halo*. Cowboy poets often express a unique view when it comes to beauty in nature.

He put me in a handstand against the bullrope pad and it was nothing but dumb luck that when I came down, his hump was under me — banged the stuff out of my pelvis.

His spin rolled under his skin, which didn't seem attached to his bones. More like a tiger, say, in a burlap bag. He tried to hook my leg and when that didn't break any bones, he dropped his right shoulder and whirled. Whiplash was involved.

I lurched hard to the outside, then overcompensated and almost fell in the well, which is the last place you want to go when falling off a bull. Flipping headfirst into the inside of a clockwise spin twists the bullrope around your glove hand and pinches the knuckles to the bull's back, locking the tail wrap tight as a noose. Imagine tying your wrist to the back bumper of a Hummer and being drug two miles through jagged rocks and cactus.

I rammed my knees into his hump and scrambled for a spur hold. We must have been near the fence because I flashed on a prosperous buckle bunny with a sky blue cowboy hat and passable tits under a yoked shirt with sequins, talking on a cell phone. No doubt making an appointment for a massage and pedicure. It pissed me off.

I screamed a word that goes against the entire cowboy code and threw myself forward with my free arm, damned if I was going to get killed while she chitchatted.

It was just enough. Ripple went into a front-end dance and came down like a Buick dropped off the third floor of a parking garage. My feet blew out, my head bounced off his ugly skull, and the Klaxon buzzed a quarter second before I pulled a face plant in the arena dirt. Ripple was so humiliated he kicked a solid shot to my tailbone before trotting off to the pen, docile as a Jersey milk cow.

I lay in a three-point stance, knees and forehead in the dirt, until the clown came up beside me. The dusty toes of his red and yellow hand-painted tennis shoes stepped into my peripheral vision. "Can you walk?"

"Possibly."

"Then cowboy up and get your ass out of my arena."

2.

The Crockett County fairgrounds men's room was this cinder block bunker with a drip wall-and-trough urinal and sheet metal mirrors instead of glass, like looking at yourself in the side of an Airstream trailer. I unbuckled, unzipped, dropped my Wranglers and jockey shorts knee level, and twisted around to view the bruise on my upper butt. My rear end hung like a pair of rotten bananas. I could make out the blue-black outline of Ripple's hoof and the split in it, off to the side of my own split.

When I was a kid my cousin Pud told me that if you break your tailbone, you'll grow a tail.

"More like a rat's than a dog's," he said.

I've broken my tailbone twice now and I know it's not true. You just don't sit down for a few weeks.

While I was taking a leak a spiffy man with the look of a real estate mover and shaker, or maybe a state-level politician, came into the john. He was dressed in Dockers and a chamois shirt with a trout and dry fly pattern. His hair had been professionally grayed at the temples.

He stood down the wall, with proper space between us, just two guys making water. He said, "God, you're a mess."

I said, "You ought to see me when I lose."

I didn't so much as glance at his tallywhacker but I have to say right here and now, the man dribbled. He had nothing like my steady flow. And, although he started after, he finished way before me. From viewing the relative uselessness of his prostate, I'd guess the man was from Denver.

He shook twice, waving his elbow like he had a flag in his hand. "What's with you little bastard bull riders?" He answered his own question. "It's a Napoleon complex, that's what it is. You think you're inferior so you have to act twice as tough as a real man. My wife has a Napoleon complex."

For the record, I am not short, at least not by bull riding standards. I'm five-seven and a half, in my boots anyway, which you have to count 'cause I'm always in them, which is basically average. Out West, when people talk about average, as in height and weight, ranch or truck size, weather, women, mean horses, ugly dogs, anything you might want to compare, they always act like the norm is more extreme than it is.

Tool in hand, I said, "I'm tall enough to kick your Yuppie ass out the door."

"See what I mean." The man Baptist-chuckled as he washed his hands at the metal sink. "That's just what Napoleon would have said."

I finished leaking, zipped it up, and headed for the door.

The man said, "In Colorado, we wash our hands after we urinate."

I looked back at him. "In Wyoming, we don't pee on ourselves."

The woman at the pay window had what we on the circuit call Provo hair set off by violet fingernails and an iridescent blouse the color of a bluebottle fly. She was reading *Dell Horoscope* magazine, an article entitled "Love Comes to Pisces," but she wasn't chewing gum. I'll give her that.

She looked across at me with exasperation. "You Rowdy Talbot?"

I said, "That's right."

"Ever'body else has come and gone. I had to stay around for you."

Bulls are always the grand finale of any rodeo, so it would figure bull riders would be the last to pick up their winnings. "How much did it come to?" I asked.

She studied me like I was on TV and couldn't study her back. "I wouldn't let my boy Donnie on a bull if his life depended on it. I'd break his legs first, save the bulls the trouble."

"My mama felt the same way."

"But she didn't break your legs?"

"No, ma'am, she cut me out of the family picture."

The cashier slid a sheet of legal blah-blah across the counter. "Sign here." As I signed, she said, "It came to four thousand three hundred twelve dollars and six cents. You win this kind of money often?"

I watched her snap open a Bass Finder tackle box full of cash. "This is the first."

"Let me ask you a question." She licked the tip of her pointer finger and started rifling hundreds. "How much do you pay for insurance?"

"Do I look like a man with insurance?"

She stopped counting to study me again. "I guess not."

She handed over a stack of bills. "I don't have a nickel. You'll have to take six pennies."

I rolled the bills tight and stuffed them into my front pants pocket where they felt pretty damn natural. I stacked the six pennies heads up for luck and slid them into my shirt pocket and tipped my hat like you're supposed to when a woman gives you money.

"Thank you, ma'am." I started to walk away, but she called me back.

"Wait a minute. You forgot something." She dug in a drawer

and came out with a white cardboard box, maybe four inches by five inches.

She said, "You earned this, cowboy," and pushed it across the counter. I turned the box over, but there was no writing or embossed corporate logo or anything. While I opened it the woman bit her lower lip in anticipation, as if she'd picked it out and paid for it herself.

Inside the box I found a silver belt buckle nestled in a cushion of white cotton balls. There was a gold raised picture of a cowboy on a bucking bull set on a black enamel background. The cowboy leaned way back with his riding arm out of position while the bull did a sixty-degree headstand. The cowboy had a kerchief around his neck, like he was planning to rob a liquor store. The cowboy and bull were encircled by gold writing that said CROCKETT COUNTY RODEO around the top and 20 BULL RIDING CHAMPION 03 underneath.

She said, "That's real silver inlay."

I said, "Thank you."

She said, "Take my advice, boy. Now you've won your buckle, quit riding bulls and get a proper job with benefits. That's what I'd want Donnie to do."

I said, "Yes, ma'am," and limped off to the truck.

3.

Back at the Super Eight, I didn't have a problem in the world couldn't be solved by a couple of Tylenol and codeines washed down with Jolt Cola followed by a hot shower. It's amazing how much pain you can be in and still maintain a positive attitude when you win, compared to when you lose. Normally, being kicked in the ass and having my head cracked on a bull's skull would have made the motel room with its shampoo tube, vinyl chair, and the TV remote bolted to the bed table feel as empty and depressing as week-long rain. As it was, the place seemed almost cheery.

I left the buckle box on top of the TV where I could see it while I watched Food Network and got dressed. Rachael Ray was whipping up swordfish cutlets. There's two cowboy fantasy outlets on the circuit—Food Network and Weather Channel—and no way will they ever understand each other. Rachael made me so chipper I whistled a Charlie Daniels song about patriotism and alcohol as I popped open a can of SpaghettiOs and ate with a plastic spoon I'd picked up at a Burger King in Laramie. One thing being on the road will make you appreciate is cold SpaghettiOs. People with homes and families can't relate.

On an impulse, I picked up the telephone and jabbed numbers. Big mistake.

Tyson answered and I could tell by his breathing he'd raced to beat his mother to the phone. In the background, I heard Mica say, "Jesus, Ty, watch where you're going."

I said, "How's my little cowboy?"

There was a moment of quiet, then, "I'm not a cowboy."

"Sure you are. You're my cowboy."

"I'm not a cowboy and I'm not yours. Cowboys are stupid."

I heard Mica say, "Is it him?" Ty must have nodded because Mica said, "Tell him he's late."

Ty said, "You're late."

I was working out the significance of *I'm not yours*. Ty was only seven, which, to my mind, made him too young for the verbal knife thrust to the ribs that was Mica's weapon of choice. So, it wasn't likely he knew something I didn't know and this was his way of dropping it on me. But then again, he might have heard Mica talking to one of her liberated friends—that gang listens to Bonnie Raitt and works themselves into a frenzy over one another's ex-husbands.

"How can you take that from the miserable bastard?" they say to one another. "I would never put up with his crapola." Then they list the sins right in front of impressionable kids who don't know there's two sides to a snake.

"I won a rodeo today," I said.

"Big whiz."

"I'm bringing you a present."

That perked him up. "What?"

"It's a surprise."

"Better not be another pair of baby chaps. Mom says we have enough cowpoke trash."

"Put your mother on."

I leaned over to the remote bolted to the nightstand and clicked off the TV. Rachael had been replaced by an ad starring a pink-faced man with flappy lips selling chicken roasters. I didn't need a chicken roaster.

The way I see the love deal, it falls off the tree either this way or that. Either the object of your emotions makes you feel better about yourself, or the object makes you feel worse. I have limited experience with the loved ones making me feel better—there was a sorrel mare back when I rode Little Britches, and I used to feel pretty good about myself around Ty, before he got old enough to resent me not being at home. Romance often starts out making you feel better but it goes the other way fairly quickly.

Dad's take, before he died, was *The kid is useless and always will be but I am a man who does his duty therefore I love him but you'll never hear me say it.* I think. Since he never said it, I'm taking the last part on faith. You can get away with wishful thinking when the person you're talking about is dead. The truth is Dad never forgave me for being short. Mama loves me the way she loves her dog, Fergie. Back in my toddler days, she's the one taught me tricks to show off for the bridge club. I could recite every word of Edgar Allan Poe's *Lenore* when I was four, but I had no idea what it meant. Neither duty-love nor pet-love is the type that makes you feel better about yourself.

Here's how my love for Mica makes me feel: I once knew a college girl named Stella who was hiking alone in the DuNoir when a grizzly sow charged out of the treeline, knocked her down, and tore off her right buttock. The bear then flipped Stella over, ripped open her belly, and proceeded to eat fourteen feet of her intestines. I never found out if it was the large intestine or small and I wish I knew because I think of the attack regularly, in hopes of composing a poem, and my mental picture is incomplete without knowing which intestine. I see Stella on her back in the short grass of the meadow between the sage and greasewood. The meadows in there are covered by elk droppings, so I see them, too. In my mental picture, the bear tears off Stella's clothes along with her butt cheek, but that's just me. It's not real. The true picture is Stella lying there in the dirt watching her guts go down the bear's throat.

Stella never lost consciousness, not while the bear snuffled around inside her and not later when a Swiss hiking club complete with bear bells and store-bought walking staffs came along and chased the bear off. They stood in a circle around Stella, in their Kelly green shorts and chunky boots, talking whatever language Swiss people talk while one of the men ran down to the trailhead and found a couple of guys from Game and Fish who, not trusting the word of a tourist, hiked back to the meadow to see for themselves. The Game and Fish guys wrapped Stella in borrowed Saran Wrap so her parts wouldn't fall out.

It was only in the helicopter on her way to a hospital in Salt Lake City, hours later, that Stella finally passed out. Her roommate who told me the story said the Salt Lake doctors spent six hours picking pine needles, sagebrush, and elk pellets out of Stella before they started sewing her back up.

I only saw Stella the once after the experience and it wasn't in circumstances where I felt comfortable asking if it was her small or large intestine the bear ate. She was having breakfast with some people at Denny's the next fall, on her way back to the DuNoir to finish the hike, only not alone this time. I waited around knocking down coffee refills until she went to the cash register to pay, but I couldn't see one buttock there where it should be and one buttock not. Maybe she had an ass transplant.

Stella's roommate, who was my friend as opposed to Stella, who I barely knew and wouldn't have remembered if she hadn't been eaten by a bear, told me that during the weeks in the hospital and months of rehab, Stella grew obsessed with the grizzly that hurt her. She felt her flesh was in the bear's flesh, she and the bear had merged on a cellular level. She drew hundreds of pictures of the bear in oil pastels and the next year, after I saw her at Denny's, she went into the DuNoir searching for the grizzly sow who ripped off her right buttock and ate a fair length of either her large or small intestine.

The way Stella felt about that sow, that's how I feel about Mica.

Mica said, "What?"

"Where's he getting this 'cowboys are stupid' idea?"

"Tyson is a smart kid. He figured it out."

The first impulse was to break glass. "You're poisoning him against me. Whenever I'm not there you say terrible lies about me and how I make a living."

"You're never here and you don't make a living."

Knife thrust. In the ribs. "Last time I was home Tyson was so proud of those spurs I brought him he wore them to bed."

"That was over a year ago when he was six."

"What's that got to do with squat?"

"He was a baby then. All babies think their daddies are great men. Then they grow up and see the truth and aren't fooled anymore. He knows the real you now."

"The real me the way you tell it."

I waited. She waited. Someday I'm going to compute how much I've spent on phone calls in which nobody on either end of the line talks. On the Sprint card, that's dead air at twenty-two cents a minute.

Finally, Mica said, "You're three months late, Rowdy. One more week and I call my Child Support Enforcement Officer."

I said, "I won today. You'll have your money. Just don't forget, Tyson is my son."

"Just because you're his birth father doesn't give you entitlement."

Lord knows which magazine or TV show Mica got the fancy word from. I looked *entitlement* up on my Internet dictionary and in this case it means rights you are born with, as in the right to talk to your own child even though his mother hates you. When she said it, I had no idea what it meant, so I reacted the way you would expect.

"You can take your entitlement and stuff it up your ass."

She made a gum chewing sound. "Every time you curse at me I

write down the date and what you said. If you ever stalk me, I'll have a paper trail thick enough to bury you under."

"I never stalked you, Mica. You're the one got pregnant so I'd marry you again."

"You are a loser and an adulterer and a deadbeat dad. Little Tyson says he'll shoot you if you are ever mean to me again." Her voice drifted from the mouthpiece. "Won't you, Ty, honey?"

From the background I heard Tyson's voice. "In the belly button."

Mica said, "Are we through?"

I hung up.

4.

When Tyson was going on two he taught himself how to sound like a pig. I don't mean *oink-oink*. I mean a real porker. With your back turned, you'd swear Ty was a piglet digging into his mama's teat. Lord knows where he heard one in the first place. We don't have pigs in GroVont and I can't make the sound myself.

Tyson was hilarious and he knew it. We had this game where he faced me, sitting on my lap, all shining blond hair, new teeth, and freckles. He would say, "How does pig go?"

And I would say, "I don't know, Ty. How does pig go?"

His little nose scrunched as far as he could take it, his cheek muscles snuffled back, and he'd, *"Snort-snort-snort."*

Then it was my turn again. "How does a hog go?"

"Snort!" This one deeper, more from the sinuses.

Then I would say, "How does Mama go?"

"SNORT!" Drawn out. Top volume. A hoot.

The first time Mica heard Ty's trick she laughed. After fifty times, she slammed the refrigerator door, snatched up her keys, and announced she was going out for cigarettes. The Mini-Mart was only four blocks down, but the trip took Mica two hours. She came back to find me and Ty sitting on the couch, watching *World's Scariest Police Chases* on cable TV.

Mica flew off the handle because Ty wasn't in his jammies and his teeth weren't brushed. She raised her voice. "Can't you ever do a damn thing around here?"

I said, "Not that would please you."

Ty pretended he couldn't hear us.

Soon after that I walked off my ticky-tack job at Purina Feed and went back to the rodeo. Which explains why five and then some years later I joined Yancy Hollister at the Gut Shot Bar and Sports Lounge to celebrate my first championship.

"I'm not an adulterer."

Yancy plugged his Blue Ribbon into his mouth and poured beer down his throat without swallowing. It's a neat trick, kind of unsettling the first time you see it. He drained the bottle then wiped his chin on his shirttail. "Who said you were?"

"Mica."

"The alcoholic, money-grubbing, sleep-with-any-man-and-half-the-women-in-northwest-Wyoming Mica?"

"That's her. She said I'm a loser, an adulterer, and a deadbeat dad."

"Loser, maybe, but I call bullshit on the other two."

"I've lived by a strict policy of monogamy when I'm in a relationship and promiscuity when I'm not."

"That's my policy, too." Yancy burped. "Or it would be if I ever had a relationship."

"And I may fall behind on child support, but I always catch up. God knows I never skipped a month."

The Gut Shot is typical of pretty much any rodeo bar in the Rocky Mountain Time Zone. Three coin-operated pool tables, five wall-mounted TVs, four of them set to rodeo and Nascar and the last one on a bar trivia contest, two waitresses ten pounds underweight and one twenty pounds over, a goateed bartender named Snuffy who has been there thirty years, seen it all, and is willing to tell you about it, truckers, working cowboys, rodeo cowboys, hunting guide cowboys, gay cowboys, veterans who never recovered from whichever war they were in, slumming fraternity boys, and a hutch of buckle bunnies who laugh too loud, smoke Marlboro Lights, and suck ice out of their rum and Cokes.

A local four-piece band that played mostly weddings until rodeo week came to town was shoehorned on a stage no bigger than a coat closet back at GroVont grade school. The dance floor, which wasn't much bigger than the stage, was chock-full of ten-steppers, two-steppers, twelve-steppers, and buckle buffers. Whenever a bunny wailed, "I'm *so* drunk," the men closed in like ravens on roadkill.

Yancy and I had a table by the unplugged CD box where we could view two girls who were definitely not bunnies. These two were shooting nine-ball and drinking shots. The one was fairly short with hair the color of a well-circulated penny. She wore a red scarf top that left her back exposed—I love the female back above all other parts—and a way-short purple skirt. Dijon mustard–colored tights covered whatever skin the skirt would have exposed. Red Keds with untied laces. Among other pieces of facial jewelry, a diamond post poked out of her right eyebrow. When she bent over to break the rack, I saw the sunrise tattooed over her thirteenth vertebra. I know it was thirteenth because a bull cracked mine.

The other girl was dark complected with straight black hair like she ironed it. She dressed all in black down to her fingernails and high-shine stiletto boots. Her layered-on makeup made her eyes look partly closed, and she didn't laugh after she missed shots like the short one. She chain-smoked hand-rolled cigarettes. She looked like a woman who would break a pool cue across your kneecap. She was also a better shot than the colorful girl. The tall one never used a bank. Her cue ball stopped on a dime, while the short one drilled the cue hard as she could, blowing balls all over hell in hopes something would eventually fall in.

"I bet they're East Coast intellectuals," Yancy said. "Lesbians who eat bull balls." There's a female dude ranch outside Darby, Montana, where women come to be empowered. At the end of two weeks, they graduate by castrating a two-year-old bull and eating his testicles raw. Ever since Yancy heard about this ranch, he thinks every woman who looks a little different is a bull-ball eater.

I said, "East Coast or prison. Why don't you wander over and put fifty cents on the table. See if you spot any jailhouse tattoos."

Yancy fished in his pocket for quarters but before he could wander over by the girls four doofuses in Colorado State sportswear got up the courage to take their shot. They had the demeanor of frat rats who had double-dared one another into coming out on the plains to mingle with the cowboy set in the false belief it would be entertaining. They didn't seem to realize they were in the last American smoke-filled room where men frustrated by love or horses and trapped in the neo-cowboy code of nonverbal communication feel that beating the crap out of strangers is an acceptable emotional outlet.

The leader of the pack was a blond giant with watered-down blue eyes and a forehead flat as a dinner plate. I took him for an offensive lineman. My guess is having the giant along gave the other three the illusion of safety.

The lineman grinned shyly and tucked his chin into what would have been his neck if he had one. "You girls look like you could use protection from the nasty cowboys." The three frat boys clustered up behind the big guy thought this was about the funniest opening line they'd ever heard.

The dark girl scowled in a way that no amount of alcohol would have led me to take as encouragement. She muttered something I didn't catch and the shorter one with red hair launched into a stream of foreign phrases, at the end of which, the dark one laughed, as in *Ha, ha, joke's on you.*

The giant jock said what jocks always say when confronted by things they don't understand. "Huh?"

The rat off his right pocket said, "It's French."

The giant said, "What are they saying?"

The weaselly-looking guy in back said, "Why don't you ask them, Homer?"

By then Yancy and I were rolling our eyes at each other, like *catch this*, and I signaled to the waitress Patty for another round of Yukon Jack with a Blue Ribbon chaser, on the theory that if this scene was headed where I thought it was headed, I'd better stock up on anesthesia.

Homer the giant spoke loudly and distinctly. "Do you understand American?"

The girls laughed and talked amongst themselves in French. Or, to be more accurate, the colorful girl laughed. She was having fun. The one doing Cher-on-PMS cracked a tiny, snake-like smile.

Homer spoke to his friends. "I guess they don't."

Weasel Boy said, "Say, *'Parlez-vous anglais?'*"

"You don't know French," said Homer.

"Any asswipe knows that much. Don't you watch television?"

There's this myth that very large people are stupid and small people are sneaky. Since a few ignorant folks consider me in the small group, I resent size profiling, but still, I can't help myself when it comes to assuming that brawn and brains are mutually exclusive.

Whatever his intelligence level, he sure as heck mangled the accent. "Parley view angles?"

The girls looked at each other and shrugged.

Homer grinned. "Would you like to touch a big American muscle?"

The shorter girl smiled and nodded the way people do when they don't understand a question but wish to exhibit goodwill. Yancy stiffened and started to rise. I put a hand on his arm. "It's none of our affair."

He didn't go on but I'm not sure if it's because I stopped him or Patty brought our drinks. I was paying, of course. I'd finished in the money.

Yancy said, "The college dildos are taking advantage."

The girls exchanged a few words. The friendly one said something that made the mean one nod and shuffle over next to her. Together, they studied the college boys with the mild interest of watching animals at the zoo.

I said, "Those two can take care of themselves."

The rat we hadn't heard from yet said, "I would like to spank your cute little bottom."

This time both girls laughed and chattered in French. This smile-and-nod tendency is why there's an actual law on the books in Wyoming making it illegal to talk dirty to a deaf woman. Not many people know about the law, but I do. Sometimes, I can be a goddamn font of information.

The weasel said, "Smile if you want me to ride you like a shit-kicker on a bucking bronco."

I stood. "That's enough, son."

Homer looked at me as if he hadn't heard properly. "Who you sonning, boy?"

"You, buffalo brains." I stepped across the gap separating us. My plan was to get in his face, but that was impossible. I'd have to say I got in his sternum. "You're just the type who gives big, ugly, stupid football players a bad name."

He said, "You're just the type that drives up cowboy fatality rates," which, I have to admit, was pretty good. Maybe he wasn't stupid after all.

"At least I've still got balls, you steroid-saturated mountain of meat."

The frat boy who wanted to spank the girls said, "Break his jaw, Homer."

I stepped around the behemoth to address his sidekicks. "How about if I ream the ape's crack first and you three after?"

Weasel Boy said, "You going to let him get away with that?"

I snuck a quick peek at the French girls to see how they were taking it. They stood, upper arms touching, leaning on cocked hips with their pool cues resting on the floor between their feet. Maybe they were waiting to choose sides. Even without the language, they had to know this hard-cock showdown was over them.

The giant's fist doubled and I flashed on that shot of Yukon back at the table, wishing I'd had the presence of mind to drink it, pre-drama.

Then, the fist opened. "We were just kidding the girls. They knew I wasn't disrespecting them." Homer appealed to the dark, angry one. "Didn't you?"

Her face was a mask.

He turned back to me. "No need to fight over it."

The short one's face twitched and formed into the smallest hint of a smile. In spite of copper hair and a face full of scrap iron, she was pretty. Let's say Sandra Bullock after an eight-day amphetamine run.

"You insulted a woman's pulchritude. That's the best reason I know of to fight," I said.

Behind me, Yancy said, "Pulchritude?" and we all fell into a silence that lasted longer than the center of a phone call to Mica. I took heart because Homer hadn't spontaneously pounded me. The longer he thought about it, the more certain I was the big ball of gas would back down.

Finally, Homer said, "No chick's worth breaking my hand over your face for. You want her, she's yours."

The weasel said, *"What?"* Yancy said, *"Yes,"* and Homer turned to walk away. I grabbed his shoulder, pulled him around, and hit him as hard as I could in the jaw.

Repercussions were about what you would expect.

The giant grabbed me by the shirt yokes, lifted me off the floor where we made an instant of eye contact, then he threw me over the pool table and into the condom machine.

I jumped up quick as I could—which wasn't that quick—ran around the table, lowered my shoulder, and plowed into him. Imagine running full bore into an upright freezer.

He said, "That's enough, small fry."

I threw the eight ball at his head, but he caught it. He said, "Idiot."

The dark French girl stuck her cue stick in my hand. To this day, I'm not sure if she was helping me win the fight or wanted to see how far I would go before he broke my neck.

Whatever her motive, I said, "Thanks, ma'am," turned, and swung the thick end of the stick like a baseball bat into Homer's thigh.

The bastard didn't even flinch. He one-handed my throat, lifted me up by the neck, and slammed me on my back on the pool table.

Breath sweet, like wintergreen Altoids, he almost whispered when he said, "Are we going to behave now?"

"You give up?"

Homer looked around at his friends, who were enjoying this more than he was. By then we had the attention of every sober and near sober soul in the bar. The band ground to a stop midway through "She's No Lady, She's My Wife." The only sound was a kid wasting Arab assassins on the Silent Scope EX game.

I felt around the pool table, searching for a ball I could use to crack him in the temple. He figured out what I was up to and tightened the clamp on my throat, so I stopped.

Once again, he leaned in close. "If I apologize, will you back off?"

I nodded yes. It seemed like time to give the kid a break.

Without taking his fingers off my voice box, the giant jock looked up at the French girls. I could barely see them over to the side of the table. The one with the tough-broad attitude still had it, but her colorful friend wore a grin. She was having fun. Her eyes did sparkly things that came across as enjoying life.

Homer said, "I'm sorry I was disrespectful. We only meant to have some fun and we stepped out of line. I truly regret my words."

The tall one didn't blink. The short one shrugged in a manner I'd never seen before—the shoulders and eyebrows moving up in unison. She put her entire body into that shrug.

Homer the giant looked back down at me. "You going to leave me alone now?"

I nodded.

"You come at me again and I'll be forced to hurt you," he said. "Neither of us wants that, do we?"

He eased the pressure on my throat to the point where I could say, "I'll let you go."

He released me and stepped away. I sat up and rubbed my numb neck. I could feel his fingerprints on my larynx.

My voice came out as a croak. "You and your buddies had better beat it back home to your coeducational brew pubs. Don't let me catch you in a man's bar again."

His hands came up in a gesture of defeat. They were big as mop buckets. "I'm done slumming. These people are crazy."

The crowd parted as the college boys filed out. The music started again, something by Dwight Yoakam. The guys on the stools turned back to the bar. The tall girl made a hand signal that I should get off her pool table so she could finish the game.

5.

My hat lay brim up on the floor next to the condom machine. It was a straw summer Stetson, not the black felt Resistol I wore for riding bulls. When I bent to retrieve it my nose dribbled blood on the crease, so I pulled a red bandanna from my back pocket and stanched the blood flow as I walked over to Yancy and the whiskey. I carry a red bandanna in my right back pocket. Most cowboys keep snuff tins in that pocket and their jeans wear through a circle there, but I don't dip or chew. I like to think of myself as a renegade.

Yancy said, "I guess you showed him." Yancy dips. It's disgusting but at least he keeps it to himself, unlike my ex-wife, Mica, who smokes.

"Damn straight," I said. "Where were you when it came time to watch my back?"

"I was watching it. Nobody touched you from that side."

"I could have used some frontal help, too."

"You said it was none of our affair."

I chugged my Yukon Jack, mellow and fruity with an aftertaste of kerosene. "That was before the jerk compared himself to a shit-kicker on a bronco."

We watched the dark French girl run the six, seven, and nine balls. They left the eight ball on the floor where Homer had dropped it. After winning the game, she blew on the tip of her cue stick and set it back on the rack. Both girls came over to our table.

The shorter of the two stood closer to my chair than American girls would have stood. She left-hand clutched a little beaded purse with an Indian design of some sort, I would say Blackfeet, as she gave a little speech in French which I took as a thank-you. When she spoke, her free hand fluttered about, with a space between her ring and middle fingers. I liked her round face and russet eyes, and the way she leaned her weight on one leg, toward me. She smelled nice, like a new pickup truck.

Between the bull, Mica, and Homer, I was feeling reckless, not so much suicidal as definitely in the mood of nothing to lose. I said, "I just got whipped defending your virtue, the least you can do is kiss my tallywhacker."

The nice-smelling girl said, "That is something we may be able to arrange."

Yancy howled with glee and the blood rushed to my face with such intensity my nose started up again.

The dark girl said, "What is tallywhacker?"

Short stuff must have known, because when she explained in French her friend looked down on me and said, "Wicked cowboy," which just increased Yancy's mirth level.

I didn't play it cool. If you're going to blurt rude to a woman, you have to back it up with more cockiness or else there's no point in being a creep. Women who go for creeps will know you were faking, and the minority of women who go for nice guys will think you're a creep.

I said, "You know English?"

The shorter of the two said, "Of course."

"The jock said you didn't speak English."

"He said so, we didn't."

I stammered around through a couple of *uhs* and a *gee whiz*.

Finally, I came out with, "I'm sorry about the kiss my . . . you know. Thing. I didn't realize."

The dark girl said, "If you are sorry, buy us drinks."

Yancy and I stood up and held the chairs while the girls sat down. I got the short one, Yancy the tall. At first, Yancy's girl didn't know why he was standing up holding the back of a chair. Once she figured it out, she said something to my girl that made them both laugh. Men are at a big enough disadvantage in courtship rituals without the women passing comments to each other in a language we don't understand.

I signaled across the bar to Patty to come and take our order. She didn't rush right over, and I firmly believe that was due to turf jealousy. Patty was the waitress twenty pounds overweight, as opposed to the others who were ten pounds under. She came from eastern Oregon and had sexy dimples at her elbows that kind of winked at a guy when she put a drink on the table. I'd heard Patty traditionally took the winner of the Labor Day bull riding home with her and I'd been eager to find out if this was true or just another small-town legend. Those dimples had been the highlight of a great daydream that afternoon in my shower.

When Patty finally reached our table, I said, "Another round of Yukon for us, and drinks for the ladies."

Patty propped her tray on her hip and waited.

The short girl said, "I would like an aperitif."

"We're all out of aperitif."

The taller girl said, "We'll take the American drink you brought us earlier."

Patty said, "Tequila."

The taller girl said, "You may keep the fruit this time."

While we waited for drinks, the four of us exchanged information. The dark one who rolled her own cigarettes was Giselle; the nice-smelling girl with the metal in her face was Odette. They were stu-

dents from the University of Paris who had been in our country for
a week, doing something scholarly up at CU in Boulder. This was
Giselle's first trip to the United States and Odette's second. When I
asked what they liked best about the U.S., Odette said, "Hotel
showers," and Giselle said, "Nothing." They were flying back to
Paris first thing in the morning and had come to Crockett County
this afternoon to take in an American rodeo.

"You were the champion today, no?" said Odette. I liked the
way she said *no* at the end of the sentence. My Patty fantasy was
rapidly taking a dive, replaced by something more French. I'd
heard stories about French girls. I mean, the kiss is named after
them. Nobody ever heard of an Oregonian kiss.

I fell back on modesty. "No. Yes. I got lucky today."

"It was thrilling when you fell and the bull stepped on you."

I said, "Pain is my life."

Giselle wasn't as impressed as Odette. "What you did was typical American cruelty. You torture animals and then rationalize your
behavior by saying they enjoy it."

"A lot more cowboys are killed by bulls than bulls are killed by
cowboys." I turned to Odette. "Do most French women have rods
through their eyebrow?"

She said, "Of course," and smiled at me. It was a nice smile. It
said, *I know you are putting me on with the rural rube act and I can play the*
game, too. It said, *Touch me, I don't mind.*

Yancy popped open his tin of Brown Mule. I've told him about a
hundred times to leave that stuff in his pocket around women. The
boy never learns. Even your hard-core bunny is turned off by the
oral exchange of wet chew. Classy French girls were not about to
be charmed by juice dribbling down the chin.

Yancy said, "I want to hear more about the part where you said,
'That is something we might arrange.'"

Patty came up with our drinks—brown shots for the boys,
golden shots for the girls.

Odette said, "We've been in your American West a week and

we must return to Paris tomorrow"—she pronounced Paris *Paree*—
"and . . ."

Giselle finished the sentence. "We have yet to experience a
cowboy."

I shot my shot.

Yancy said, "Experience?"

Patty translated. "She means fuck."

Yancy said, "Oh."

Giselle shot her shot. I don't think Patty would have left our
table if the place was on fire.

Odette leaned close to me. "You were so chivalrous with the college fellows." She touched the visible vein on the inside of my wrist.
Her fingernail was cool and warm at the same time. It's hard to
explain, but no one has touched me quite like that before. Her eyes
took on the sparkle I'd noticed while Homer was pounding me.
"We hoped you might be willing to oblige us."

Yancy leaped to his feet. "Hot damn."

Giselle spoke. "Not you."

Yancy's face pulled a classic *What?* Odette used the break in
conversation to shoot her shot of tequila. Patty stayed put.

Giselle nodded toward me. "Him. The conquerer of bulls."

Yancy couldn't believe it. "Both of you?"

Odette drew a nail across my wrist. Her fingernails were glittery gold with red stars in them. "Think you can satisfy two curious
girls from France?"

I reached over, took Yancy's shot, and drained it. "You got any
friends? I'll take care of their cowboy needs, too."

Odette smiled. "Only us two."

"I can make do with that."

Giselle, Odette, and I stood up to leave. Patty didn't move a
muscle to get out of my way.

Yancy was on the verge of a panic attack. "But two on one
ain't fair."

Odette picked up the beaded purse. She said, "Only an American would think sex should be fair."

Yancy turned his eyes to me, pleading. He said, "Buddy."

I nodded. "What she said."

Odette and Giselle moved off through the crowd, neither one looking back to see if I was following. Yancy was ready to cry. I said, "Can you pay for that last round of drinks? I'm a little short."

6.

The night smelled of hot dust and horse dung. The dung came from trailers scattered about the parking lot and the dust rose from wherever it rises from on the plains. You'd think the dust bowls that blow through every few years would eventually scrape the earth down to rock, the way it did the Badlands. Besides the horse trailers, there were maybe twenty ancient Cadillacs — old cowboys love old Cadillacs — and seventy pickup trucks of every size, make, and age settling into spongy asphalt like dinosaurs sinking in tar pits. Not a single SUV in sight, praise the Lord. The only non-pickup, non-Cadillac on the lot was a little green Daewoo with a National Car Rental sticker on back. Doesn't take deep insight to figure whose car that was.

"We will follow to your hotel," Odette said, from the driver's seat.

"It's a motel," I said. "Super Eight."

Giselle said, "How authentic."

I pointed over to my '86 Mazda short bed with the off-color driver's door and the front bumper tied in place by pigging string. "I could give you a lift in my outfit. Bring you back whenever we get through."

Giselle said something French I took as disparaging about the size of my truck, because Odette looked over at it and laughed.

"We fly from Denver early tomorrow. It would be more agreeable if we had our own car with us."

I fell back on the cowboy version of *whatever:* "Suit yourself."

The thing about three-ways, in my experience, is they're never as exciting in reality as they are on paper. I mean, the anticipation between when you know you're in there and you're actually in there is a hoot — *hot damn, I'm scoring double* — and the social status at the chutes the next day is deeply satisfying — tall saddle bronc riders look at you with respect, even awe if the girls were presentable — but the actual oral and genital stimulation of the moment tends to lose itself in technical positioning.

"Lie there. No there. On your side, facing my feet."

"It won't go that way."

"Yes, it will. I've seen it in the manual."

"Jesus, when was the last time you cut your toenails?"

There are timing issues. Not everyone finishes together and those who get done early or late drift off into bored motions. Unless it's purely recreational fun between strangers, the emotional geometry gets too convoluted to follow.

Not that I'm Mr. Been-There, Done-That. The fantasy has only reached fruition twice. First was with two Big Springs pole benders in white hats and leather fringe who said they were nineteen but I found out later weren't. Those girls were dumb as gravel only more irritating to sit on naked. They giggled. We started in a Holiday Inn hot tub and afterward they made fun of my wanger, which is bad enough one woman at a time. They bounced humiliating metaphors back and forth without knowing what a metaphor is until they settled on my thing looking like a road-killed weasel.

The other time was with Mica and her Pilates teacher, who only went with me to get to her. It's no fun watching someone lay atop your wife, even if you are under her. Love has no place in sport sex.

Which adds up to why I was deeply divided as to whether I wanted the girls to turn right and follow me onto I-76 headed east, or I would rather have them cross the overpass and take the ramp back to Denver, laughing all the way. Part of me said, "Those girls are French. They'll know things Mica never even read about in *Cosmo*." The other part of me knew I could tell a better story tomorrow if we skipped tonight.

Okay. *Hell.* I'm blowing smoke and I told myself I wouldn't. Of course I wanted to nail the French girls. I'm not nuts. I wanted more than to anticipate nailing, and I wanted more than to say I had nailed. I wanted to nail. Honesty is a bitch. What happened was I cranked down the window and held the side mirror straight, which is the way to get a stable look at what's behind me. I flipped the right turn signal that was working because I'd changed the fuse in Cheyenne. There was a two-second dark pause, while I held my breath, then the Daewoo right signal blinked, on, off, on. The thrill was palpitating.

The spaces along the motel wall were filled up so I had to park out in the lot. Nobody talked as we walked through the over-warm night air to my room. The cicadas were kicking in like chain saws. Northwestern Wyoming where I was raised doesn't have cicadas, so they grated on me, like you'd expect chain saws at night would. Locals who live with the bugs don't even notice. You mention the incredible screech peeling your spinal cord and they don't know what you're talking about. There's a lesson in life for you.

I thought I ought to hold hands with one or both girls as we walked to the room. I'd been taught that you're supposed to hold hands with a girl you're fixing to nail. But I didn't know which one, and holding both at the same time felt like campfire songs at church camp.

So I said, "Right here. Room one-fifty-eight."

And Odette said, "I like your number."

I said, "Me, too."

Inside, Giselle sniffed around, checking out the trash can, using the toe of her stiletto boot to lift dirty T-shirts off the floor, looking under them. I don't know what for. She picked up my Saddlerock spurs and spun the rowel, making that *clickety* sound.

Odette sat on the edge of the bed and gave it a test bounce. She kicked off her tennies. "Motels are nice."

"They're just hotels without hallways," I said.

"Does it have cable? Our hotel has cable but only thirteen stations."

"In America, we call that basic service."

Odette smiled at me and said, "Lovely."

I emptied my keys, billfold, checkbook, bandanna, and cell phone on top of the TV, next to my buckle box. Then, I got worried that these two did this for a living and they'd hit me on the head and steal my winnings, so I picked up my billfold, only I didn't know where to put it. I slid it back into my pants pocket, casually, but not so casually that Giselle didn't notice.

She touched the tip of her thumb to a rowel point. "You use this to inflict pain on the bull?"

"I use them to hang on with."

"By digging this point into the bull's flesh."

"Listen, lady," I said—wrong way to start out if you want a lady to listen—"rodeo stock have the easiest lives on the ranch. I wish I only had to work eight seconds a day."

Odette crossed her legs. "How much do you work a day?"

That brought an awkward silence while I came up with an answer. The girls watched me, waiting.

Giselle said, "Well, bull rider?"

"Depends on who you listen to. Woody Guthrie said, 'A cowboy's life is his occupation.' That would mean I work twenty-four hours a day, even in my sleep. Mica says I don't work any."

Odette said, "Mica?"

"Ex-wife."

Giselle said, "May I please use your toilette?"

French girls can make English words sexy. I tried saying toilet the same way she did. "My toi*lette* is your toi*lette*." But it came out different.

Giselle went into the can, leaving me and Odette alone. We looked at each other a long time, sort of adjusting to the fact that we were here together as strangers and before long we'd be naked and I'd be plugged into her body. At least, I was adjusting. She may have been thinking about clothes.

I opted for the most original line I could think of, considering the codeine, Blue Ribbon, and Yukon Jack. "How'd a French girl like yourself come to Colorado anyway?"

When she recrossed her legs, left over right, the mustard tights made a sexy whisper sound. "Giselle and I are philosophy students. We came to your university in Boulder so that I might deliver a paper on William James."

All right. Something in common. "Will James? I love Will James. Got every book he ever wrote."

"I am impressed." Odette leaned forward, toward me. "I would not think an American would find pragmatism stimulating."

"I'm modeling my life after James. Whenever I'm in big trouble and don't know what to do, I ask myself, what would Will James do if he was here? It always works."

"I once followed Santayana—"

"Carlos Santana?"

"George Santayana. But after reading James, I changed my outlook on religious experience."

"Me, too."

We proceeded to have a lively literary discussion. Odette was informed and opinionated. She cared passionately and a woman who cares passionately about something outside her weight and romantic prospects has always excited me. I kept wishing I had an excuse to move closer to the bed so I could smell her again.

"*A Pluralistic Universe* is his most mature, focused work," Odette said. "It shows a mind operating at its full capacity."

"My favorite's *Smoky the Cow Horse.*"

Her face did this thing where the eyes flipped inward. She said, "William James did not write *Smoky the Cow Horse.*"

"It's his most famous book, that or *Sand.*"

"We are discussing William James, the philosopher and psychologist, who lectured at your Harvard at the dawn of the twentieth century, no?"

"You got your years right, and Will James was a philosopher if I ever heard one, but he never went to Harvard that I know of. He was a cowboy."

Her shoulders drooped. "My William James is not your William James."

"I guess we don't have anything in common after all."

Odette looked sadly down at the floor. "I guess not."

I stood and went over by the TV, watching Odette sink into sadness. She must have been thrilled to find an American who understood her passions. You think you have a solid basis for a relationship, then it's whisked out from under you. Same thing happened to me when Mica told me she hated barbecue.

A flush came from the bathroom, and it occurred to me that Giselle could hear every word we were saying. After all, this was a Super Eight. And my war bag was in there. I hoped she wasn't messing with stuff women aren't supposed to mess with.

Odette stood, lifted her skirt, and pulled off the mustard tights. I got one quick look at black bikini panties before the skirt fell back into place. What was more interesting than the panties were the letters tattooed on Odette's toes. One letter per toe, facing out, toward me.

I pretended to drop my cell phone so I could get a better look — AIMEZ ❤ MOI, with the z and ❤ on the big toes.

"What's it say on your feet?"

She looked down at her toes as if the tattoos were so old she'd forgotten what they meant. *"Aimez-moi."*

"What's that mean in English?"

"Love me." She sat back on the bed and crossed her feet, LOVE over ME. She leaned back on one arm, what I would call a seductive pose. "You knew the big boy in the *salon* would back down if you continued in a relentless fashion."

I said, "Yeah."

"He may have hurt you permanently. How did you know he would not do so?"

Several decent stories popped into my head, but I chose the truth. I kind of liked this girl. She had a strong neck, and I enjoyed the way her brown eyes snapped when she saw something that interested her. Lies are for sleeping with girls you don't like.

"He's on a football scholarship."

"How do you know this?"

"I can tell these things. Football players aren't supposed to be in the Gut Shot, much less getting into fights. If the police had been called, he'd lose his scholarship."

She nodded, processing the information. I wondered if she'd been in the States long enough to know football isn't soccer.

"You took a risk," she said.

"He insulted you. Letting that slide goes against the code of the cowboy, like cheating a friend or hitting a woman. There's certain things we don't allow."

"But he admitted his error and he was leaving. Why did you hit him?"

Why indeed? "I wanted to show you what a real bull rider is made of."

Giselle stepped out of the bathroom, wearing my Resistol hat and chaps and her spike shoes with my spurs clamped onto the heel, above the stilettos. Nothing else. Her nipples were big as truck stop coffee cup coasters and the hair around her crotch formed a map of Michigan. A mushroom tattoo grew out of the Upper Peninsula. I noticed that right off.

She said, "Take everything off, then put your boots back on, cowboy. Let's see what you are made of."

I looked from Giselle to Odette. Odette smiled.

. . .

Twenty minutes later I was on my back atop the bedspread with Giselle straddling my crotch and Odette on my sternum, both facing front, toward my head. Giselle had her chapped legs draped over Odette's bare thighs, which put Giselle's heels—and my spurs—under my armpits. For a woman who claimed rodeo ignorance, Giselle knew how to rake a pair of spurs. The pain was unique in my experience. Odette of the nice eyes and beautiful throat leaned forward until her boobs bounced against my cheekbones. Her left breast had a golden hoop through the nipple. She smiled all glittery and warm, and whispered, "Hi, ho, Silver."

Then they switched around with Odette on the stick and Giselle in the front seat. Giselle was a good deal heavier than Odette had been, but Odette was livelier in the saddle. This riding-double-on-a-horse move wasn't a position either the pole benders or Mica and her Pilates teacher had known. Mostly, with them, it had been a mouth-to-genital progression, what the manuals call a "daisy chain." In the pole bender case, the chain was straight; with Mica it had been a triangle. Both times had been almost all oral with no penetration. Down South they wouldn't have even called it sex.

Giselle placed her palms against my shoulders and pressed down, pinning me like a wrestler. I'm not so good at interpreting looks, but from the firmness of her lower lip and the crease of her eyes, I'd have to say she gave me a look of pure loathing.

I said, "Did anybody ever tell you you have a nice smile?"

Giselle growled. Odette came.

After that, they tried a number of tag-team positions, all of which entailed me lying flat on my back stiff as a two-by-four with a protruding spike, not the most comfortable posture for a person who's recently been bull-kicked in the behind. I wasn't allowed to move. Once, with Odette on the nail and Giselle on my nose, facing back toward Odette, I got into it a bit and gave a squirmy little thrust.

Giselle snarled. "Be still."

I suppose they were necking up there above me. I don't know. My view was blocked by Michigan. After a while, Giselle giggled—a sound more frightening than her snarl.

Later, while Giselle rolled a cigarette, Odette did some hand work and I squirted on my belly. This got both girls laughing hysterically, like I'd done something vastly entertaining. Odette jumped out of the bed, ran off, and came back with a hand towel from the bathroom.

She said, "The cowboy has a premature gun."

"Hell, I lasted an hour. What do you want?"

Odette held my penis with what I took as tenderness, or, at the very least, curiosity. Her thumb was aligned along the top, as if grasping a fly-fishing rod. If I'd had my way, we'd have called off the rest of the party and I would have gone to sleep with her holding me. She said, "How long does *le pistolet* take to reload?"

I said, "I'm not sure. My girls are generally satisfied the first go."

Giselle bent down to remove her stirrups. "We're not. Why don't you move over to the chair and play with yourself."

I crawled from the bed, dug a pint of Jim Beam out of my saddlebag, and washed down a couple more codeine. An hour later, it felt silly sitting with my sweaty, blue-black ass stuck to the vinyl Super Eight chair, so I pulled off my boots and put on yesterday's jockey shorts. Then I slumped back into the chair, idly watching Giselle work on Odette while I nursed the Beam. It was interesting without being poignant, like watching reality television. Fingers and tongue here. Fingers and tongue there. Odette came again, louder this time than she had with me in her. As I drifted off to sleep, Giselle finally had an orgasm. The shriek came at me from far off, like a mountain lion celebrating her kill.

7.

*Bang*ing. At the door —*bang*ing. Would not go away. My head hung off to the side so my neck *crick*ed weirdly when I opened what I could of my eyes. A fist *bang*ed on the door.

Yancy Hollister: "Hey, *peckerhead.*"

I spit a disgusting clot and tried to rise but my back had sealed to the vinyl. Took two grunts to make it upright. Standing hurt my bruised butt. Breathing cracked open spur sores along my ribs. What the heaven's name had I done last night?

Yancy was not willing to walk away. "I know you're in there."

As I veered across the room, stepping over the Beam bottle and a pair of chaps, some of yesterday came back, then some more. By the time I opened the door to Yancy and sunlight that cut like a skinning knife, I had a pretty good idea what I'd done to feel this bad.

"What took you so long?"

"God, Yancy, what time is it?"

"Almost nine, peckerhead." He barged into the room. I turned to watch him case the place. My spurs hung from the overhead light fixture. The Tony Lamas were toe down in the trash. There was a tampon on the floor, which brought a couple questions to mind.

"Did they put out?" Yancy asked.

One thing about drinking yourself to sleep is you wake up with a tremendous need to pee. As I broke for the bathroom, Yancy said, "I'll bet a bundle they were teasers. Got you over here and made you bark like a cow dog, then didn't come through."

I pulled down the band on my shorts. Didn't bother with the toilet lid. "French girls don't tease, Yancy." The piss was wonderful. Good enough to write a poem about.

Yancy followed me into the can. "So were they into kinky positions and sadism or what? Sadism is named after a French guy. Bet you didn't know that."

"Marquis de Sade."

"Yeah. Him. Were they contortionists? The little fox looked like a contortionist."

"It's all geometry." I shook and tucked without Yancy seeing me. "You figure it out." I went past him back into the bedroom. "Where's my pants?"

Yancy said, "Don't be a douche bag, for Chrissake. I gave up my fun to let you have them —"

"Yeah, right."

"Least you can do is tell me what they did."

I tried putting on my Wranglers standing up — the hop-on-one-foot method — but wasn't up to the task. I said, "They were enthusiastic," thus confirming Yancy's worst fears.

"I knew it."

I sat on the bed, pulled the jeans over my feet and knees, then stood back up to finish the job. "It's every girl's dream to sleep with a bull rider. Last night, Odette and Giselle had their dreams come true."

"One at a time, or both together?"

"Both together, then one at a time, then both together again."

So sue me. He wouldn't have believed the truth.

Yancy said, "It could have been me."

"I doubt it."

I checked my billfold. The money was still there. "I wonder if they gave me AIDS," I said. "Those girls were experienced. They could have been professionals."

Yancy paced, like a coyote on a choke chain. "Did you anal them? You can't get AIDS from a female unless you anal her."

"Who told you that?" I headed for the TV to collect my pocket change, keys, phone, and checkbook.

"I read it on the Internet."

"And you believed what you read?"

"They don't let people put stuff on the Internet that isn't true. Whole thing would be worthless if they did."

"Whole thing is worthless." I yanked the TV stand out away from the wall. *"Jesus."*

Yancy stopped pacing. "What?"

"It's gone."

"What's gone?"

Nothing behind the television but a *Book of Mormon.* "My Crockett County Champion Bull Rider belt buckle. I won it yesterday and it's gone."

Yancy peered at the floor, under the window unit air conditioner. "Maybe you lost it."

I dropped and searched under the bed. "I didn't lose it." Dust bunnies galore. Super Eight doesn't necessarily vacuum under their beds.

"The French sluts stole my buckle."

"That's no way to talk about girls you just nailed."

"I was asleep and they took it." I pulled my boots out of the trash can to find an empty SpaghettiOs tin and a plastic spoon from the Burger King in Laramie.

Yancy said, "They didn't take your money or your hat. Why steal your buckle?"

" 'Cause they're French sluts." I found a plastic packet tucked in my day planner in my saddlebag, under a sheaf of poetry.

"What's that?" Yancy asked.

"Passport. I picked it up before the Calgary Stampede in case I finished in the money. They won't pay out in Canada without a passport."

"If you thought you might finish in the money at the Stampede, your fantasy life is more insane than the sluts."

There were two fairly clean shirts in the bureau drawers. I stuffed them into the saddlebag, on top of the passport and my poetry, along with two pairs of undershorts and socks and the dregs of the Beam. He who travels light comes back.

"I'll meet you in Dalhart Friday, before the Grand Entry. Don't let them turn my bull out."

"Where you going?"

I flipped the saddlebag flap shut and tied it down. "To get my damn buckle back."

8.

I once got into a fight over Will James. This idiot calf roper from Medford, Oregon, said Louis L'Amour knew more about horses than Will James, which was such a stupid statement I almost let it go by. There's no glory in a rough stock rider punching out a timed event cowboy, you might as well beat up your granny. But then he said Will James couldn't shoe a mule and that was the end of the rope. I'll bet nobody's ever gotten in a fight over William James. Two professors, maybe, exchanging rapier wit.

The thing is, I didn't fly out of that Super Eight like a bat flies out of Texas. The impulse was to haul ass for Denver International in hopes of catching the girls at the gate, but that came across as too unlikely to act on. They'd be long gone by now. Besides, I'd have to purchase a ticket to get through security, and the tampon on the floor made me wonder what had been sitting on my face last night, so I stripped down again and showered. Put on clean underwear this time. After all, I was going to Europe.

I checked out and hit a 7-Eleven to buy a money order for seven hundred fifty dollars. That's what three months' back child support adds up to. I would have paid a month ahead if Mica hadn't poisoned Ty with that cowboys-are-losers garbage. As a teenager,

Mica idolized cowboys. She read rodeo magazines for entertainment. Our first date was a reward for giving her a Lane Frost autograph. Now, she has my son doing glorified yoga. She'll no doubt turn him into a vegan.

I bought envelopes at 7-Eleven but had to go three places to find a stamp. Ended up back in the lobby at Super Eight. Guy there with muttonchop sideburns begrudged me the last stamp they had 'cause it was Labor Day and he couldn't buy more.

"These are for guests," he said.

"I was a guest last night."

"You aren't today."

Faced with hitting or tipping, I tipped. Gave the jerk a dollar for a thirty-seven-cent stamp. Sometimes I'm so reasonable I make myself sick.

Then came breakfast at IHOP. After four cups of coffee the waitress quit offering refills and I had to track her down, cup in hand.

Denver long-term parking is way the hell and gone off from the terminal. I piled my war bag and duffel onto the cab seat, even though the passenger door doesn't lock. My Mac laptop went behind the seat, along with the wire cutters, pigging string, stink bait, unmatched gloves, vise grips, sleeping bag, piles of maps, a crowbar, and my library. Leaving goods in a truck bed is like passing out invitations.

"I'd like one ticket to Paris, France, please." I worded it that way, to avoid confusion with Paris, Texas.

The Delta ticket lady had on a name tag that said DIERDRE. Her hair was piled up on her head and held there by a pair of laquered chopsticks. "Round-trip or one way?"

"Do I have to say now?"

Her fingers danced across the keys. "It's cheaper if you do."

I said, "Round-trip."

The lady talked with her eyes on the keyboard instead of me. I find that extremely irksome, but it's modern America for you. Not much you can do. "When do you plan to return?"

"I've got a rodeo in Dalhart Friday night."

"When do you plan to return from Paris?"

"Friday morning."

"You have to leave Paris Thursday night to be in Denver Friday morning."

"Sounds reasonable."

"How many bags are we checking?"

"We are checking none."

She hesitated, then typed some more. "What credit card will you be using today?"

"Am I allowed to pay cash?"

She finally looked up at me. Her eyes were green but you could tell it was from tinted contacts, not nature. "You can, but security will flag you. It's less hassle with a card."

"I'll pay cash."

My long-term plan is to ride bulls until I can't anymore, then I'll hit the cowboy poetry circuit. The living won't be great, but it can't be worse than what I make now. The only poem I've read in public, so far, was at open mike night in the Ten Sleep Laundromat—a piece called "The Bull Rider's Lament." The subject is airport security.

I consider myself a fairly average bull rider—except I don't put a pinch of anything between my cheek and gums, I read, and I don't use Jesus as a rabbit's foot. Otherwise, I'm normal, which means I carry more or less two pounds of metal enclosed in my body. Rods in my legs, and clips in my right shoulder, thanks to Ripple. A little titanium in one ankle. I know guys with a lot more, including stainless steel skull plates. I'll do whatever it takes to be the real cowboy, but, for me, metal on the brainpan is the rodeo version of a pink slip.

I've heard at Code Orange a penile prosthesis will set off the detector in Reno. That would be interesting to explain to the guy with the wand.

Anyway, I've had airport experience enough to carry X-rays and letters from various orthopods. Here's how much X-rays help— zip. None. You buy a ticket to Europe with cash, show up with no luggage other than a saddlebag, and make the metal detector sing like a mining town lunch whistle, and the gate security agents do not give flying whiz for a note from your doctor. Added to all that, in my haste to catch a plane I forgot the Udap Bear Deterrent wrapped in a bandanna at the bottom of my saddlebag.

"What's this?" the black woman with cornrows at the hand search table asked.

"Deodorant."

"Step this way, please."

She took me to a room without windows and left me in the care of two incredibly sober men in thin ties, white short-sleeve shirts, and wrestling-coach haircuts. After X-raying every part of my body—no doubt giving me testicular cancer thirty years from now—and bags, they took my clothes to test them for chemicals and stuck a flashlight up my butt.

I grinned and said, "That feels pretty good," even though it didn't.

The man with the flashlight said, "Are you going to be reasonable?"

"You're the one makes his living looking up assholes."

In my poem, I include a list of lines I've learned not to say at security. The most important thing not to say is, "Do I look like a terrorist to you?" Other mistakes I've made: "Is what you're doing legal?" and "Touch me again, I'll wrap that wand around your neck."

Next time I rewrite the poem I plan to add, "Have you guys had a girl with copper-colored hair and a golden hoop through her nipple come by today?"

Despite what you've heard from everyone you ever talked to, the security people don't mind jokes, so long as they aren't sarcastic quips threatening violence. Even I'm not stupid enough to say, "Don't pull the red wire."

But chattering teeth in your carry-on, that's okay. It lightens tension. Rubber puke generally rates a chuckle. I caught grief once for setting a mousetrap in an electric razor case. Not everyone has a sense of humor.

"Why are you going to Paris?" said a man with a gun.

"None of your business." I could have explained the part about Dad dying without ever noticing that I'm a real cowboy, and how my son is growing up thinking his father is a failure and the only way I could show Tyson the truth would be to give him a buckle with CHAMPION written right on the front. I could have told the man at security that champions are not losers. I could have, but he wouldn't have understood.

The man said, "I don't have time for jerks."

"I'll let you strip me naked and X-ray me and light my shoelaces to see how fast they burn"—I know, I don't wear shoelaces, but I was on a roll here—"if it'll make America safe, but so long as I'm not breaking any laws, it's none of your damn affair why I do what I do."

The upshot was they kept my bear spray, refusing to write out a receipt, and I missed two flights to Paris. The plane they put me on left in the evening and I had to change in Chicago. What with time zones and all, I didn't arrive in Paris, France, till Tuesday morning.

Paris

9.

If I was the bureaucrat in charge of hiring employees to work the booth where folks line up to trade their dollars and pounds for local cash, I believe I'd hire someone who speaks a little English, just to simplify the process. That's my opinion, which, I admit, is American-centric. Maybe putting angry single-language bureaucrats in the money booth is the French way of establishing the rules, their way of saying, "Adjust, jerks. It's not our job to accommodate you."

I noticed a certain level of pissiness even before I reached the money line, right off the plane. You walk down this long hall of dead space and come out at Customs, where there's a bunch of lines with signs that say EUROPEAN UNION, and two lines for the rest of us. The woman at Customs was wearing black like everyone else French except Odette and she was sitting down, which would never happen in the U.S. She asked me what I was doing there and I'm not as green as you might think, so I said, "Tourist." I know what happens if you say, "I'm here for justice." Or "vengeance." Or whatever your purpose is other than to spend money.

She looked me over slowly and said, "Clint Eastwood."

"He's an actor. I'm the real Rowdy."

Her eyes had that expression you see on women when a double amputee with infected sores on his face asks for spare change. Or maybe I'm overly sensitive, coming from a town in Wyoming that makes its living off tourists. I know how much tourists are held in contempt by those who feed off them.

And anywhere you travel, you'll find two types of tourists—those who try to blend in and fail miserably, and those who strut their ignorance. I don't know which is worse, but I do know the majority of Americans in line at the money-changing booth were of the ugly variety. Underdressed, over-loud, suspicious, arrogant, with no control over their kids—nothing like a cowboy. Up ahead of me a couple groups a man wearing plaid shorts had a T-shirt that read I DON'T GIVE A DAMN HOW YOU DO IT HERE, I WANT ICE. His wife had flesh hanging off her arms and their son wore a Teletubby knapsack. From my days with Tyson, I would guess Tinky Winky. I remember Tyson curled up on my lap in his Roy Rogers jammies. As the Tubbies flew out of a hole in the ground, we'd both shout their names—*Tinky Winky! Dipsy! La La! Po!*—then we'd fall over in a giggle heap. We don't do that anymore.

Ninety percent of the passengers jumped on cell phones the moment the plane touched down. God knows, they had to inform the world they were back in touch. The guy directly in front of me in the money line wore a DUKE cap and talked continuously on his phone while his dazed wife stood at his side in what I took as a Xanax fog. He shouted the way people did when telephones were first invented. "Don't tell me what I already know! They'll cheat us blind every chance they get! They hate our guts here!"

His wife gave me an embarrassed smile. When her husband stepped to the window to deal with the money changer, she said, "We've only been in Paris twenty minutes and I can already tell this trip isn't going to save my marriage."

I said, "I'm sorry, ma'am."

She nodded twice, and her face took on a sad, walleyed smile. "I'll go shopping."

When my turn came, I said, "I'll take five hundred worth," and slapped my bills on the counter.

The guy with a rubber on his right thumb chattered to himself, counting, or maybe he was chattering to me, thinking I understood. The money was different colors and sizes for different denominations. I suppose the sizes are so blind people can tell a one from a ten. I don't know what the weird colors are for. Looked like Monopoly money to me. And the cash isn't called francs, like it is in stories. It's euros. I probably knew that already but I tend to ignore information that doesn't relate to bulls. Now I wish I'd paid more attention to all those *USA Todays* I've read in truck stops over the years.

I said, "Thanks, pard." See how I was already falling into the act. You do that in strange places where they expect certain behavior. I'd never call a man in Wyoming "pard."

The man said, "Cow-boy," and pretended to shoot me with his rubber thumb and index finger.

He said, "Bang, bang."

I said, "Never shoot anything you don't plan to eat."

De Gaulle Airport gave me the same feeling I get deep in the Teton Wilderness, up on Fox Creek Divide. Up on Fox Creek, or any of the divides along the Yellowstone border, there is the illusion of solitude. No one is going to tell you where to sleep or what to eat or which lake's water will give you the trots. There is no one to point the way down to safety. No one to hold your hand and say, "Calm yourself, honey. It'll be okay." Break your leg back there, and you're dead.

De Gaulle felt the same way. Even though it was full of people, I was on my own. Not a soul in there cared whether I got out of the building alive or not. For me, it was a mass without communication.

Luckily, I found McDonald's. Hot oil and meat smells covered by Lysol, plastic garbage cans with flaps, life-size statue of Ronald himself in his yellow playsuit. Home. McDonald's may be as close to stability as most people who live on the road ever come. Even bat poop tastes good when you can count on it.

The de Gaulle McDonald's had breached the language barrier

by having a menu that was pictures of what you were buying. I pointed and the boy behind the counter rang up the bill. Couldn't have run smoother had it been in California. The hamburgers were more overcooked than stateside, if that's possible, and the fries dripped, but they made up for their shortcomings by selling beer. There's not a McDonald's in the Rockies sells over-the-counter beer. I tried a bottle and it was tasty.

Chowing down on my burger, I looked around at the families and cute Goth couples and European businessmen in McDonald's who were instinctively giving me more room than they gave one another and I thought to myself, piece of cake.

Remember how I said I'd tell the truth or shut up? Well, truth be told, I'd never ridden in a taxicab sober before. Not that I'd ridden in hordes of them drunk, but the two or three I had been in, I was more or less poured into the backseat. I had no experience at flagging one down from scratch. I tried the way they do in movies because movies is where I learned most things about getting by in unfamiliar situations. In movies, they stand on the curb and hold up their hand like asking a teacher to be excused.

This doesn't play in Paris.

After a bit, I wandered up the airport bypass there until I found a line of taxis stretching one way and a line of people the other. They converged at a bike rack–looking thing where people were loading into one taxi at a time. The taxis waited their turn. The people waited their turn. Nobody walked down the taxi line and hopped into an empty.

They were mostly mid-90s black Mercedeses, nice car for a taxi. I seem to recall my drunk-ride-home taxis as being yellow. The one came up when it was my turn had tires you wouldn't brag about and a radio antenna dead center on the roof. The license plate was black on yellow and four feet across. Inside, the heater blasted even though it was about eighty-five degrees already, and there was a dog gate between me and the driver, whose name started with two As. Aahuad. Aachma. It was hard to read the card on the passenger visor. He was short, by any standards, and southeast Kansas mud-colored, and he wore a nice suit and tie he must have bought in the boys' department.

He knew on sight that I spoke English. "What is your destination, please?"

I said, "The University of Paris."

"Which one?"

"Crap."

He waited patiently for me to pull a destination out of my ear hole. "How many are there?"

"Six, maybe. Seven. I do not know."

"The one where they study William James."

That seemed to satisfy him.

Once you leave the airport, the deal goes foreign. There was a sign — *!* inside a triangle. What's that supposed to mean? And the speed limit was 120. The fog was inky, not the fluffy low-flying clouds we get in the mountains, and the highway was packed with cars driven by Ritalin freaks who acted as if they had X-ray vision. My driver was right there with them, whipping in and out of lanes, passing on the right, on the shoulder, on the white line between lanes. We're talking aggressive. It came to me that saying *piece of cake* was somewhat premature.

I broke the cowboy code of strong and silent. Fear does that. "You lived in Paris all your life?" I asked.

He held up his thumb. "One year." I had no idea what the thumb business meant. "I was born in Libya," he said, without slowing down a bit. "I came across after Gaddafi's men kill my brothers and rape my sister."

"Is that true, or a line you tell the tourists?"

He said, "I do not understand?"

"Back home we make up stories like that for the tourists. I tell them my grandfather was a Cheyenne warrior nailed to a tree by Kit Carson."

I think maybe I hurt his feelings, which is the last thing I'd want to do with a low-end wage earner. I'm generally a sensitive fella, when it comes to pride issues. Or maybe some other car passed us and he took it as a challenge. Whatever caused the attitude change, little Aahuad or Aachma's bad driving got worse. We drove hell bent for leather into a tunnel. I hate tunnels with more passion than I hate almost anything else in the world, and I knew a Paris tunnel was where they ran Princess Diana to ground. Suddenly, red lights blazed like when some drunk stabs you in the eye with a lit cigarette, and the Libyan driver stomped his brakes. Traffic came to a dead stop. Imagine an L.A. freeway going from full blast to gridlock in six seconds.

My driver leaned back and lit a cigarette. "Are you a musician in the United States of America?"

I said, "Not me," and rolled down the window, careful to keep my feet off the floor. When I was a kid, Dad told me his own personal self-evident truth, which was you must hold your breath on bridges and keep your feet up in tunnels. That was practically all the preparation Dad gave me for life, so I go along the best I can.

"Why do you ask?" I said.

"Americans dressed as you very often play the musical instrument in a band. Or they gigolo."

"I'm not a gigolo, either."

He seemed to take that for granted. He tilted his little head back and blew smoke at the ceiling. He had the look of a man there for the long haul.

I rolled the window back up, figuring cigarette smoke would take longer killing me than exhaust fumes from a traffic jam in a tunnel.

I said, "If Chad attacks Libya from the rear, do you think Greece will help?"

He said, "I do not understand." Then, he didn't say anything else the rest of the drive into Paris.

10.

The University of Paris isn't a real university, not in the American sense. Real universities have a student union and a quad for Frisbee and sunbathers. Dormitories. Even Casper College where I went for one semester on a rodeo scholarship had that much, only we called the food court a commons instead of the union. Every college I ever saw has grass and a rock students paint before basketball games. The University of Paris doesn't have any of that. I couldn't find dorms anywhere. How can they call themselves a university without dorms? Mostly what they have is long hallways painted glossy gray, classrooms that smell stale, and a couple of auditorium-type things. No gym that I saw. I wandered the halls looking into the faces of girls for an hour or so. The smile-to-frown ratio was horrendous. No one I saw in the French educational system was having fun.

To go in and out you had to pass through a line of depressed radicals giving out xeroxed flyers on issues or some folderol. If it'd been Colorado, I would have taken them for religious lunatics, but I think these were more politicized. I went outside and came back in, working my way from zealot to zealot until I found one spoke English. She had real short hair, not bald, more in the way of a crew cut, and a mole on her neck, looked pre-cancerous. Her nose had a crook to it I tried not to look at.

She thrust a washed-out yellow sheet of paper in my face and said, "You are responsible for your government's actions."

I said, "Not me. I'm from Wyoming."

"Meaning?"

I hate politics and will as a rule belch in the face of anyone tries to talk it, but this girl spoke English and I needed cooperation. "I could dynamite myself in the town square and it wouldn't affect Bush any more than a rock tossed in the Pacific Ocean."

"That is the mind-set of a German under the Nazis."

The thing makes me burp in the face of political fanatics is they ignore any logic that says what they think matters doesn't. The crook-nosed woman jumped into a rant about globalization and Kyoto and the arrogance of imperialism. I missed most of it. The bottom line was the United States wants to turn the Third World into customers for Wal-Mart.

I said, "No, duh."

She made a fist, leaned toward my ear, and shouted, "The Egg McMuffin shall never displace the omelet!"

I told her I agreed wholeheartedly and I would write that in my day planner first chance I got and she said if that's true I should take up arms. I said I would do so soon as I got back home but first I had to find the literature department. I asked if she could help.

"I am here to fight American aggression, not be a tour guide."

"I promise I'll help your cause soon as I find the literature department."

"French, Russian, or English?"

"American."

She used her sheaf of flyers as a pointer. "One floor up, east wing, end of the hall. The door is green. You can't miss it unless you are color-blind."

I said, "Much obliged," but by then she'd turned to inflict her views on someone else.

. . .

You would not believe how good it feels to be eighteen and a real cowboy. The spit and sizzle of it. The incredible joy brought on from just being outdoors and breathing. The future stretches forward like a string of Christmases, an all-you-can-eat buffet of bulls and women, women and bulls. The possibilities are endless and you, you are the very thing you admire most.

I went off to college flush with confidence, two good knees, a full set of teeth, and a hot, young wife. Five months later, I limped out of town with none of the above.

The rodeo coach and I disagreed right off. He said I held my spurs too far back on the bull, at an improper angle. I called bullshit. He said I had an attitude. I was eighteen and he was thirty and so racked with arthritis he couldn't saddle a big dog. To me, the man was a dinosaur.

And here's what I learned in Casper: Relentless wind blows love away. It simply wears you down. Mica couldn't forgive me for dragging her out of her niche. There's kids whose deepest desire is to get the hell out of their hometown, and there's kids who want to stay put, and the two should not marry each other.

Mica and I were fighting so hard I couldn't be bothered by classes, except for an English lit class I went to because the fox teaching it winked at me once on campus, thus fueling enough creative visualization to keep my tail in her class. She knew it, too. She held her educated snatch out like a carrot, leading me into Graham Greene, Somerset Maugham, and Evelyn Waugh, who is a guy, by the way, in spite of his girlish name. My preconceptions of Paris came from those three, especially Maugham. In *Razor's Edge* he says a martini is nothing but a common cocktail until you add a splash of absinthe. Of course, bull riders don't drink martinis, so I'd never had one and still haven't, but absinthe sounded like it met cowboy standards. I was hoping someone in Paris would offer a splash.

By Christmas, Mica was long gone, back to GroVont. I blew my

ACL on a practice bull no meaner than a Holstein, and the coach pulled my scholarship. I was too embarrassed to go home, so I drifted down to south Texas and worked a car wash till my knee got its flex back. That summer, I tried British Columbia under the false hope cowboys there would be less competition.

Then Mica sent me a letter, saying how much she missed me and how she wanted to try again because now she knew our love was pure and everlasting, so I drove home and got married a second time. Until the letter came, I didn't know she'd annulled the first go. All that year, I'd thought I was committing adultery.

What brought this stroll down memory lane up is the similarity of the English lit office in Paris to the English department at Casper College. The both of them ooze institutionalism — walls, desks, and file cabinets, all standard issue — and they must have a farm where they raise women to work in those places. Genetically engineered and corn fed for maximum anuses, bureaucrats who live for rules and get a charge out of crushing students in the name of policy.

In the Paris situation, there were two of them, an older one in a tight silk blouse doing her nails, and a young one dressed as a matron playing computer solitaire. A Nordic-looking doofus in the twenty-five range was feeding paper into a copy machine. He was white-blond, lanky as a bareback rider, cheekbones that cast a shadow. With each page, he pushed a button, then slapped the copier on the side and waited till it spit out a copy. Through an open door at the back of the office, I made out another office where a man who must have been the boss was eating a sandwich about two feet long.

The matron ignored me — she was concentrating on her cyber cards — but the old lady dressed for allurement looked up and blew on her nails. She asked me a question in French.

I said, "I'm looking for two students named Odette and Giselle. They came back from a William James seminar in Boulder, Colorado, yesterday."

The old one looked at the young one, who grimaced. *Grimace* is not a word I use lightly.

I said, "You understand American?"

The old woman chattered at me in French. French people talk fast. Imagine walking through the woods, pissing off squirrels.

I tried the line I'd learned from the Colorado State frat boy. *"Parlez-vous anglais?"*

This got the matron started, then the old one kicked back in and they overlapped. Whenever two or more French people speak, they overlap.

I said, "This is the English department. How is it you don't speak English?"

The secretaries jabbered. The kid on the copier slapped at his machine. The man eating the sandwich came to his door to watch.

Finally, the older woman who took herself as spokesman turned to me and said, "Clint Eastwood."

11.

There was an empty plastic mop bucket out in the hallway, the yellow, rectangular kind with the squeegee attachment. I turned it upside down and hoisted myself on top so I was above the general gaggle of students.

"Who all out here knows English?"

I probably shouted louder than need be because up and down the hallway people stopped whatever they were doing. It was like that freeze shot at the end of *Butch Cassidy and the Sundance Kid.*

"Somebody out here must know English," I shouted.

This bespectacled boy of about fourteen held his hand up shoulder height. I took him for one of those child geniuses goes to college when he's twelve and doesn't have the social wherewithal to lie when asked if he knows something. I hope Tyson isn't way-gifted like that. Those kids all seem to have nervous acne. Most are asthmatic.

I pointed at the boy. "You. Come with me."

Back in the English office, I gave him the rap. "Tell them I'm looking for two of their students. Odette and Giselle. They were in Boulder, Colorado, at a conference and came back yesterday."

The women looked at the boy, who looked on the verge of tears. I said, "Now."

The boy launched into a translation that took quite a bit longer than my original statement. After a while, the old secretary jumped in, and then the matron. They talked all at once. The older one waved her arms in the air, as if speech wasn't enough to get her point across.

The man in the doorway aimed his sandwich at me and said something of a gruff nature. His women shut up.

The boy who spoke English said, "They have no students named Odette and Giselle."

"Do they have anyone who's been to a seminar in Colorado in the last week?"

This didn't take near as long to translate. The man in the doorway said, "No."

The boy turned to me and said, "No."

No translates as *no*. "Are they sure? Maybe they lost track."

"None of their students have been in the States recently. This is the first week of the new term. They would know if they had a student at a conference."

I looked from the secretaries to the man in the doorway. He bit into his sandwich. Dead end.

I went out to the hallway to turn the mop bucket back rightways and consider the options. At the moment, I couldn't see any, other than standing next to the green door there like a wooden Indian waiting for two women who no doubt lied to me about being students at the University of Paris. Or maybe I was at the wrong U.P., if the Libyan cabdriver was to be believed. The thought of traipsing around Paris from school to school, reliving that mess I'd just gone through, depressed me no end.

The bespectacled boy slid out of the office door and hugged the wall as he passed by me. He had the skittish look of a person who's come through a narrow escape. I supposed if I was going to make the rounds of every English lit office in every college in town, I should nab him, but he was such a quivery mouse, I let him go. I could recruit new translators.

The blond fence post who'd been slapping the copy machine came from the office, carrying a pile of papers. He made off a few steps down the hall, then he turned and came back.

He spoke in a Southern accent. "Hey, Slick, William James is philosophy."

I was momentarily at a loss, like you are when you expect an answering machine and a real person answers the phone. "What?"

"Henry James is English literature. William is philosophy."

"I thought Will wrote books."

"Philosophy books."

"Oh." With that blond hair I should have guessed he wasn't French. Not that French are never blond, but his hair was longer than I'd seen so far, and his face wasn't squinched up in disapproval. He had the relaxed posture of a snowboarder after two bowls.

"Do you know where the philosophy department is?" I asked.

The kid nodded, northward. I think it was northward. I never did get my Paris bearings straight. "North wing. Ground floor."

"Will you take me there? I'll need a translator."

He hesitated, looking me up and down like you would a salad bar in a cafe where you don't trust the freshness of the ingredients.

He said, "Why not?"

I said, "Much obliged."

"We don't get many cowboys through here. It should be interesting."

"I've been told foreigners are fascinated by the American cowboy."

"That's not what I mean."

Real cowboy style may look snazzy but it's based on riding a horse a long ways over uneven ground. The getup isn't worth much indoors. You got your pants—Wranglers that fit when you sit in a saddle, as opposed to Levi's invented by a miner for miners. The shirt must be long-sleeve, tuck-in, buttoned right at the cuffs 'cause cowboys knew about melanoma decades before the rest of the country. The hat is your basic hands-free umbrella, great if you've got space in front of and behind your head, but hell on airplanes or even pickups with a headrest. The code won't allow taking it off in public except for two occasions: during the national anthem at sanctioned events or when your horse dies. I don't know what son of a bitch made up the code, probably some dime novelist didn't even wear a hat.

The least convenient cowboy attire is the boots. Cowboy boots have pointy toes to go through stirrups and a heel so they don't go too far through. If you're not on a horse, they're nothing but vanity. Like a woman's party heels, they're okay for dancing, somewhat handy in a fight, but painful as your second divorce when it comes to walking a distance on pavement or a hard surface such as the floors in the University of Paris that go for miles without so much as a throw rug to soften the step.

By the time we reached the north wing, I was ready to screw the code and buy tennis shoes.

Early on in our trek, my guide stuck out his hand and said, "Michael Gunner, Orlando, Florida."

"Rowdy Talbot. PRCA. Why didn't you speak up back there when I needed a hand?"

"It wasn't my business. Everyone in the office knew English."

He walked dead center in the middle of the hall, like he owned the building and couldn't be bothered with weaving through the little people. I rethought my stoned snowboarder impression. Michael was more of a star quarterback on an Ivy League football team, that is, a major stud within the confines of an extremely small arena.

"Jerks," I said. "Do they always fake stupidity?"

"Only if they think you're being rude."

"I'm well known for my politeness. Ask anyone on the circuit."

Michael chuckled in the soft, Southern style that makes you think of the laughing-with or laughing-at deal. "When you came in, the first thing you should have said was 'Bonjour, madame. Bonjour, monsieur.' It means *good morning*. If you say that every time, they can be fairly cooperative. If you don't, they treat you like a rat."

I had to step around a clot of students blocking the hallway with their books clutched up against their chests like they were braced for a robbery. Michael sailed through without a swerve.

I said, "How can they talk? The French are famous for being the rudest people on Earth."

He smiled. Imagine Mona Lisa's mouth on a boy. "They have high standards in Americans."

"We don't have any standards for them."

"A Frenchman justifies his rudeness by saying you were rude first."

Besides extreme foot discomfort, I reached the north wing with a bad case of nausea from the prevailing fumes. The walls smelled recently painted, and the coeds I dodged in and out of were wearing perfume would embarrass a Tonopah whore. Some bunnies wear perfume—generally Corral West's finest—to cover the cigarettes, but I never smelled anything like what a Paris woman uses as the daytime norm. I swear, I smelled it on some of the boys, too. Give me the stockyards, any day, over a building packed with French students.

Michael the would-be stud pulled up in front of a door I took to be our destination. He said, "Think of yourself as an ambassador for your country. It only takes one thoughtless remark to turn these people against our entire nation."

I didn't much care if Parisians hated Americans or not. I didn't like Americans outside the middle two time zones that much myself. Coastal Americans value what television tells them to value.

"Most important," he said, "always assume they know what you're saying, even if they pretend they don't. It saves on embarrassment."

I said, "Embarrassment never hurt anybody."

"You're not from the South, are you, Slick?"

"Wyoming."

"That explains it." He looked at me, as if apprising my chances of survival in the big world. "Odette and Giselle, right?"

"I need to find them."

"Okay," he said. "You want cooperation, meet their eyes, smile, and radiate goodwill."

"I always radiate goodwill."

"Bonjour, monsieur," Michael said.

"Bonjour, monsieur," I said, although it didn't sound the same. Michael and a man in a sneaky mustache shook hands, formally, like chess masters after a match. When my turn came it was shaking hands with a slice of white bread.

Michael and the man exchanged pleasantries before Michael launched into the question. I waited, patient guy that I am.

The philosophy department was as institutional as English had been, only with more square footage. More file cabinets. There were three minions—one male, two female—instead of two, and they were actually working, none of that nails and computer solitaire in philosophy. They had a window. English lit hadn't had a window.

I don't get philosophy. It's the study of Deep Thought, right? Thoughts made up in the philosopher's brain, from scratch. They make a product out of no raw material, which is my definition of a scam. I mean, I think Deep Thoughts every day but I wouldn't go telling other people what I think. It's like religion or politics or true love or just about anything else. Think about it all you want, but for God's sake, keep it to yourself. Words never changed anyone's mind. Studying Deep Thoughts people other than you came up with is like studying their stool to figure out how to cook what they ate. It may be possible, but it's not worth what you have to wade through.

So Michael's talking to this man whose very reason for being I would deny. That's bad enough, for a first impression, but the man also has a mustache looks like a nightcrawler crawling out of his nose. He might as well have had a tattoo reading SNEAK on his face. You won't see a cowboy wearing facial hair that gives away his character.

As Michael went on, Mustache Man got up, walked to a file cabinet, and pulled out a file. His answer to Michael was fairly long and unintelligible, except every now and then a word popped out — *Colorado, James, Odette Clavel.*

This one female secretary who was keyboarding like a house on fire looked at me and smiled. I smiled back. Her little pink tongue flitted out and touched the tip of her upper lip. American girls don't do that.

I said, "He knows them."

Michael nodded. "He knows Odette. Never heard of Giselle."

"Where is she?"

Michael listened, then said, "He's not about to help us track her down."

I spoke through my smile. "What if I bust him in the face?"

Mustache slapped the folder closed and cut it back into the file. Michael said his piece, and Mustache said his piece. The girl with the cute tongue went back to typing. She was through with me.

Michael said, "He thinks you're a stalker."

"I'm the frigging avenging angel if he doesn't hand over an address."

Mustache picked up the phone.

Michael sighed. "What did I tell you about assuming they speak English?"

I gave the cowboy's refrain. "Yeah, yeah."

"Security is on the way."

The file cabinet he'd been digging in was across a counter and against a wall. I could leap over the counter, stiff-arm the mustache, fling open the file, but then what? No doubt the file was in French. Whatever information I might find wasn't worth a stungun situation.

"Is there enough time to break his furniture?"

Michael ran his hand through his blond hair. "It would jeopardize my fellowship at the university."

Two men in avocado-colored uniforms ran through the door and stopped. The one came across as a student working his way through law school, but the other emitted the aura of professional roller derby. His neck muscles throbbed. He had the haircut preferred by lesbians and Toby Keith fans.

Michael said, "Please don't do anything that might get me deported."

Mustache spoke to the security guards. The skater thug smiled and wet his lip, not unlike the cute secretary.

"Okay," I said. "For you, because you helped me."

"Awfully nice of you," Michael said.

"You know a place where we could get a cup of coffee? I haven't had coffee all morning."

12.

Crepes a Go Go had outdoor seating and three kinds of sugar, none of it artificial. Three kinds of real sugar! How bizarre can a country get? We sat at an iron table with a view across the plaza of stone steps going up to double doors into the university. A stream of students wearing black and carrying books and bags flowed into and out of the building. Scarves galore. No berets. No laughs. Fanatics of every sort stood on the steps, trying to pass out tracts, but hardly any students would touch the pages thrust in their face. They acted blind. It was like walking down the Strip in Vegas, pretending not to see the waifs passing out whore flyers.

"You think they'll use that door?"

Michael glanced up from a paperback book he was reading. The moment we sat down, he had pulled the book from his daypack. The cover was pastel, all words, no art. I couldn't read the title because it was in French.

"The university has many doors, but that's the one closest to philosophy," he said.

A waiter in a white shirt and an ironed apron hovered over our table, not saying anything. In the States, his haircut would have proclaimed him either gay or a missionary. In France, it probably meant *guy*.

Michael said, *"Bonjour."*

The waiter said, *"Bonjour."*

Michael said something and the waiter looked at me.

I said, "I'll take a cup of coffee. Black."

Michael said something more in French and the waiter walked off.

"You forgot to say *'Bonjour,'*" Michael said.

"I didn't forget. I tried it in my mind and it sounded silly."

"They would rather you try and sound silly than not try at all." Then Michael launched into this discussion of the difference between French and American mentalities. Over the next couple of days, I was to discover most everyone you meet in Paris is itching to tell you the difference between French and American mentalities.

"The French are suspicious, reserved, and big-hearted," Michael said.

"Like New Yorkers," I said.

"That's right. Imagine an entire nation of people from Brooklyn."

Michael's theory was that Americans are romantic pragmatists and French are pragmatic romantics. Odette had used that word *pragmatic*, too, and I didn't know what it meant when she said it, either.

"Does that explain no fake sugar and three kinds of real?" I asked.

"Exactly."

The waiter whose mother would have been proud of his posture returned with a ceramic mug of coffee and cream for Michael and a little girl's tea party–sized cup of what appeared to be coal mine runoff for me.

I forgot the part about being an ambassador. "What the hell is this?"

"Your coffee," the waiter said.

"I don't want a shot, I want a whole cup."

Michael gave his superior blond-god smile that was beginning to grate. "It's espresso."

The waiter turned and left. He didn't care.

"I don't want espresso. I want coffee."

"That's what coffee is in France." Michael explained the workings of an espresso machine—hot water under pressure forced through packed grounds or some such hooey. "Be glad you aren't in Greece. They use half the water and leave the grounds in, in Greece."

I tried a sip. It tasted like coal mine runoff, too. "I can't get by without my coffee."

Michael sipped his. I swear, he did the thing where his little finger stuck out, away from the cup. "This is the best coffee in the world."

"How come yours is regular sized?"

"Mine is café au lait—espresso with steamed milk."

"I want what you have, only without the milk."

"What I have without the milk is the same as what you have."

I gave the coffee another chance. It wasn't so awful the second go, tasted kind of like campfire coffee where you boil the holy beJesus out of grounds and throw in an eggshell. "Yours is nothing but a tiny amount of coffee and a large amount of milk?"

He nodded.

"Might as well drink dirty milk." I downed what was left of my shot in a gulp, then chewed on loose grounds from the bottom. I'm not big on chewy coffee. Back in high school, on camping trips, I stuffed my grounds in a sock before boiling them. That eggshell trick works better in stories than real life.

"Do they charge for warm-ups? I won't go to Starbucks except for emergencies because they charge for warm-ups."

Michael's superior smile spread into a superior grin. To him, I was an inexperienced hick. I'd like to throw him on the back of a bull and see which of us is inexperienced. People always think other people who don't know local stuff are stupid.

"The concept of a free refill is beyond the French mind," he said.

"Jesus, what kind of country is this?" I signaled to the waiter, who ignored me. Michael signaled to the waiter and he came over.

"Listen, bud," I said. "Bring me four of those mini-coffees and an empty mug like his. I'll pour them all together."

"The espresso is three euros fifty, a cup," Michael said. "Plus, each espresso carries more caffeine than a grande of American Starbucks."

"What's your point?"

The upside of spending twenty dollars before ingesting a reasonable amount of caffeine is that you can stay there all day if you feel like it. None of this "spend money at least once an hour or move along" attitude you get in American coffee shops. And the weather was nice. I have to give Paris that much. That morning was blue and just far enough above room temperature that you noticed the way the sun warmed up your skin. There were fountains in the plaza. Young people dressed Goth sat on the sides of the fountains, necking. Others ate and still others read books. Some people ate and read at the same time. Except for me, everyone who wasn't necking ignored everyone who was.

My translator proved nosy. "These girls you're looking for, Odette and Giselle, why do you want them so much?"

"They took my property," I said.

"Must be valuable property to cause you to jump on a plane and fly to France."

I chose not to go there. I had enough to keep up with watching the university doors and the social scene around the fountains. I saw no reason to justify myself to a tall person.

Michael leaned my way with the book between his knees. It was a prop. He didn't read a page the whole time we sat there. "Did you sleep with one of them?"

I looked over at his pink face, that permanent sunburn you see on womanizers at ski resorts. "What kind of question is that?"

He wet his chapped lips and stared at me closely. "Here's what I'm thinking. This isn't about property. Believe me, Slick, these French women know how to drive a man insane."

"That's your excuse, not mine."

"They get off on the power. Whichever one of these twats you slept with will treat you like you're a dead corpse—if you pull off a miracle and find her—but secretly, she'll be delighted. French women keep score."

Sounded like crapola to me. "Is that why you're in Paris?"

"I'm in Paris to research André Gide. Now there's a winner in the game between the sexes."

"Bicycle rider, right?"

"The greatest French novelist ever. Gide puts Flaubert and Proust to shame." Michael ripped into an extended rave about some writer I never heard of. I mean, French writers weren't covered in the class I passed at Casper College, so I hadn't heard of any of them, except the guy who wrote *Count of Monte Cristo,* and I forget his name. I saw the Disney *Hunchback of Notre Dame* with Ty, but I suspect Disney screwed with the story. Gargoyles didn't sing in the French book.

Michael was hot on Gide, even hotter than Odette had been for William James. When Odette went on about her dead guy, she was interesting. Michael was just another bore, but then I'd been waiting to take Odette's clothes off. Self-evident Truth #3: *Foreplay changes the nature of interesting.* In hopes of shutting Michael up, I tipped my hat way down over my face and propped my feet on a chair, in nap mode.

He didn't take the hint. "Gide created the myth of the modern French female. Because of Gide, every girl in Paris feels compelled to flaunt her sexuality."

I said, "Yada, yada."

That's something I picked up from TV. It's a short and meaningless response to a long and meaningless statement. I've been told it's Yiddish for *whatever.* Michael said more but I tuned him out by watching the neckers. Tuning out wasn't that hard. The weird coffee had my ears ringing.

The neckers were interesting. They stared intently into each other's eyes between hugs and kisses, which for the most part were not the openmouthed, tongue-on-tongue variety. They weren't French kisses, more like movie kisses. I noticed that with each couple, one person was more possessive than the other. And one person—not necessarily the more or less possessive one—was happier to embrace while the other pushed for aggressive kissing. The timing was slightly off, all around the fountain. I couldn't recall the last time I necked in public. Or necked anywhere, for that matter. In America, when nailing regularity goes up, kissing regularity goes down the tubes.

One of the neckers was a pretty girl with brown hair streaked blond where it framed her face. I couldn't see the boy's face, only the oily back of his head, but between smooches, the girl looked over his shoulder at us and smiled. I got the idea the boy was being played for a sucker.

"That's Isa," Michael said.

"She's paying more attention to you than her date."

"Isa's a good kid. I could arrange for you to fuck her, if you want."

"You're a pimp?"

Michael laughed. "Of course not, Slick. I'd see it as a favor for a fellow American. We don't want your trip to France to be a total waste."

"Tell you what, bub. You call me Slick one more time and we're going to show these folks what a violent country the United States is."

Michael closed his book with a snap and blinked rapidly. "I was only trying to be friendly," he said.

"You failed."

The thing is he had touched a sore spot. Bull riders pull that giving-girls-to-each-other number all the time. If they aren't outright loaning a bunny to a friend, they're selling her for a six-pack.

Mostly it's bluster and if the girl found out she'd slap the both of them, but it still pisses me off. Men should not arrange other men's lays.

"You don't have to go all huffy on me," Michael said.

"I'll go as huffy as I want."

The pretty girl ducked her face back into the boy's shoulder. She seemed nice. Had Michael said, "I'll introduce you," instead of "I'll arrange it," we might have hit it off. But now the relationship was ruined before she even knew we'd had one. After that, I ignored the son of a bitch, although it made me feel like I wasn't doing all I could to express my disapproval. Self-evident Truth #4: *You can't hit every asshole you run into.*

13.

Students, artificial students, tourists of various nationalities and religions, men in coveralls with green plastic brooms—the lunch rush came and went like the tide. They ate and smoked at the same time, stubbing their butts out on half-eaten sandwiches. A professor-looking guy with a beagle on his lap pontificated to a couple girls in black sweaters and matching book bags. I say he was a professor because he wore corduroy pants.

Michael ordered this thing looked like pigs in a blanket. I was hungry but damned if I would order off a French menu while he sat next to me, willing to help. I knocked down a couple more mini-coffees instead. The cafe had alcohol, but I was in Paris on business. It wasn't the time or place for recreation.

I kicked my saddlebag under the table so it'd be less of a temptation and stood up as the waiter came outside carrying a pink drink on a tray. He took the drink to a man wearing a parka even though it wasn't cold.

"You got a men's room?" I asked.

Mr. Braille himself could not have read the waiter's face.

I said, "Bathroom?"

Blank stare.

"Restroom? Comfort station?"

Michael chuckled and I knew he was waiting for me to ask him to step in, but I wasn't about to. Michael was an idiot.

I tried again. "Toilet?"

The waiter woke up. "Toilette."

"Yeah, toilette."

He led me inside and nodded toward spiral steps that corkscrewed down a hole no wider than a well. I truly hate being in wells or coffins or any other form of underground, and this didn't look like any place for a can. It was worse than an outhouse hole without the outhouse. But the waiter must have known what I was asking. Giselle had used that toi*lette* pronunciation, too. Nothing less than a deep need to pee could have taken me down those steps.

At the bottom of the corkscrew I found an open room with two urinals on the right and two doors marked w.c. on the left. One w.c. had a female silhouette and the other a male. In the middle of the room, a flat-chested woman of eighty or so sat on a folding chair next to a card table crowded with paper towels and aquamarine soap and bottles of smell. She had a hand-drawn sign that read ¢40.

She said, *"Bonjour, monsieur."*

I said, *"Bonjour."*

A guy was whizzing in one of the urinals, right in front of her. It looked to me like that was the drill. Seemed odd to whiz with a woman at your back, but what the heck, in a foreign land you have to be flexible. I started for the vacant urinal and the woman cleared her throat. Made a popping sound, like a sage grouse. I looked at her and she clicked her fingernail on the ¢40 sign.

"You want me to pay to take a leak?"

She clicked her nail on the sign again. I'd assumed it was the price of cologne or whatever she was selling, but, evidently, the old girl expected cash for going. Never one to be difficult, I dug two quarters from my pocket and said, "Keep the change."

French men don't use urinals the way we do. I'd noticed it first at the airport and then in the college. They stand six inches closer

than us. This guy, in black sweats, a nylon jacket, and Nikes, was
hunched up almost inside the urinal, with his knees on either side of
the lip. Looked like he'd bang his wanger on the porcelain, and, for
certain, he was set to catch splash. Maybe it's on account of a
woman nearby, only no women had been present at the other toilets
I'd visited. Maybe French children are trained that way and they
grow up thinking everyone does it the same. You never know what
people will think is normal in different parts of the world. Makes
me wonder about Wyoming.

I was standing the standard American distance out, releasing
my fifty cents' worth, when the woman squawked. Without cutting
flow, I turned to see what the fuss was. She held my two quarters in
the palm of her hand, this horrified look on her face, as if they were
poison mushrooms. The woman let loose a stream of invective in
my direction. It's funny how language is not an issue when a
woman is livid. I would have known what she meant had she been
saying it in Swahili. She didn't want U.S. change.

"I'm whizzing," I said, "and if you want to stop me you can come
over here and try." So much for flexibility.

The Nikes man flushed and washed his hands excessively.
When he went to the card table for paper towels, they exchanged a
few words which I figured were about me. She had a strong opinion and he agreed with her.

I zipped it up and washed my own hands since I've been told
foreign germs are worse than ours. I passed on the paper towels.
Pant legs are plenty absorbent.

The woman glared, hawklike, as I headed up the corkscrew
steps. She spit words—*Abruti d'Américain, va.* I didn't need a translation.

When I came back to the table, Michael was long gone and his
place had been taken by an old man in cutoffs and a denim vest
over a sleeveless T-shirt. Skinniest legs I've ever seen on a male.

Flip-flops. Silver ponytail of the type worn by senior citizens in the galleries along Canyon Road in Santa Fe, New Mexico, and basically nowhere else. Cured leather tan. Confederate gray eyes set in crow's feet. The ragged-cut shorts branded him as American as much as my hat did me. At his feet, a wire-haired Scottie dog sniffed my saddlebag, but I don't know enough Scottie lore to tell if he was looking for food or a place to go. All I know about Scotties is they're fairly useless on a ranch.

"Sir, do you mind if Monty and I share your table?" the crasher said in the whiskey voice I associate with sheepherders and aging disc jockeys.

I looked around at the eight or nine empty tables in the vicinity and shrugged. "Suit yourself."

"You are quite kind." He held out his hand. "Pinto Whiteside. And this is Monty Clift."

My attention stayed under the table, unsure how the man would take it if I gave Monty Clift a nudge. Dog pee is hell on leather. "What's that?"

"In France, when we meet a stranger we give our name and shake hands. My name is Pinto Whiteside."

I studied Pinto Whiteside, deciding if this was going to be more trouble than it could possibly be worth. A cigar stuck out from the pocket on his vest. That was a bad sign, and the way he leaned forward gave me the feeling I get when someone is about to pitch a new long-distance plan. Or maybe term life insurance. He was definitely leading up to a plea for time or money or both but, let's face the truth here, I was in need of help, and in no position to go snippy on an old-timer.

"Rowdy Talbot."

As we shook, Pinto said, "I once knew a family of Talbots in Puerto Vallarta. They ran a business selling mail-order cancer treatments."

"I doubt we're related."

"Pity," he said, although I have no idea why. He signaled the waiter, who seemed to know what the signal meant. "The family marketed a syrup that when ingested caused the patient's toenails to turn vermilion and flake off. It actually brought about remission in some cases."

My fears were confirmed when Pinto pulled the cigar from his vest. He went into the lighting ritual.

"You going to smoke that, go somewhere else," I said.

"I beg your pardon."

"There's tables you can claim for your own. If you plan to smoke, move to one of them, far from me as you can get."

Pinto Whiteside twirled the cigar between the thumb and index fingers of both hands. His straw eyebrows arched and stretched independently, as if each brow was controlled by a separate side of his brain. "You must be a new arrival." He slid the cigar back into his vest. "I predict over time you will discover attitudes are far different here than in the Wild West."

"I won't be here over time," I said. "And if Monty lifts a leg on my gear, neither will you."

Pinto sniffed, clearing a runny nose. "I daresay you lead a miserable, frustrated existence if you must search out things that can go wrong but probably won't."

The waiter brought Pinto a drink while I worked out what he had just said. I needed a comeback, and *"Oh, yeah,"* was the best I could do until I figured out what he meant. The drink was emerald green, served in a glass shaped like a funnel.

Pinto said, *"Merci."* He held the drink up and looked through it, toward the fountains, before he sipped. His lips moved, as if in prayer.

"That's not absinthe, is it?" I asked.

"Midori."

"I read where absinthe is green."

"So is Midori. May I ask you a personal question?"

Monty the dog circled twice clockwise and settled on his master's flip-flops. Not for the first time, I wondered if cow dogs in Australia circle the other way.

"Is there much I can do to stop you?" I said.

"What is your frank opinion of turquoise?"

The question didn't hit me as all that personal. "Pretty color. There's lakes in Alberta are turquoise. None in the lower forty-eight that I know of."

Pinto's second sip took in more liquid and he swished before swallowing. "I mean, turquoise the gemstone."

"Old ladies in Phoenix wear a ton of it. And square-dance callers. You never run into a square-dance caller without a turquoise bolo tie."

Pinto cradled his glass with both hands. I concluded it was his first alcohol of the day and he needed it. "The Navajos believe turquoise thrown into a river will cause rainfall."

"They must not throw many rocks into rivers. I've rodeoed on the reservation plenty, and never seen a drop of rain."

"Turks claim a man wearing turquoise will never fall off his horse."

"They got anything for bulls?"

"I firmly believe turquoise will soon replace gold as the international monetary standard. By next summer, turquoise will be more valuable than diamonds."

"You sound like a fella sitting on a pile of turquoise."

I've never known a man's mood to plummet so quickly. His gray eyes slicked over and the hands on his glass trembled. I hate it when you meet someone new and right off they weep. Happens fairly regular, at night, in a saloon, but we were outdoors, for God's sake.

Pinto let out an almost, but not quite, silent moan. "Over three hundred pieces of the finest quality rock. Lander Blue stone. The best you can buy anywhere. It's worth a fortune, but I can't give it away." He stared at the spot on his glass where his thumbs met. "Or, maybe, I could give it away, but these Parisians won't pay half what it cost me in New Mexico."

"I guessed you were from New Mexico."

"Taos. I had it worked out perfectly. Buy in bulk in the South-west then bring it to the fashion capital of the world and make a killing. I've been to every haute shop and jeweler in the city. No one wants turquoise." He changed his voice to a French snob's pitch. "Two thousand three is the year of lapis lazuli."

I was in this hotel bar in Taos, New Mexico, once with a bunch of Yancy's buddies, calf ropers, mostly, and through the first two drinks I thought we'd stumbled into a Georgia O'Keeffe lookalike contest. I said as much to the others but none of them had heard of Georgia O'Keeffe, which tells you all you need to know about calf ropers. The bar was packed with skinny women in flowing white dresses and flowing white hair, having profound conversations, drinking bottles of red wine. You've never seen so many squash blossom necklaces.

The old ladies packed away alcohol faster than the cowboys, and they were aggressive. Long stares. Winks. Poochy-lipped air kisses. The guys at my table made a wager where we each anted up fifty bucks and whoever slept with the oldest woman won the pot. You're thinking sexual predation, I know, but that isn't true. The ladies heard us making the bet. They knew the stakes and played along. I wouldn't be surprised if the old broads didn't have a bet going on their own.

The dowager I ended up with said she was seventy-four. We loaded into her LX 470 SUV and drove up the side of a mountain to this glass-and-rebar monstrosity filled with tasteful objects. She must have spent a lifetime and a million dollars collecting stuff. Her bedroom was upstairs in a glass turret. Before we started, I made her show me a driver's license and I'm happy I did because she was only sixty-eight, two years younger than the authentic Zuni princess one of the calf ropers was supposedly nailing. I got out of there and walked back to town. Took all night and that afternoon my bull threw me first jump.

Pinto cleared phlegm from his throat. "I've been told the Swiss are obsessed by Western regalia. If I could take the stones to Switzerland, I could make a profit."

"So take the stuff to Switzerland."

He looked up from his thumbs to meet my eyes. "I can't. My wife is a prostitute."

"Mine's a whore but I wouldn't let that keep me from going to Switzerland."

Pinto finished off his green drink and nodded to the waiter, who'd been waiting by the door with another one. "You do not understand. My wife is not a whore in the fashion that every American calls his wife a whore when he is angry with her. Mrs. Whiteside has a position in one of the most respected houses in the eighteenth. Her clients include gentlemen at the highest levels of commerce and government."

"Why do you call her Mrs. Whiteside if she's a whore?"

"She is a courtesan, not a whore. And Mrs. Whiteside is her name."

It didn't make sense to me, but this was a foreign country. If I came in expecting people to make sense, I would soon enough find myself hosed. I said, "Eighteenth what?"

Pinto Whiteside ignored the question. He was too upset over having a hooker wife who, turns out, controlled the purse strings. "She gives me thirty euros a day as an allowance to stay in Paris. Thirty euros barely keeps me in comestibles and Midori."

I almost felt sorry for the guy. I've known cowboys who depend on women with jobs, and they tend to walk slump shouldered. Modern equality is a good deal—I'm all for it—but it rarely works out with women supporting men.

"Does it feel weird, having a real hooker for a wife?"

Pinto reached down and picked up his dog. "That is not a question I care to discuss."

I figured I knew the answer by the way he held the dog on his lap, like Monty was his last friend. "Does she enjoy it, when you service her?"

That whipped his mood around—more of a lateral change than up or down. "What difference does that make?"

"I've always wondered if whores"—he gave me a nasty look—"courtesans enjoy their husbands."

"I satisfy her, if that is your insinuation. Love is an emotional issue. Not physical."

"I'll bet all whores' husbands say that." Across the way, Odette stepped out of the university doors.

"Holy Hannah." I dug in my pocket for cash. "There she is."

14.

Odette was joined on the steps by another girl and three gangly guys. They seemed to be discussing which way to go next. I threw three twenties on the table, grabbed my saddlebag, and took off, past the fountains and across the street. One thing you don't want to do in France is run across a street without looking both ways. Cars honked. A little Peugeot hit its brakes and slid into me. No blood, no foul, except the driver didn't see it that way. I could hear him spewing French anger even though his windows were rolled up.

I danced over the curb and across the sidewalk. One of the guys Odette was with saw me coming, but she didn't.

I said, "Odette."

A flash of fear crossed her face. Just a flash. If you weren't looking close, you would have missed it.

"You walked off with something of mine the other night," I said. "I need it back."

The tallest and spindliest of the boys said something to Odette in French. She did that full-body shrug I'd seen in the Gut Shot.

I moved to the sidewalk, right below Odette, where I could grab her if she broke for cover. I spoke to the others, politely. "Will you excuse us? Odette and I have some business."

The three guys and girl were dressed in black, in sharp contrast to Odette, who wore a maroon, flowing top over a brown skirt. Same bright red Keds as Sunday night. She had on glasses. That was different.

The tall kid more or less barked, *"Tu rêves quoi,"* which I took to mean *Get away from us.*

Odette nodded in agreement with whatever his specific words were. While, visually speaking, she showed nothing but disgust at my sudden appearance, I thought I detected a twinkle coming from the corners of her eyes. The Michael character had been right— outward contempt for me, inward delight at the proof of her power.

Odette spoke in French. The girl with her said something that made one of the boys—not the tallest one—snicker. I reached out for Odette's wrist. At touching her, the group tone darkened. I lost my entertainment value.

"You try this I-don't-speak-English scam on me, honey, and what could be clean and simple is going to turn nasty."

Two of the boys, including the tall, protective one, stepped in closer. The other girl in the group looked on with the interest of a kid watching a bug die. The third boy ducked back into the building.

Odette spoke to the tall guy, who had an Adam's apple big as a doorknob and four days' growth of beard wire. He put a hand on my shoulder. Using more force than necessary, I flung his hand away.

"Don't try it, Jack."

Jack said what I could tell was a dirty word.

"Are you the boyfriend?" I didn't wait for an answer. "You ought to keep your woman on a leash. She's got sex mixed up with Cracker Jacks. Thinks it comes with a prize."

Odette watched, wide-eyed. The glasses were incredibly clean and had oval frames that did exotic things to her eyes. The browns in her irises kind of shimmied, like shaved ice in sunlight. I could feel the pulse in her wrist, where I held it. Her pulse reminded me of her body, naked, sitting on my chest, which was an inappropriate thought at the moment. Tyson was depending on me.

"Where's my champion buckle?"

She replied in French. At least she was talking to me now, instead of her friends, although God knows what she was saying. She went on for a while.

When she stopped for air, I said, "I'm willing to think you didn't know the buckle was vital to me and taking it was an accident. Give it back and we'll call the last three days wasted and done with."

"This behavior is over a belt buckle?"

I turned to find Pinto Whiteside had followed from across the street. He carried Monty under one arm, the way I'd seen Parisians carrying bread.

"You speak the language. Tell Odette I want my buckle."

The third boy came back out of the building, accompanied by the same security guards who had thrown me out of the philosophy department. A veritable hullabaloo of foreign noise exploded, all the players talking at once. Only Odette kept silent. And me. I stared at her face while she stared at the ground. Then, she raised her brown eyes to meet mine. It felt like that first high dive out of the gate. The gut drop. The band on my chest. The adrenaline.

The guard I'd taken for a roller derby thug stepped between me and the boyfriend, facing me. He grunted — *Lâchez-la* — and I let go of Odette's wrist.

Pinto said, "You need a new story, cowboy. Nobody is going to believe you crossed the Atlantic Ocean for a belt buckle."

"Tell her it's not worth the mess. Tell her the buckle means nothing to her but if she doesn't give it back, I will turn her life into a nightmare."

Odette blinked.

Pinto said, "Do I hear a threat?"

"You hear a promise."

That's when the policeman arrived. The gendarme. Blue suit. Silly cap. Serious as a stroke. Everyone shut up while the less imposing security guard explained the situation to the gendarme. The cop listened, then the boyfriend jumped in and gave his side.

The gathered crowd exchanged views. From the mutters, I'd say public opinion was not swinging my way.

The spare girl asked Odette a question. I don't know what she asked, but it ended in *Clint Eastwood*.

Odette smiled. In daylight, and wearing glasses, her smile was less complicated than it had been in Colorado. I'd call the nighttime booze-and-seduction smile detached. Ambiguous even, although that isn't a word that comes up much on the rodeo circuit, so I may be using it wrong. Her daytime glasses smile was open. Crinkly lines radiated from her eyes.

"Her boyfriend insists that you be arrested," Pinto said. "He says stalking is accepted in the United States, but in Paris it is considered rude and therefore illegal."

I tore my eyes from Odette's. "Being rude is not illegal."

Pinto and the gendarme got into a discussion. Odette continued staring straight at my face, only once I'd looked away, I couldn't look back. It was disturbing. My ears grew hot and when I swallowed, battery acid burned my throat.

"I'm trying to convince him you are a pitiful cowpoke," Pinto said.

"Thanks."

"He's not buying it."

After hearing everyone else's version, the gendarme turned his attention to Odette. She talked. Pinto translated over her words.

"She says she was raised in Polynesia, that her father owned a pearl diving operation there, and when she was fourteen, he sold her to you for six thousand francs."

My face must have shown how aghast I was because Odette shot me an interesting look — I'd call it a challenge — as she went on.

"She refused to marry you," Pinto said, "so you stripped her naked" — Odette's hands flew, showing how I stripped her — "at a rugby match and shoved her onto the playing field. Thousands of Polynesians saw her shame."

A hunched-over old lady from the crowd hissed. I've been

booed plenty of times, by impatient fans, but never hissed. It caused a squirrelly sensation in the spine.

"Still, she refused to marry you, so you bought the bank note on her father's boat and foreclosed. You destroyed the family business."

"That's a good thing, right? I mean, her father sold her. Wouldn't ruining the old goat be considered good?"

"Family is sacred in Polynesia. Odette loved her papa and what you did was villainous."

"But I didn't do it."

"Tell her that," Pinto said. "She claims you did, and I don't see why she would lie."

Neither did her friends, the security guards, the gendarme, or the crowd. I was a stranger in a strange land.

"Penniless," Pinto said, which is a word I'd never heard in conversation, "penniless, she fled to Haiti and in despair she became mistress of a plantation owner. But you followed her and when the owner would not give her to you, you threatened to expose them to his mother."

"Mother?"

"And wife. The plantation owner was forced to cast her out into the wilderness."

"Awfully Old Testament of him."

"He was black."

By now the crowd was transfixed. Odette was putting on a goddamn Greek drama, one of those plays where by the end everyone beds down their mama and pokes out their own eyes.

"She escaped in a refugee boat that sank off the Florida coast. All but Odette drowned. She was rescued by drug smugglers who forced her to mule dope into Miami." Pinto paused to listen. He asked Odette a question. She answered and went on with the hogwash.

"You caught up again in Bogota, but she hid with nuns until they could smuggle her to Paris, where she is now trying to start a new life."

Pretty Odette gave me a look that said, *Top that, sucker.* There was a moment of silence. Had we been in Iraq—or Wyoming—I would have been hung.

"That's the most bizarre story I ever heard. No one could possibly believe that malarkey," I said.

Pinto said, "It makes more sense than chasing her down over a belt buckle."

The gendarme placed a sympathetic hand on Odette's forearm. She sniffed back tears, murmured, *"Merci,"* and nodded as the gendarme spoke gently.

Pinto shifted Monty to his other arm. "The policeman wants to know if your friend Odette would like you arrested."

"I haven't broken any laws," I said.

"That is meaningless here."

After the gendarme said his piece, Odette's lower lip quivered. She clasped her hands, as if in prayer. The girl was good.

"Non," she said.

"Looks like you lucked out," Pinto said.

The gendarme gave Pinto the lowdown and Pinto passed it on to me. "He's willing to let you go if you promise to stay away from the girl."

"In a pig's ear."

"The alternative is arrest and tomorrow they place you on a plane for the States."

"Okay."

"Okay, what?"

"I promise."

Pinto passed this back to the gendarme, the security guards, and what by then was a good-sized mob. The mob wanted me in chains. The guards wanted to beat the stuffing out of me. The boyfriend made the most noise. He couldn't believe I was being cut loose to terrorize another day. I don't know his exact words, but the gendarme asked Odette if she wished to reconsider.

Her eyes met mine again. She said, *"Il ne ferait pas de mal à une mouche, ce cowboy."*

She turned, reeking with dignity, and walked away, her friends at her side. Grumbling, the security guards retreated back into the university. The crowd broke up with nothing worse than the old hag lady spitting on the sidewalk, there next to my boot. The gendarme gave me a long stare, as if memorizing my mug, then he, too, moved off, leaving only Pinto and Monty as Odette reached the corner and, without a backward glance, disappeared.

I kept my eyes on the spot where she had last been visible. "What'd she say there at the end?"

"She said, 'The cowboy wouldn't hurt a fly.'"

"I need your help."

Pinto Whiteside looked at me with some humor in his face. What might be called a simper. "You should have thought of that earlier, when you were flaunting your Western arrogance."

"You have to help me find out where she lives."

"Think about it a moment and see if you cannot discover a polite way of asking."

My future ability to live with myself depended on getting that buckle back. Tyson was more likely to grow up strong and decent if he had hard evidence that his father was not hopeless. "Please."

Pinto held the miserable dog up. "Monty wants you to say please to him also."

I would rather snort barbwire than talk to a dog as if it's human. God knows I've talked with horses, and the occasional bull, but I draw the line at dogs. Talking to other people's pets is stupid.

"You're humiliating me on purpose, aren't you?"

"How much do you want to find the girl?"

I looked at Monty. I swear, the dog had the same sappy, beat-down-by-gravity face as Pinto. Leather cheeks. Broom eyebrows. "Please, Monty. Can your master help me find that lying tramp who stole my champion belt buckle?"

Pinto smiled. "Only if you let me smoke."

"Christ."

15.

Pinto Whiteside took off down the sidewalk at a good clip, Monty under his arm, flip-flops flapping loudly with each step. I hustled to keep up. One thing I've noticed is there's a direct relationship between the speed people walk and the size of the city they live in. I walk GroVont, Wyoming, speed, which puts me to the rear of most folks.

"You slept with this girl you claim is a lying tramp?" Pinto asked.

I circled a three-wheeled car parked on the sidewalk. Paris doesn't have parking rules. "Her and a friend of hers. They were a double."

Most men get curious when you mention doing a double, but Pinto didn't bat an eyelash. Maybe doubles are commonplace in France. "Did your lover give her name?"

"She's not my lover. We had sex, and she only gave a first name, Odette, but the man in the philosophy department said Odette Clavel had been in Boulder."

"That's a start."

A funny little taxicab sat parked diagonally across the corner point where two streets met. The body was mustard yellow, same color as Odette's tights the night we met, and the top was electric blue. It had a silver racing stripe and PERNOD painted red across the side panel behind the back door. The car was Pinto's destination.

As he unlocked the passenger door, I said, "What's this?"

"What?"

"You drive a toy."

"It's my car. If you wish to find the girl, you'll get in." The car had a swept-back look, the shape considered futuristic about fifty years ago. I could picture Buck Rogers driving this car on Mars.

"Not the front seat," Pinto said. "Monty Clift rides in front. Paying customers ride in back."

"Am I a paying customer?"

"Cabdrivers can't give free rides. It's against city ordinance."

The backseat was covered by the same material as my aunt Delilah's davenport. "What year is this thing?"

"'Sixty-seven. I traded thirty cabochons for it. Quite the bargain, in my humble opinion."

"Depends on what a cabochon is."

"Unit of turquoise." Before Pinto started the car, he lit the cigar he'd threatened me with earlier. "That was the last year Citroën built a classic automobile. After 1967 they modified the profile to mimic the more pedantic Mercedes."

I rolled down both the backseat windows. "Does it run?"

"Of course she runs." And to prove his statement we bumped off the curb and into traffic. For the second time in my life I found myself sober and in a taxi. Just when you think you've done everything you'll ever do and the rest of your days will be variations on the familiar, experiences start popping out at you. Life is similar to riding bulls, in that respect. Self-evident Truth #5: *If you don't stretch regular, the falls will break you.*

Monty stood on his back legs with his front feet on the seat back, watching me and drooling into that facial fur you find on Scotty dogs. I leaned over the front seat to roll down his window,

too, and while I was lurched forward I got a good look at the oper-
ator license card on the passenger visor. The ID photo showed a
turkey-necked black man with a tattooed lower lip.

"This isn't your taxi," I said.

Pinto glanced at the picture of the black guy. "That's the owner
I bought it from. He quit driving to become a drug dealer. Special-
izing in North African hallucinogens, as I recall."

Back in my own seat, I said, "So you don't have a license."

"I have a license. In New Mexico."

"Why is the speed limit eighty? That seems kind of quick, for
city streets."

Pinto snorted smoke out his nose. "The signs are for kilometers
an hour, not miles."

"That explains it."

We turned the corner past a Gap store. The other three corners
on the intersection were held down by an Athlete's Foot, Wendy's,
and a Southern Baptist Church. "That's the fourth time you've
turned right," I said.

Pinto said, "I wasn't counting. Are you certain you don't wish
to purchase a piece of turquoise? What's a cowboy without
turquoise?"

"You're driving back where we started."

"Paris isn't laid out in rectangular blocks like Boise or wherever
you are accustomed to. Seen from above, the streets here resemble
a fireworks display. Intersecting sprays."

"That's the second time we've passed the old lady with the bird-
cage."

"You would be astonished at how many women in this area
carry birdcages. The city is rife with them. Listen, cowboy, I must
talk to you about something important."

"Is this as personal as your what-do-I-think-of-turquoise
question?"

"I believe my wife is cheating on me."

A suicidal maniac on a bicycle cut in front of us. The Citroën bumped his rear tire, spinning the bike rider into a three-sixty and over an outdoor bench where a couple was holding hands and gazing into each other's eyes. The bike rider did an ass plant, then he bounded up and flashed us what I took as the French bird. Monty barked, but I don't think Pinto noticed any of it.

"But your wife is a whore," I said.

"She is a courtesan. France would have no history without courtesans. No culture. You have a banal American sensibility about the subject that is completely off base."

"Your wife screws for cash."

Pinto blew a smoke screen at the windshield. "What is your point?"

"Doesn't a woman who screws for cash cheat on her husband, by job description?"

Pinto puffed smoke and made more right turns. I sat back and watched Paris. The neighborhood reminded me of the once I was in Memphis, Tennessee. Same humidity. Much more ethnic diversity than we have in Teton County.

Finally, Pinto said, "I think Mrs. Whiteside may be talking to someone other than me, revealing subjects close to her heart. Life, art, beauty."

He blew more smoke. Even with the window down, forward visibility was limited. I politely pointed out that the only conversational subjects worth the bother are subjects you can do something about, and life, beauty, and art don't qualify. I said, "A sentence without information is a dead sentence."

Pinto went on as if I hadn't said a word, which more or less shows I was right. "She has a customer who comes to her three afternoons a week, after lunch. I have no proof, but I believe they are not having sex."

"So she's finishing in the money by not doing the job. You should be proud."

I'm not sure if he heard me. Pinto Whiteside had a way of disappearing, as if he could shut off his senses, like with the biker Monty and I saw but he didn't.

"I've been there after he left the premises, and the bed looks artificially mussed. I strongly feel Mrs. Whiteside shook the sheets to make it look as if they'd been rolled in. And her bidet was dry."

I remember the first time I realized Mica was getting plowed on the side. She drove her truck into the ditch and called me on the cell phone to come pull her out. When I got there, I found tracks—size twelve, at least—leading off in the snow toward the Stagecoach Bar. She denied anyone had been with her, even after I found a torn condom foil in the ashtray. Silver Sheaf. Ribbed. I circled the far side of the ditch until I found the rubber where someone had tied a knot in the top and thrown it over the fence. Mica still denied it. Said she'd never seen that rubber before in her life.

That was the end of marriage number two with Mica. Number three started up a year later when she got pregnant with Tyson. Don't get drunk and sleep with an ex-wife for old times' sake is so self-evident you shouldn't even have to write it down.

I said, "For me, personally, a wife who doesn't screw someone else is better than a wife who does."

"Not if they talk intimately." Pinto slipped back into the funk I first saw when he admitted being saddled with unsellable turquoise. He had this way of moving in and out of deep funks. I've known women whose every mood swing showed on their face, but Pinto was the first man.

"Does your wife talk to you about life, art, and beauty?" I asked.

Cigar clamped between his teeth, Pinto drove with his left hand and rubbed Monty under the chin with his right. "Of course. She is my wife."

"My wife never talked to me about stuff like that."

"It is no wonder you are obsessed by a belt buckle."

Pinto pulled straight into a parking spot that was supposed to be parked in parallel. His rear end stuck out in traffic, but not enough to concern him. He turned off the car and shrugged around to face me.

"That'll be twenty-two euros. Common practice is to tip fifteen percent."

Pinto took me to a post office that looked like your basic stateside post office—Orem, Utah, to be specific—except the clerk sat behind a cage like in an old-time bank. I was once arrested in the Orem post office for threatening a clerk who wouldn't take a thirty-four-cent check. They only held me an hour. The arresting officer had played football against the clerk in high school. He said the guy had been born a bureaucrat and would die one. The cop wound up buying me a beer.

Another difference was the Paris post office had a public computer. I don't know what kind. It didn't look like any computer I'd seen before, but that's what Pinto said it was.

"Every post office in Paris has a computer. You can find anyone in the country, if you know how to use this machine."

"I'm hoping you do."

He took on a sly, silver-ponytail look. "I don't allow myself to touch a computer each day until I have sold at least one gemstone. It's an element of my strict self-discipline."

"Back home, that's called extortion."

"In France, it's *laissez-faire*."

"What's that mean in a language I know?"

"Free enterprise."

I checked out the machine to figure the odds of me working it without help. The directions were in French. The keyboard looked nothing like my laptop keyboard. I didn't have a clue.

"How much?"

"Thirty euros for a beautiful cabochon, ideal for the cowboy bracelet or a lady's necklace. The veining is wonderful. The color is so blue tears formed in my eyes the first time I saw this piece."

"Laying it on a bit thick, aren't we?"

"I am being honest."

I considered the alternatives. "Ten."

"Twenty-five."

"Ten. You want more, I'll walk the streets till I find someone who knows English and French both. There must be a lot of them in Paris."

"Not that will admit it to a tourist."

I waited. I'd seen his hands tremble when he put down that first Midori. Pinto was a drinker with his alcohol intake controlled by a woman. He was not in a strong bargaining position.

Sure enough, he caved. "I paid ten at the mine."

"You got robbed, same as I'm getting robbed now."

He fished in the front left pocket of his cutoffs and came out with a pretty turquoise oval, maybe an inch across. It was nice, even though I've never understood the lure of shiny rocks. Mica put a lot of stock in rocks. She bugged me for a diamond clear through three marriages. Damn things cost as much as a truck. I told her if she wanted a diamond she could buy one herself. Rocks are something you throw in water.

"Everyone takes advantage of the expatriate," Pinto said.

"I don't much care what you used to be." I stuffed the rock in my back left jeans pocket where it would no doubt get me strip-searched at the airport.

Pinto pushed buttons and studied the screen. "The name is Odette Clavel?"

"Right."

"One L or two?"

"How the heck should I know? The man in philosophy didn't spell it out."

"You are fortunate Odette is an old-fashioned name. Not common anymore." He clucked his tongue and pushed another button. "In Paris and the suburbs, we have four with one L, and one with two."

"I hope this doesn't mean miles of walking."

"There's a new listing in the fifth, near the university. The others are all quite a distance out."

"Fifth what?"

"I will write down the address." He pulled out a card that said TURQUOISE TAXI and *American Owner* above a silhouette drawing of the '67 Citroën and a phone number with ten digits—five pairs. He flipped the card over and scribbled on the back. "It's on rue St. Jacques."

"Can you point me that direction?"

"I can drive you."

"No, thanks, I can't afford any more of your help."

16.

The apartment building on St. Jacques was across from a monster of a church surrounded by a ten-foot wrought iron fence with spikes on top and a locked gate to keep people out. Next door to that was an Internet cafe and next door to that was Chinese takeout. I went into the takeout place and bought two egg rolls because they were the only food I recognized in the display there, except for a tray full of chicken feet. I wasn't flexible enough for chicken feet. The Chinese man working the counter was friendly. He called me Clint Eastwood, and meant it the good way. We got along fine with me pointing at the egg rolls and him writing the price on a pad of paper. His number 1 looked like a check mark pointed up. I don't know if that's French or Chinese.

I sat outside in the sun, watching Odette's door and eating egg rolls, hoping she would come along with my Crockett County buckle. I wondered what Tyson would do with the buckle when I gave it to him. Throw it away, maybe. Or trade it for an Xbox. I didn't care so much what he did with the buckle, so long as I gave it to him, and, later, when he's old enough to escape Mica, he can remember he once had it. I didn't want to die with him thinking about me the way I thought about my old man.

Shit and piss on myself. I'm lying again. I hate it when that happens. The truth is, I didn't want to die with Tyson thinking about
me the way my old man thought about me when he died. I didn't
need disappointment from two directions.

Dad didn't believe in hugs. To tell the truth, I don't recall ever seeing him touch a human being. He must have. I mean, I was born,
which implies touching Mom, and I figure he hauled me around or
somesuch, back when I was a baby. But I certainly don't remember
him hugging me, or squeezing my shoulder. Tousling my hair. My
theory is being a male in Wyoming had turned him emotionally
catatonic.

Most of the time, Dad worked, although I suspected that was
more getting away from Mom than any great labor ethic. He
smoked Larks and read *Fur, Fish & Game* in the bathroom, dropping
the butts between his legs into the toilet. Once, when he drove me
to school during a blizzard, we were stopped at the red light in
GroVont and he leaned forward to wipe condensation off the windshield. While he was leaned forward, he looked over at me and
asked how old I was.

I said, "Ten."

He nodded and said, "I would have guessed nine." The light
turned green and he put the truck in gear.

I said, "How old are you?"

Dad said, "Don't matter."

That's the last conversation I can remember having with him.
I've played it over in my head a thousand times, trying to read love
between the lines.

After a while, a woman with a bouquet of flowers approached
the glass door from inside. I wiped my fingers on my jeans and
crossed the street. She pushed a button on the wall and there was a
buzz in the door. I held the door open for her while she backed

through with the flowers. Big purple blossoms of a type I didn't recognize.

She said, *"Merci."*

I said, "You're welcome," and went on in. There was the one door off the lobby there. A bank of mailboxes took up part of the wall. The elevator had two doors instead of one. The outer door was on hinges, but the inner door was expandable steel, like a toddler gate. When I looked in I saw the elevator was tiny, maybe a yard square, big enough for one person if he wasn't hauling much stuff or two if they liked each other a heck of a lot. Too much like an upright coffin for me. I have a thing about coffin-shaped enclosures.

I walked up two flights of dark stairs to a hallway with a runner rug and no lights. The hallway smelled like Pine Sol. The door off to the left had a 2 on it. I knocked and waited. The door had three locks, which seemed excessive. Even foreigners must not trust foreigners. It took quite a while for whoever was in there to twist open the locks. Finally, the door opened a half inch and a female voice said, *"Qui est là?"*

I said, "Rowdy."

"Qui?"

"Don't pull that speak-no-English on me again."

"Je ne vous connais pas."

I threw my shoulder into the door and blew her back across the room.

Frenchmen sprouted from all over the place—the couch, the kitchen, a door I think led to a bedroom. In two seconds, seven of them ranging from five to eighty-five clustered together over by the flickering TV that was set on a game show where three girls tried to get a date with one boy. Big eyes ran in the family. High foreheads. Five females and two males stared at me in various degrees of fear and disgust, and the most disgusted of the bunch was the matriarch. I've observed that Paris has an amazing number of old women under five feet tall, with curled spines. I have two theories:

(1) French women lose more height as they age than Wyoming women, or (2) hardships during World War II caused an entire generation of stunted growth. Whatever the cause of her seahorse shape, that old woman wasn't about to take any guff off me.

Soon as the old lady paused for breath, I said, "Odette Clavel lives here, right? Where is she?"

All seven cut loose a maelstrom of language. The littlest girl was asking questions of the father, who seemed to know the answers until his wife told him he was wrong. The girl I'd bounced across the room with the door looked eighteen and pretty. Where the family eyes made Grandma owlish, on the girl they created an open, innocent face, like you see on velvet paintings.

Because she was the prettiest person there, I addressed her. "Whoa, dammit. I'm not here to hurt you. I need Odette Clavel. This is twenty-four-oh-six rue St. Jacques, apartment three-oh-two, right?"

Amid the squawking, a boy of twelve or so was pushed to the front. He wore khaki shorts and a tan nylon jacket with a school emblem on the breast. Turns out, he was the only member of the family to speak English. The kid was a brave little cuss. I don't know if, at twelve, I would have stood up to a madman who broke through the door.

"Sir, my father and mother wish to know why you have crashed into our home."

"I'm looking for Odette Clavel." I showed the boy the address on the taxi card. The others gathered around, throwing in their two cents.

I said, "Apartment three-oh-two."

A murmur ran through the collective family. "We live in two-oh-two," the boy said.

"How can that be?"

The teenage girl jabbered to the boy, who nodded, then turned his attention back to me. "In France, the ground floor is ground floor. The story above that is number one."

I counted in my head. "So, the fourth floor is the third floor?"
The boy said, "That is so." The old lady scowled.
I said, "Oh."
"Your quarry must live one story above us," said the boy.

How embarrassing can you get? I looked from face to face, the
old dwarf to the father to the pretty girl to the child. Not a one of
them saw the humor of my mistake.

"Wrong apartment." I backed on out, checking to see if I'd dam-
aged their door. Luckily, it looked fine. "You folks go back to whatever you were doing."

Why would an entire nation call the second floor the first? Anyone
might have made the same mistake, only it wasn't anyone. It was
me. I'd not only knocked on the wrong apartment, I'd used violence to gain entry. I felt like slime. That little girl could well have
a tainted view of Americans the rest of her life. I don't mind her
hating the United States if she bases her hate on our government, but this hate would be based on me, personally. That's not
good.

As I walked up the stairs, I tried to come up with a way to make
it up to the family. I could give them money, but that seemed like
such an American way to apologize. I could go back and actually
apologize, only I didn't think they would open the door to me now.
They'd had enough.

Nobody was home at the real 302. I knocked. I waited. No
answer. Odette's door only had two locks and I might have been
able to kick it in, but that felt like a bad idea for a man who claims
to learn from his mistakes.

Instead, I sat on the fourth—their third—floor landing and
fished through my saddlebag for a Bic pen and a receipt from Starbucks in the Denver airport. I wrote *I am sorry I intruded. Please forgive my lack of tact,* which is all will fit on a Starbucks receipt. I went
down a flight and slipped the note under their door. There was just

enough of a gap to push it through. Before I let go of the receipt, someone inside snatched it from my hand.

The lobby door across from the post office boxes had a doorbell. I rang it and, from inside, a dog went ballistic. I can't stand little house dogs who go insane at the knock on the door or ring of the bell. My mom has a dog like that. Fergie. Long-haired, fat-lipped, pug ugly. More loved than me. Mom knits her sweaters. Every time I'm home I want to stick a dowel rod up Fergie's butt and mop the floor.

The woman who answered the door had a mustache. Sagging arm skin exposed by a sleeveless blouse with a used Kleenex stuffed under the shoulder strap. Unfiltered cigarette held between her lips by a snarl. Yellow fingers with painted nails. Your typical apartment manager anywhere in the world.

"I'm a friend of Odette Clavel's. She lives on the fourth floor. I guess, third to you."

The woman slammed the door shut.

I counted to ten so as to prove I hadn't lost my temper, then I rang the bell again.

17.

Odette Clavel rattled her first key in the bottom lock, turning it two full turns counterclockwise. She pulled that key out and stuck another that looked like an old skeleton key in the top lock, which turned the other way, one full circle. She picked up the beaded purse at her feet and pushed open the door. Light sliced into her small apartment before she entered and kicked the door shut, plunging the room back into relative darkness.

Odette cooed softly, *"Robert, Robert, Je suis là."*

A cat meowed from her bedroom. Odette dropped the keys into the purse and shrugged her sweatshirt off over her shoulders. *"Robert, mon minou, tu t'es ennuyé?"*

Robert, the white Persian, stretched into the living room/kitchen combination, his tail held high. He strutted to the couch and sharpened his claws while Odette clunked her purse down on the counter. A wooden match flared, then settled into a steady flame that Odette used to light a tapered candle. She blew out the match and said, *"Pauvre bébé, tu m'as manqué aussi."*

Robert rubbed in and out of Odette's ankles while she crossed to a bookshelf and flipped a switch on the CD player. The room was filled by Miles Davis making love to his trumpet. Odette swayed in the music while Robert's *mews* grew louder, more in the way of demands. To the beat, Odette kicked a red Ked past the lamp on the end table into the corner. The other Ked flew into the shadows.

"Ah, Robert, t'es un chat super."

Odette put one hand on her belly, Napoleon-style, and danced into the bedroom. A few seconds later, she danced back into the living room, minus the skirt. Wearing only bra and panties now, she thrust forward to the music, swinging her hair to the front, then leaned back and boogied her breasts from side to side.

"Allez, Miles!"

The music was "So What" from *Kind of Blue.* Odette wrapped herself in the notes, swaying gently, her eyes half closed. She tossed her glasses on the counter, then danced into the kitchen side of the room, led there by Robert's insistent mews.

Her body undulating like willows in a stream, she opened the refrigerator. Soft light reflected off her skin, throwing shadows on her ribs and the shallow dent of her collarbone. She bent at the waist to search the bottom shelf. *"Voilà, minou."*

She pulled out a pint bottle of heavy cream, popped the top, and poured a stream into the flat-bottomed bowl on the floor beside the refrigerator. Robert let out a *meow* and stuck his nose up against the cream's surface, his tongue darting in and out, lapping away. Odette put the cream back in the refrigerator, hip-bumped the door shut, and dropped onto her belly beside Robert.

Together, they shared the cream, each lapping from one side of the bowl. Odette's tongue slipped out, in, out. Her eyes closed, savoring the texture of cream.

Miles wailed. Odette and Robert lapped. "So What" ended and "Freddie Freeloader" started. Odette flipped onto her back on the linoleum floor. Her arms flowed to the music, up, around, wrists swiveling somewhat like a horizontal hula, or maybe a belly dancer. She dipped fingertips in the cream bowl and let droplets run into her belly hollow. She picked Robert up and set him on her crotch,

on her panties, facing her head. As Robert darted his tongue in and
out of the cream on her navel, Odette closed her eyes and shud-
dered. She dipped her fingertips again and sprinkled a trail of
cream drops up her flat stomach across her sternum and into the
cleft between her breasts. Robert licked his way into cleavage.

I turned on the lamp. "That's about all I can take."

"You." Odette sat up, which upset Robert's balance, causing
him to bury his claws in her flesh, causing Odette to yelp and flail
at the cat stuck to her chest.

"You always practice animal rituals when you come home?" I
asked.

Odette extricated the claws with a minimum of scarring. "Only
when I am alone." She stood and grabbed a dish towel to blot her
breasts. The bra was the sexy kind that left skin exposed above the
nipple and the exposed skin was pink, lighter than the skin on her
arms. It looked soft as a bubble gum bubble.

Odette dropped the towel onto the counter and waited with her
arms at her sides, staring at me where I sat on the couch with my
hat in my lap. I'd been napping. We held the mutual staredown a
full minute.

"I paid money to take a leak," I said.

"What is leak?"

"Piss. Can you believe that? And the coffee in this country
tastes like melted-down snow tires."

"Our coffee is the finest in the world."

"If you folks are so proud of your coffee, why not sell a whole
cup at a time?"

I studied Odette closely. I hadn't gotten a chance to look at her
good the night we had sex. The bra and panties were black, so she
didn't totally go against the French color scheme. Her legs belonged on a teenager while her neck was the neck of a woman. Had
the circumstances been better, I would have loved her for her neck
alone. She had nice-sized breasts, for a short girl. A lot of your
short girls are fairly breastless, not that it bothers me. I'd lots rather

see a woman's bare back than her boobs. Sometimes, I'll sleep with a bunny just so I can look at her back.

"Where's my buckle?"

She slid her glasses back on. Apparently, they made her feel more dressed. "It's not here."

"I know that much."

With the couch lamp on, Odette scoped out the apartment, which had obviously been searched. I didn't trash the place. I'm not that kind of boy. But I did search thoroughly and not everything was put back exactly as I'd found it.

"You have flour on your face," she said.

I did what anyone would do and rubbed a hand over my cheek.

"Your chin," she said. "And a spot on your forehead. I can't believe you thought I flew back from Colorado and hid your belt buckle in the flour bin."

"You might have come home this afternoon, after you knew I was in town."

"I didn't. Are you planning to rape me because if you're not I'd like a cup of tea."

"You're not in any danger."

"I know." She opened the refrigerator and took out a bottle of Glacier water. She screwed off the top and emptied the bottle into a cast iron teapot on the stove. "I could have had you deported this afternoon."

I stood and walked to the counter so it was between us, but I could still see all of her. My legs had gone numb while I slept, sitting on her couch, waiting. "Why didn't you?"

She glanced up from the bulk tea she was spooning out of the tin. "You have the nice bottom."

She spooned the tea into this wicker cone thing with a handle. It seemed like an odd way to make tea.

"You didn't have me arrested and booted out of France because you like my bottom?"

"I like the way it fits your denim jean."

When the water boiled, she turned off the heat and dropped the cone in the pot so its lip balanced on the pot lip. It didn't look as efficient as a string stapled on a bag, but you have to give foreigners credit for ingenuity. She took a lemon from the refrigerator and opened a drawer to pull out a tiny knife.

"I think you wanted me to find you," I said. "You expected me to be here when you came home."

"I thought perhaps you would be hidden outside the front door." She pointed the knife at my neck. "I certainly did not expect you on my divan. How did you get in?"

"The woman downstairs has a set of keys."

"The concierge?"

"She didn't tell me her name."

Odette cut the lemon into eighths. "Mademoiselle Frangot despises everyone. Why would she let you into my apartment?"

"You'd be amazed what people will do when you threaten to kill their dog. I have to search you now."

Odette's mouth formed into a hint of a smile. She held her arms out at her sides, the cutting knife still in the fingers of her right hand.

"Okay, cowboy. Search me."

I felt stupid threatening to search a woman wearing nothing but a bra and panties. These weren't the kind of panties Mica used to wear, either, the cotton kind where you could hide small items, like a cigarette. If Odette had had a quarter stuffed in her panties I could have called it, heads or tails. She stood there, smiling slightly, waiting to see what I would do. She was considerably more comfortable in her underwear in front of a stranger than I would have been.

"Where do you think I have your precious buckle secreted?"

"Your purse there. I'll have to look through your purse."

"If you must."

Odette got out china cups and saucers while I dumped her beaded purse onto the counter. The thought of drinking tea from real cups on saucers kind of excited me. It was like being sophisticated.

"Do you take cream?" she asked.

I flashed on drops of cream across her pink belly. "Uh, no, I guess not. Whatever's standard around here. How do you drink it?"

"Without."

"That's fine by me."

Miniature Kleenex pack, birth control wheel, key chain from Disney World, address book, leather wallet too small to hide a championship buckle, cell phone, Advil, Altoids, William James's *Emotions* in a heavily thumbed paperback, fancy ink pen, a hotel key card from the Boulder Inn, nail scissors, a nostril stud, a small bottle of perfume with French writing on the label — no buckle. Robert jumped on the counter to walk amidst the clutter. I rubbed the cat behind his ears and tried to picture what Odette was like based on her stuff. She wasn't a barrel racer or a bunny, and that put her outside my range of experience.

Odette brought my tea over and we stood facing each other across the counter. I started to put junk back into her purse, but she said, "Never mind. I know where it all goes."

The tea was okay, I guess. Basically, it tasted like weak coffee. Miles Davis ended and Chet Baker started. I'll wager there's not one bull rider in a hundred knows Chet Baker when he hears it.

"Where's the boyfriend?" I asked.

"Bernard and I had a fight. On account of you."

"Bernard? I can't believe you're sleeping with a guy named Bernard."

She eyed me through her tea steam. The more I got used to them, the more I liked what the glasses did to her eyes.

"He knows enough English to catch your insinuation this afternoon."

"I thought I was pretty direct."

She blew across the surface of her tea. "I told him I like you."

That was the most amazing statement I'd heard all day.

"From your comments he realized we made love."

I snorted into my tea. "Made love? Your English is weak, honey. I've had a fair amount of sex in my life—average for a bull rider my age, anyway—and I can say with no doubt that was the worst fuck I've ever been involved in."

"It wasn't so bad."

"I've had baseball gloves were more emotional."

Odette's eyes flashed. I'd hurt her feelings and she was one of those women who reacts to hurt feelings with anger. "You criticize me based on Giselle. I was emotional. If you'd stopped ogling her for five minutes you would have known."

She snatched up my cup even though I wasn't through. "I can't believe you didn't notice I was flowing with emotion."

"I missed it."

She rinsed the cups, savagely. "No one has ever before said I am bad sex."

"Well, I'm saying it."

"What do you expect? You make love like the dead. My husband is American and he doesn't lie there as if he is a sculpture. Maybe it is a cowboy technique." Her husband being American explained a lot about the way she talked.

"It's what you and Giselle told me to do."

"When having sex, do you always obey orders from the woman?"

That surprised me. "Yes, as a matter of fact, I do."

"No wonder your wife left you."

The conversation had turned on its head. I had gone from the righteous party whose precious property had been filched to the defensive one, accused of not satisfying my wife. I would have explained if I'd known the truth, but the fact is I don't know. Odette might be right. Mica enjoyed creative lovemaking as a teenager. Senior year, she'd been a damn nymph. Queen of the lunch break quickie. The best I ever met at giving head in a moving four-wheel-drive. Throughout our first marriage and midway into the second, she'd been enthusiastic when it came to off postures and cavities, but about the time she turned twenty-three her sexual growth spurt ground to a halt, at least with me. God knows what she did with her Pilates teacher. With me, sex had the spontaneity of a rodeo parade — do this, do that, Mica comes, do that the other way, I come, she says, "Get off, you're crushing my boobs," I roll over, sleep.

The last time we had relations she wore headphones and listened to a book on tape throughout the event — *Women Who Run With the Wolves*. It took one whole side of a cassette to get her off. I don't think she would have ever made it had it been a CD instead of a tape.

"If you will excuse me," Odette said. "I am going to bed." She walked out of the kitchen, turned off the music, and went into her bedroom. Robert and I followed.

In contrast to the semi-neat living room, the bedroom was a pit. The closet was small and she made up for the lack of space by piling clothes on the floor. If the piles had a system, I didn't see it. There was a bookcase crammed two-deep with books that were ninety percent French. The few titles I could read were philosophical and of no interest. Her desk was so cluttered with papers and catalogues I'd been into my second search before I found a laptop buried under the junk.

Odette undid the front clasp on her bra and let it drop to the floor.

"So, where's my buckle?" I asked.

She opened the closet door and took an ankle-length cotton nightgown off a nail. "Giselle kept it. She's the one who stole it in the first place. For a souvenir of our adventure. We didn't know it was important to you."

"It said BULL RIDING CHAMPION right on the front. How could you think it wasn't important?"

Odette stepped out of her panties and pulled the nightgown

on over her head. The hem caught on her nipple hoop for a moment before it dropped to her ankles. She was remarkably unself-conscious about her body. Even at the height of our compatibility Mica would have pulled on the nightgown first before dropping the panties.

"We figured you had dozens," Odette said.

"That's an understandable mistake," I said. "Knowing me."

She walked on into the bathroom and I followed. Robert stayed curled on the pile where her bra had landed. Odette loaded her toothbrush with this French toothpaste—a red gel.

I sat on the side of the tub. I'd expected to find a bidet because I'd seen one in a movie, but the bathroom was basically American, all except the flusher hung on a chain up by the ceiling and the tub had a two-foot rubber hose clamped on the nozzle. "It doesn't make any difference. You wouldn't ball an actor and rip off his Oscar, just because he had two."

She looked at me in the mirror. "Giselle might."

After brushing, Odette cleaned her face with a circular pad thing. She was quite thorough. She leaned close to the mirror and concentrated on her skin with an intensity men don't give to details. I enjoyed watching.

"Where is Giselle now?"

Odette rubbed cream on her neck and thighs. "I do not know."

"Where does she live?"

"She won't be home tonight. She is at a meeting."

I didn't believe that for a minute. It was two A.M., for Christ's sake. Nobody goes to a meeting at two A.M. Not even AA.

Odette hitched up her nightgown and sat on the toilet. "She will probably be at the Pléiade Cafe in the morning. She usually is. We could go there and search for her. In the morning."

I found myself staring down at the LOVE ME tattooed in French across her toes. It seemed an odd message to permanently affix to your body, as if Odette needed more attention than the rest of us. She reached for the toilet paper and front wiped. I hadn't heard any pee striking water, so the toilet must have been designed for female rim shots.

"Do you have a location from which to sleep?" she asked.

"I'll bunk on the couch out there, where I can keep an eye on you."

"You no longer trust me?"

"Let's say I know which drawer you keep the knives in."

She stood and let her nightgown settle. "Rowdy, you are the most suspicious person I ever met. You must be terribly unhappy."

18.

Odette loaned me a well-used quilt — alternating squares of chickens and sheep. I finished off the dregs of my Beam, then stuck my boots under the legs of her chair there, by the couch, so she'd be less likely to steal them. My folded-up clothes, all except the undershorts I slept in, went on the chair with my hat, brim up, on top. I used the saddlebag for a pillow.

I've never been one to have trouble sleeping, but that night I got to worrying over Tyson. I thought about what it would have been like to grow up with my dad around, and, frankly, I think it would have been nice. I might be a normal guy now, happy with backyard barbecues and televised sports. I'd own two guns and a dog. If Dad hadn't died, I would probably have a 401(k). Even when he was alive, I didn't see so much of him. Dad worked for county electric all day and spent his evenings at the Elks Club, except in winter, when he plowed most nights. That's how he died, from plowing. Avalanche took him out. Mom woke me at dawn and told me Dad had gone to a better place. I thought she meant San Francisco.

Now Tyson was growing up, not just without me to show him how to throw a rope or drive a truck on ice, but with a woman whose voice oozed bile at the mention of my name. Ty was pretty much the only good thing I'd done so far with my time. It seems a shame for the only good thing a man does to think of him as a clown.

Odette's door opened. She padded into the living room, barefoot, lifted the quilt, and slipped in next to me. We spooned on our sides, with my back to the back of the couch, one arm under her head and the other across her shoulder. The couch was plenty wide for two. It didn't take me long to fall asleep.

I dreamed I was at my funeral. I mean, I'm not sure where the I who was dreaming was. I often have dreams that are like watching a movie in that I'm not in them. I only see them. The I I was dreaming about was in a cheap coffin at the front of the Presbyterian church there in GroVont. Ty sat on the first pew. His feet didn't touch the floor, and he had on my belt buckle. He wasn't crying but his eyes looked like maybe he had been recently. Mica was holding hands with the Pilates teacher. Mom had Fergie on her lap. Dad sat in back, smoking a Lark.

The preacher knocked on my casket three times—*Knock, knock, knock*—and said, "Here lies a man who never quite woke up."

The next thing I knew a key was rattling in the lock again, only this time it wasn't Odette. She had rolled over in her sleep and we were now facing each other with our foreheads touching. She had nice breath, a little sagebrushy. My arm was still across her shoulder and her knees were between mine. It would have been a pleasant way to wake up had a French crap-storm not broken out when Bernard the boyfriend found us.

He shouted something that brought Odette to. She blinked a couple times, processing the who and where, then she yelled something back and they both took off. Arguments in foreign languages sound so much more vicious than arguments in English. Maybe

English isn't the language of domestic discord. My squabbles with Mica started out interesting enough, but they soon degenerated to her yelling, *"Fuck you,"* and me yelling, *"Fuck off."* I can't say, not knowing the French word for *fuck*, but Odette and Bernard seemed more articulate. Near as I can tell, Bernard claimed they had a mutual exclusivity deal when it came to sleeping on the couch with someone, and Odette thought Bernard was a horse's ass. I imagine they were both right.

I fished in my saddlebag for my toothbrush and wandered off to the bathroom, where I took a morning leak and checked out the red gel toothpaste. It didn't taste like Crest. Had a hint of spearmint, maybe some sage, which would account for Odette's sleep breath.

I reentered the living room in time to see Odette slap the beJesus out of Bernard. Her fingerprints showed through his stubble. He reared back a fist and was on the verge of knocking her senseless when I stepped in. I touched the index and middle fingers of my right hand to Bernard's chest.

"Whoa, pard," I said, thereby using the P-word twice in two days. It felt right this time. I decided to use it whenever I could in Paris. "There's a time and place for that behavior and this isn't it."

Bernard looked confused.

Behind me, Odette said, "What?"

"Odette and I have an errand to run. You want to beat her up, come back later. *Parlez-vous anglais?*"

Bernard looked from me to Odette and back. He didn't know what to do. He had maybe six inches' height on me, and thirty pounds of weight, but then again I was a cowboy and he wasn't.

He barked, *"Salope!"* at Odette, which any idiot alive could translate as *cunt*—same thing an American male either thinks or says when he loses a fight with a woman. Then he left.

Odette put on her glasses. "There is a time and place for the striking of women?"

I smiled at her. "In a fair fight, you'll rip the sucker's throat out."

. . .

An hour, a shower, and two jiggers of French mud later, Odette and I walked across this park next to a castle, looking for breakfast. I think it was a castle; it might have been a palace. We don't have either in GroVont, so I'm not sure of the difference. It was one hell of a big building. Maalox-colored, with doodads around the top. The park was what used to be the castle's front yard, back when the castle was a private house. Now, the castle was a museum or something governmental, and the front yard was a park.

There was a circle pond with concrete sides. Little boys raced screaming around the pond, poking toy sailboats with sticks so the boats would sail away across the water, only to bump against the far side where the boys with sticks waited to turn them around again. The game looked like something Ty would enjoy. I wondered why American kids never got the imagination to think of it.

About a hundred mothers and nannies stood around baby carriages, watching the boys. Black grandfather chairs had been set up two or three deep around the pond, but only a few intellectuals reading books sat in them. I saw a couple of deadly earnest journalers. In one area, by a wall, a dozen old men were smoking and playing chess. They had that concentrated posture you run into in a Texas domino parlor. I finally saw my first beret.

"Do you love your wife?" Odette asked. She was wearing stretchy pants that came down to her calves and a brick-red sweater with a matching scarf. Sparkly barrettes kept the hair off her face. I was wearing what I had on yesterday.

"What kind of question is that?"

She led me off toward a grove of trees where there was a stand she said sold breakfast. "It is a simple question. The night of our tryst, you spoke of your former wife. I wonder if you love her."

We had to step off the walkway to let joggers go by. We'd only been in the park five minutes, but we'd already been passed by at least fifty joggers. Most of them ran openmouthed. Not a one met my eyes, much less said, "Hey."

"There's nothing simple about that question," I said.

Odette switched on her high-beam look. "You seem lonely."

Which is a hell of a thing to say. I was eight time zones from home where no one knew squat about bulls or the scoring system for riding one. I didn't know the language, and what these people thought of as normal was anything but normal for me. I mean, they expected you to pay to pee. Of course I was lonely. I was alone.

"Listen, Odie."

"Odie is Garfield's dog. I am Odette. My grandmother was Odette. Her grandmother was Odette."

"Odette. What we have here is basically a hostage situation. You're stuck with me until we find Giselle and my buckle. This love talk is not appropriate material for chitchat."

"Did the union result in a child?"

"Nosy question. I don't do nosy questions."

We walked on past these stubby ponies that were hooked up four abreast and pulling carts full of what I automatically assumed were brats. I always assume that at pony rides. Don't ask me why. The horses were Shetlands, although not the American strain. More like potbellied Welsh ponies with strange pinto patterns I hadn't seen on Shetlands out West. They had jumpy gaits, useless for anything more strenuous than pulling kiddie carts in city parks. Baskets were mounted off their little rear ends to catch scat.

"I have a boy. Tyson. He's seven years old now. He's a good kid."

She talked without looking at me. "Does he have his father's appearance?"

"I don't remember. I don't see much of him."

Odette made a *Mmmn* sound, like that explained everything, which it didn't. "Do you love your son?"

"Of course I love my son. Do college girls ask stupid questions?"

"It is not a stupid question. My father does not love me."

"How do you know?"

"He told me."

"Your father said he doesn't love you, out loud?"

She nodded. "The night I became a woman."

Took me a while to figure out what *became a woman* meant. In Wyoming, getting laid doesn't make you a grown-up. "He was just pissed off. He wouldn't have said that on a regular night."

"He would have thought it."

The weather had clouded up since yesterday. It still wasn't cold, even though most people we met wore coats and sweaters. Scarves galore. The business-looking men carried umbrellas, which is something you almost never see in Wyoming. We have snow and wind, but not enough rain to make an umbrella a worthwhile purchase. What I wondered was the percentage of children who grow up thinking their parents don't love them compared to the percentage of parents who don't love their children. My guess is we're talking a wide spread.

Odette stopped walking and turned to face me. "Maybe if you saw your son more you wouldn't fly halfway around the world to retrieve a clothing accessory."

The breakfast stand was more of a sheep wagon with wooden wheels, a counter, and a fifteen-inch, flat frying pan where a pretty girl with dark waves in her hair and thick eyebrows made crepes. It was interesting to watch her ladle the batter and spread it in a spiral to the very edge of the pan without any runoff. She poured on the topping—chocolate for Odette, Grand Marnier for me— then did this thing with the spatula I'd never seen done before and the crepes came out like a tortilla turned into an ice cream cone, the pointy-bottomed kind, that she put in white paper and handed across.

I couldn't understand how she got away with selling Grand

Marnier in a park. "There's little kids come to her stand," I said. "Are they allowed to buy crepes soaked in Grand Marnier?"

"Of course. Why shouldn't they?"

"Does she have a liquor license?"

"You don't need a liquor license to sell crepes. You need a crepes license."

Odette didn't see the moral difference between chocolate syrup and Grand Marnier. All I know's if they sold booze-saturated pancakes in GroVont there'd be teenagers lined up down the block. Mine tasted great, although it was somewhat insubstantial for breakfast. I hadn't had any meat or potato since hitting the country. No wonder the French are skinnier than Americans.

"Why're French people so nuts for crepes?" I ate mine by sucking out the juice, then biting off the breading. "They're just pancakes without baking powder. I was in a place yesterday and it seemed like that was all anyone ate."

"Why are Americans so nuts about hot dogs?" Odette asked, as usual switching the question so I was on the defensive end of the deal.

"'Cause we like food you can put ketchup on." I didn't believe that. I only said it because that's what a French person would expect me to say. I'd been in town twenty-four hours and I was already acting more American than I acted back home. It's like I was pouring myself into a preconception. Pretty soon, I'd be saying "Yep" and "Nope" and calling cattle *doggies*.

We ate our crepes as we walked on down the park past another raft of joggers. Some wore Walkman headsets, but a surprising number were jogging with hands-free cell phones that must have made them pant like obscene telemarketers. Every fifty feet or so we walked by a statue on a pedestal. Olden people in states of near nudity, mostly. Lots of rape scenes. Your cowboy poets are obsessed with human and animal excretions, which is gross, but child's play compared to rape-as-art.

Odette did a handstand. The girl seemed to enjoy doing

unpredictable stuff with her body. She walked five or six hand-steps, then sprang back-over-front onto her feet.

She said, "Try it. You'll have a new perspective."

"I like my old perspective."

We crossed a street without getting run over and Odette took me to a building with glass brick walls, like a Southern bus station. Just past the entrance, a wide staircase went underground. "The Pléiade is in the ninth," Odette said.

I said, "Ninth what?"

Same as yesterday, when people threw numbers around, Odette thought I was kidding. "We'll take the metro."

At the top step, I balked. "I don't do well in mine shafts."

She made it two steps down the stairs before she realized I hadn't followed. "It's not a mine shaft. It's a metro, like a New York subway without the urine. You've ridden subways, no?"

"No."

She came back up and pulled me by the arm. I resisted. "Underground is where you go when you're dead. If God wanted us underground, we'd be born dead."

Odette was not entertained. "You ride the bulls and are unafraid."

"I'm plenty afraid when I mount a bull. Man would be an idiot if he wasn't."

"But you climb up on the bull anyway. You conquer the fear."

I nodded. This wasn't the place to explain adrenaline addiction and how time expands during danger.

"Why do you fear the metro?" she asked.

"I'm not afraid. I just think it'd be quicker to flag down a taxicab."

"A taxi would cost you thirty euros, if we could find an honest driver."

"I met one yesterday. He's American."

She pulled on my forearm, leading me down. "Come," Odette said. "I will protect the cowboy."

19.

Okay. I'd planned on skipping the early life nonsense—there's nothing more pitiful than writers who blame the way they are now on what happened before—but if I leave this part out, you'll take me for a shavetail and we wouldn't want that. Uncle Ed. Family Republican. Thinks truck drivers are cowboys 'cause they wear the boots. Taught his kid to swim by tossing him off the end of the dock. Pride of his life is the condition in which he keeps his knives.

"Show me a man's knives and I'll tell you all you need to know about the man." When Ed got married for the third time, he carried a Colt AR-15 rifle down the aisle.

Mom, who couldn't keep a secret if the future of America depended on it, told Uncle Ed I slept with a night-light. This was after the avalanche nailed Dad and before I climbed on my first bull. Ed decided it was shameful for a ten-year-old boy to need a night-light and he was going to cure me. He shut me up in a kindling box, padlocked the door, and threw blankets over the top so no light came through the cracks. A kindling box is no better than a coffin except it has air holes. You can't bend your knees or lift up your arms. There's spiders and centipedes. Mice. You want to warp a kid but good, lock him in a kindling box overnight. I learned how to sleep without a light, but, for me, the price was not worth the gain. That was the last time I cried, before Paris, and I never let Mom find out I was afraid of anything ever again.

So, here I am a wimp when it comes to enclosed darkness and here is Odette dragging me underground. She had me at a disadvantage. I walked with my eyes straight ahead, like crossing a creek on a log. Every now and then I told myself to breathe. Whenever I thought, Gee, I hope the ceiling doesn't collapse, I would knock on wood, so I was constantly knocking on wood. At the ticket place there, I found a pencil stub for the purpose and took it. Self-evident Truth #6: *You can never knock on wood too often in a tunnel.*

Odette showed me how to stick the ticket in a slot in a machine, then it shot through and out again and the turnstile turned when you pushed through. You had to be quick or people stacked up on your backside and grumbled. We walked down a long tunnel with tile walls and down steps and through another tunnel. There were splits and side tunnels with the directions in French for where they led. Odette could have run off and ditched me and I imagine I would have died down there. One thing you don't want is to get dependent on your hostage for survival.

I heard music and we came out in a big cave room with spoke tunnels leading all over. Two black men dressed in traditional Muslim attire were playing music — saxophone and a waist-high drum thing you hit with your hands like a bongo. They were incredibly good. Even in my late stages of panic attack, I could tell they were way better musicians than what we have back home. They were playing a free-form jazz thing, I don't know what it's called. The drummer closed his eyes and at the end of a saxophone riff he cried out, *"Ha!"*

"Do these guys live down here?" I asked Odette.

She hadn't been paying them proper attention. "I imagine they go to the streets when they are not working."

"So they stay underground all day and only surface at night?"

"It's their job. You have a job. They have a job. You work where you must."

I dug in my pockets and had Odette take some euros over to drop into the open saxophone case. She tried to make me do it, but I preferred staying where I could hold on to the rail along the wall there.

Odette called me a "silly cowboy" and she kissed me. Not much of a kiss. Nothing wanton, but it was on the lips and did signify goodwill. I watched her walk over to the musicians and drop my money into the case. She said something and pointed toward me. The saxophone player nodded acknowledgment. The drummer kept his eyes closed. I was frozen in place, wondering why Odette had kissed me when she knew full well I was afraid.

We went down more steps to a platform by a drop-off into a ravine that had two sets of train tracks running along the bottom. I stayed as far from the drop-off as I could get, for fear the vertigo would pitch me onto the tracks. I knew from reading about New York that one rail down there would kill you dead if you touch it, but I didn't know which one. Now I know how city folks feel camping in grizzly country. It's not the danger, it's the damn ignorance that makes you shake.

Pretty soon a train came *whooshing* down through the tunnel. The double doors opened with a hiss of air, like the vacuum tube at a drive-up bank, and a horde of people surged off the train. The horde going on the train didn't wait till the ones getting off got off. The getting-on bunch charged right into and through the getting-off bunch. No one looked at anyone else. I have no idea how they did it, but Odette was right there amongst them, with me in tow.

Once inside, we had to stand much closer to other people than the cowboy code allows and hold on to this pole in hopes of not falling when the train took off. I couldn't have fallen anyway. There were so many bodies around us I would have come up against someone who was against someone all the way back to the wall. It was like a mosh pit you see on MTV, only with umbrellas. Odette was watching me, a smile kind of flickering across her face.

"How can people live like this?" I asked.

She leaned toward my ear to talk. "The Paris metro is safer than your American streets. Just watch out for pickpockets."

I automatically felt for my billfold, which, I suppose, was a mistake since anyone watching would now know that I kept it in my front pocket instead of my back. I'd left my passport and American money at Odette's, hidden under one of the clothes piles in her room, but I had a good deal of my French money and my PRCA card. I didn't want to lose that.

The train started up and, sure enough, the forward thrust pulled the crowd back into an even tighter pack. Odette's lips brushed my earlobe. I liked that. She said, "Like cows on the trail drive, you think?"

"More like canned sardines," I said.

A man off my elbow broke the don't-look rule and glared at me. He had on a black suit and carried a leather briefcase with initials on the front—CJC. If he was half as important as he looked, he should have been in his own car.

"I didn't mean you. Don't be so sensitive." I turned to look away from him and my hat knocked a lady's eyeglasses off. She lit into me like a hornet and I was happy not to know the language. I bent over to retrieve her glasses and offended someone behind me. I never saw who, just felt the stab at my butt and heard a *hmmf.* When I came up, Odette was laughing. She put her hand over her mouth.

"I hope you are entertained," I said.

She said, "Immensely."

We went on three or four stops and each stop more people came onto the train than got off. I stood there thinking no more would surely fit and here came two women pushing strollers, a batch of American college kids with sixty-pound backpacks, and a guy looked like Buffalo Bill Cody with a sheepdog on a leash. The only plus was each time it got more crowded I had to inch closer to

Odette until her right breast pressed into my left ribs and her face was up against mine. I have to admit she'd become a distraction. I was in Paris to find my buckle and get the hell back to Denver in time to reach Dalhart before they turned my bull out, but every time I thought I knew where I was headed and why, this woman started breathing in my face.

She smiled at me from four inches out. Her eyes were the brown of half-and-half cream in fresh coffee. They were highly curious, compared to most eyes I've looked into. I turned my gaze away from Odette before we fell into one of those meaningful eye contact moments that get you in trouble no matter what you do to get out of them. I looked at the toddler down at knee level because toddlers are a safe place to look in a crowd. Anywhere else can cause problems. This one was blond and chubby and about Ty's size back when I last lived with him on a regular basis. Ty used to straddle my boot and play horsey. I imagine I enjoyed it more than he did. There was a song I used to sing while he rocked, about the old gray mare not being what she used to be. Mica hated it.

"We leave at the next station," Odette said.

The crowd was so thick I almost didn't make it out the sliding doors in time. Odette had to hold my hand and pull. I'm not adept when it comes to forcing my way through strangers.

I was never so glad to surface in my life. "Let's don't do that again," I said.

Odette said, "Do what?"

We came up at a six-way intersection that didn't look any different from where we went down. Fancy women. Thin men. Tiny cars. I had no idea which way was north or the direction we'd come from. Think of yourself as popping up in Oz.

Odette turned right and took off. I followed.

I said, "Do you love your husband?" Okay, I'm a turd for asking her what she'd asked me. Odette was the villain in this deal. She'd stolen my stuff, and I had no cause to get involved in her personal life. But we'd slept together on the couch, and — Self-evident

Truth #7—*Sleeping-next-to is at least as intimate as banging.* Besides, I'd been underground with her and come back alive.

"Of course I love my husband."

"Then why aren't you with him?"

Odette stopped walking and her arms shot out in a *Give me a break, you nitwit* gesture. "Because he took advantage of my trusting spirit and broke my heart. He is an American." She started walking again, faster than before. "I was a fool. Ever since William James I have believed Americans when they tell the same lies that I would never believe coming from a Frenchman. It is my tragic weakness."

She gave me a fierce look. "You had better not break my heart."

"Cowboys break hearts," I said. "Bull riders show women the full potential of life itself. Then we move on down the road."

"I am already familiar with the full potential of life itself."

She pointed catty-cornered across the street to a cafe with dark green windows and a single, unoccupied table out front. "Armand's apaches meet him here every morning to learn their assignments."

"Armand?"

"Giselle's man. He is charismatic. You must beware of his magnetic force."

"And Armand has a football team?"

"I do not understand."

"I know he doesn't have a tribe of Indians."

Odette stepped into the street and we crossed diagonally, which is another way to irritate French drivers. "*Apache* is a French word. It means ruffians. Sabots. Armand sends his followers out to do battle with American imperialists. I myself have cut tires on Pizza Hut delivery scooters."

"Back in Wyoming everyone says Pizza Hut is a front for imperialism."

"The American franchise system is a relentless assault on indigenous culture throughout the world. McDonald's is much more insidious than the CIA."

"That's true."

Odette put one hand on the door, but she didn't go in. "You be polite, once we are indoors."

"Why do people keep telling me to be polite?"

"These are not football players who will lose their scholarship for beating you into soup."

20.

The tables and chairs hadn't been replaced since Ernest Hemingway liberated Paris. Soccer flickered from two wall-mounted televisions more expensive than all the other furniture combined. Groups of men huddled at the bar, staring up at the televisions, a cigarette in one hand and a drink — coffee more likely than alcohol — in the other. A few looked me and my hat over, but the soccer match interested them more. A woman behind the cash register with eight-inch earrings dangling down to her armpit fuzz watched me longer than the men did. Her watching was not what I would call a welcome. There wasn't a tourist in sight, not that I could have seen one had he been there. Visibility ended about fifteen feet out.

"You think they're using a machine to pump in smoke?" I said to Odette.

"Do not exaggerate. The French abhor exaggeration."

"Maybe something's on fire."

She took hold of my hand and led me down an aisle between students and blue-collar guys in coveralls, eating lunch. The wall opposite the bar had a bunch of banged-flat tin signs that said stuff in French. There was a painting of two toddlers nursing on a wolf. God only knows where that came from.

Odette released my hand. "There is Armand now." She indicated a round table at the far end of the room.

"Which is Armand?"

"Next to Giselle," which wasn't much help because seedy-looking gentlemen sat on both sides of Giselle. "The snake is Remi, and the rugby lock is Leon. He is more bodyguard than politico. You know Bernard."

That left the man on Giselle's right as Armand. All in black, one-day beard, eye sockets you associate with vegetarians, sneer, deeply receding hairline, skin that made you think of Charolais tits. Had I run into Armand anywhere on Earth, I would have hated him on sight.

Giselle spotted me through the smoke. She nudged Armand. I nodded, the way I would to a gate puller before a ride commenced, and jumped in.

"Hey, Giselle, long time no see."

She glowered, which I took as encouraging. Nine out of ten failed rides fail in the first two seconds. Survive that first two seconds, and there's a reasonable chance you'll make the bell.

"Yo, Bernard, beat up any helpless females today?"

Bernard wouldn't look at me. From the lack of shock and awe at my appearance, I figured he'd warned the group that I was on the way. His eyes stayed down on a map of what I figured was Paris that was spread on the table there, the corners held down by beer bottles. More bottles and overflowing ashtrays littered the table. A pile of black shirts sat before the one named Remi, who looked more like a badger with pointy sideburns than a snake. I fingered the collar on the top shirt. It had a golden arches logo on the breast.

"You fellas selling hot McD uniforms? I'll bet there's a good market from guys trying to pick up chicks."

Remi muttered something ugly and negative. Odette launched

into her spiel. The henchmen and Bernard inspected their beer bottles while Armand stared at me, dead-eyed, unblinking, the look obviously developed in front of a mirror. Nearby customers cut their eyes at our group, seeing without looking.

Giselle interrupted Odette. Whatever she said was the equivalent of a verbal slap to the head. Odette said words back, Giselle let loose a torrent of scorn. I began to regret that I'd given Giselle the benefit of my dick.

Odette said, "Giselle claims you are a spy. You are CIA, working with Starbucks to destroy the Parisian antiglobalization movement so they can brutalize our culture."

"I'm here for the buckle."

Bernard mumbled, "Only the CIA would provide such a transparent cover."

I have no use for mumblers. "I'm PRCA. So is the buckle."

Giselle sat up straight, leading with her knockers. "You presented the buckle to me, as a gift."

"You are a lying tramp."

Armand went off in French for quite some time. While he rattled, I checked out the map. There was a red sticky star at an intersection by a bridge over the river. My impression was they were planning intrigue.

"Armand says his woman does not lie," Odette said.

"Took him a lot of words to say it."

"I summarized."

"Does he know his woman is a bisexual, sadistic fame-fucker?"

"He knows English. I would remain civilized if I were in your position," Odette said.

Giselle said, "No buckle. You understand that much English, cowboy?"

Remi and Leon brought their heads up to show me how surly they could be. Leon had a golf ball–sized lump on his forehead and a pearl-colored hearing aid in his right ear. Bernard focused his wrath more on Odette than me. He had his own issues. God knows what they expected. I sure as heck hadn't flown across the ocean just to say, *"Never mind,"* and fly back home.

I rested my fingertips of both hands on the edge of the table. "These boys remind me of a bunch of northern Idaho survivalists. Same body odors."

Next to me, I felt Odette bristle, as if she knew the gist of what was coming and didn't approve.

I went on. "Deep down, they can be reasoned with, but you got to get their attention."

Without asking, I pulled a chair over from the next table. Instead of sitting down, I used the chair to climb up on the round table. "You mind?" I said to Bernard as I borrowed his beer. He didn't mind, out loud, anyway. Careful not to kick over any bottles or ashtrays, I stepped onto the map, with my boots pointed toward Armand, the bar behind him, the bottles behind the bar, and the mirror behind the bottles. Not a one of the butts in the ashtrays had a filter.

"First, let me say that I am an ambassador for my country."

I paused for that to sink in. If my goal had been to get attention, I had done that. Everyone in the place was looking up at my show, even the soccer fans.

"Second, I did not give Giselle, the iron twat here, my Crockett County championship buckle as a gift, although she did sit on my face and probably does deserve compensation. I earned that buckle by staying on a bull was one hell of a lot tougher than you pud pullers."

Remi muttered. Leon growled, even though I would bet he didn't understand a word, except maybe *pud puller*. Armand smiled.

Odette said, "Rowdy."

"Third, I want my buckle back. Now!"

I threw Bernard's bottle into the mirror, which exploded. The bartender and waiter hit the floor in a hail of glass. I whirled and kicked Leon in the head knob.

Repercussions were about what you would expect.

. . .

I went for Leon first because he seemed the dangerous one of the bunch, in a fight, anyway. Remi no doubt had a knife hidden somewhere, but I figured he wouldn't pull it unless he could stick me in the back. Armand was a politician. He would order others to rape, maim, and kill, but he wasn't likely to do so himself. And Bernard didn't bother me.

Of course, these calls were based on one-on-one, which wasn't the case here. The case here was, you bring enough coyotes to one location, they'll take on a bear. Remi grabbed my leg that was in midair from booting Leon, and he lifted it. Bernard grabbed the other leg and pulled. Armand swung a bottle into my ACL. I went over. The table went over. Chaos reigned supreme.

Real fights are nothing like movie fights, especially old cowboy movies where John Wayne could throw a man through a picture window without slicing an artery, or a guy in a black hat could wallop Audie Murphy over the head with a bottle and break the bottle instead of Audie's head. People almost never get hurt bad from fistplay in movies. Happens fairly regular in life.

I was on my back on the floor, not the place to be. Remi kicked me in the mouth. I bit his ankle to the bone. As I rose, Bernard pummeled my back. Leon did the charging bull thing. Caught me in the ribs and knocked me through a little table where two berettype codgers were sipping liqueurs. They saved their drinks but lost the table.

Most of the customers stampeded away from the action but a few decided to play kill the cowboy. The ones coming and the ones going got in each other's way, giving me time to bust up more furniture. I karate-chopped Armand in the Adam's apple. He went over backward and rolled quickly onto his knees. He looked up at me with his mouth open, shocked that someone would dare hit him instead of his minions. Or maybe he was shocked he'd been karate-chopped by a cowboy. John Wayne didn't use karate moves. I learned mine from Jackie Chan movies.

That Leon was a tough bastard. He lifted me off the floor and tossed me into the bar. I bounced and kicked him in the crotch. He didn't care. I figure steroids had turned his nut sack to stone. Whatever, he was more pissed than incapacitated.

Bernard had a brandy bottle raised and ready to splatter. Odette two-handed a chair leg into his wrist so hard he dropped the bottle and fell to his knees. Odette let go of the chair leg and looked over at me.

I said, "Thank you, ma'am."

She smiled.

Giselle ducked out the back door.

I yelled, "Hold on," and took off after her. Made about three steps when Remi coldcocked me with a textbook. Four hundred pages, right in the nose. I fell and lay on the sticky floor, facing the book. It had an English title — *Synergy of Global Economics.*

Remi and Leon each took a side and yanked me to my feet. Leon twisted my right arm up behind me. Pain shot through my shoulder and I screamed, "*Yow!*" He pinned me to the wall like a bug on a windshield. Armand was in my face, spewing French invective. He held his hand out toward Remi and I was right about the knife. It was the kind you open with a button. *Zip.* Remi handed the knife to Armand. Armand stuck the blade to my throat.

He said, "We kill CIA spies here."

"I swear to God, Armand, I'm not a spy."

He grinned big and I think the son of a bitch would have cut me had the cavalry not arrived. Whistles screeched and gendarmes came pushing through the crowd, yelling things I didn't understand. Armand touched the knife button and, *zip,* the blade disappeared.

Armand breathed into my face. "Go home."

Leon let go and I fell. Next thing, the gendarmes were lifting me off the floor and the apache bunch were long gone. Only one stayed to watch was Bernard.

I said, "Boy, am I glad to see you guys."

The gendarmes didn't see it as a rescue. They took me as the perpetrator, to the point where one of them slapped handcuffs around my wrists.

"Some hoods tried to mug me," I said. "I'm an innocent tourist. Here to spend money."

Several patrons broke into explanation. They pointed at me and up in the air to show how I stood on the table, then over at the busted mirror. A guy in suspenders demonstrated my kick.

I squirmed against the cuffs. "This won't look good for your public relations. I was attacked in broad daylight."

Bernard was smug. I didn't see Odette.

I yelled, *"I am an American!"*

The cash register lady spit in my face.

21.

The French police castrated me. Symbolically. They took my boots, belt, and hat. The belt isn't important unless it's held together by a champion's buckle, and while the boots belong to the code, they're valued more by hunting guides than me, but to take a man's hat — that's cruel punishment. My hat is my soul.

Or balls, depending on the metaphor of the day. The arresting gendarmes were your typical humorless neighborhood peace officers, clean young men who lift weights and overreact to belligerence, but the booking sergeant or whatever that position is called in France was the friendliest fella I'd met in two days. Scotch-nosed, triple-chinned, a truly amused man. Happier than even the Chinese takeout guy. He leaned across the desk and shook my hand. Everything I said struck him as hilarious, even though, so far as I could tell, his English was limited to "Tommy Lee Goes to College" and "Teen Choice Awards," both of which he said several times while I emptied my pockets. One long question in French ended with "Jessica Simpson?" I think he was asking if I knew her.

I said, "We used to ball at church camp."

They had this high-tech inkless fingerprint machine, like a grocery store price scanner, that compared me to a database of terrorists. I'd been fingerprinted once before. Back in high school, on the way to a rodeo in Bear Lake, I couldn't find anyone to give money to at a gas station in Montpelier, Idaho, so I left. Ten miles later, the highway patrol came down on me like a kidnapper of children. An hour later, I was printed and dumped into a drunk tank with a man who told me he was the prophet Elijah. I was too scared to call Mom or anyone back home, so they held me through the weekend and cut me loose with no paperwork.

Maybe the no paperwork is why I didn't show up on their database cross-check, or maybe Montpelier lies outside the terrorist radar system, because the happy man read his computer while I waited, then he clapped me on the shoulder and said, *"C'est bon, vous n'avez pas de casier."*

I said, "I could have told you that."

The hang-up came when they realized I didn't have a passport on me. The booking man clucked his tongue, as if I'd disappointed him, and called someone else into the room who called someone else. A severe woman with twin hair buns covering her ears came in and glared at me while she talked on a cell phone. I explained that I hadn't planned on crossing any borders when I went out that morning. They either didn't know what I said or it didn't matter. Seems foreigners are supposed to haul their passports wherever they go, like Arizona is with green cards.

Finally, the nice fella shook my hand again. He made a big deal over showing me the cardboard box where he stuck my stuff for safekeeping. He put my hat in brim down and I had to explain that the head hole goes up, whenever you set a hat down. He acted as if it doesn't matter even though it does. He shook my hand a third time and one of the gendarmes who'd arrested me led me down a hallway designed to showcase the functionality of fluorescent lighting and shoved me into a cell. Like I say, the arresting officer was not nearly as relaxed as the booking guy.

. . .

The cell wasn't anything like you would expect if your concept of French jails is based on *The Count of Monte Cristo*. No rats, no prisoners who hadn't bathed in a decade, just regulation bars and a cell with three sets of bunk beds and your toilet-under-the-sink combination they use in American jails. Three French-speaking degenerates played cards at a wooden table, a man whose face I never saw slept on a top bunk, facing the wall, and a teenager from Chillicothe, Ohio, who said his name was Jesse, paced up and down, back and forth, cracking his knuckles and neck and ranting.

"When they busted my ass over on Rivoli I had to eat forty tabs of crystal and they threw me in here with no one who speaks English. I've been climbing walls for three days with no one to talk to."

I sat on a bottom bunk, elbows on thighs, head hung low. I was depressed no end. It's a shame for a man's identity to get so bound up in his hat that without it no one knows who he is or what he stands for. The hat had taken care of first impressions. It spoke so I didn't have to. Now, I was a nameless nonentity lost amidst millions of people who didn't care whether I existed or not. And, I was no closer to retrieving Ty's buckle and gaining my dead father's respect than I'd been at the Super Eight in Colorado. I felt ineffectual, which is not the way a bull rider wants to feel.

"I'd just as soon you not talk to me, either," I said.

Jesse had reddish hair, a pink face, and copper-colored braces on his teeth. Excessive freckling. If I'd had my hat, he would have known me saying, "I'd just as soon you not talk" was code for "One more word and I'll rip out your throat." Cowboys speak in understatements, taking for granted people will know they mean business, but this kid didn't know diddly because he didn't know I rode bulls and there was no way to tell him without telling him, which, of course, I couldn't do and still be a bull rider.

So he cracked his neck and plowed on. "Except the first day there was this fag from Bermuda. He talked fancy English, like a butler or something, but I stayed away from him. I'd rather talk to frogs who don't understand what I'm saying than a fag who does."

"They're Frenchies, not frogs."

"I've heard them call each other frogs all over town."

"It doesn't matter," I said, temporarily giving up on silent depression over letting Ty down, again. "Black people call each other nigger, but that doesn't make it okay for you. Same with fags, Okies, and goombahs. You have to be one to say it. You've been here three days?"

The kid climbed up a ladder to a top bunk. "Haven't slept a minute." He climbed back down. "They're dumping me on a plane tomorrow, shipping me back to Chillicothe." He walked around the card table, checking out each player's hand. I don't know why they didn't throttle him and be done with it. "My dad's going to kick my fanny down the stairs. I'm supposed to be studying sculpture, but I never made it to a class."

Your rodeo cowboy accustomed to all-night driving will often take diet pills or methadrine to stay awake. Personally, I'd never been able to tolerate the stuff. I'd rather guzzle coffee and pee at every rest stop than pop pills and feel like my head's being flayed.

"They usually deport Americans they arrest?" I asked.

He did pull-ups on the vertical bars, not an easy thing to do. "Unless you killed somebody. You didn't kill anybody, did you?"

"I'd rather not say. The cell might be bugged."

That got Jesse's attention. Once again, had I been wearing my hat, he would have known dry humor is my style. Bareheaded, he couldn't tell, which made him nervous and that's not a good thing if you're artificially jacked up.

He lowered his voice. "See the guy playing cards, in the middle there."

One cardplayer was Arabian, I think. He was dressed in white robes, like a suicide bomber. His hair appeared to have been Brylcreemed. No doubt, they'd taken his headgear and pride also. Another one gave off the vibes of a hard case—greasy T-shirt, antique tattoos, nose that had been broken on a regular basis. From the way he held his cigarette, you could see he didn't need a hat to convey attitude. In the middle, between those two, sat the guy my speed freak buddy was talking about. This boy was effeminate in all senses of the word. He had the eyelashes, cheekbones, and throat. Straight or gay, he would have been in big trouble in an American jail.

Jesse bounced closer to me where he thought the others couldn't hear. His meth breath was atrocious. "He's not really a guy. He's a chick. She told the booking officer that her name is Claude and they stuck her in with us. She's hoping her boyfriend will show up. She expects him to be arrested any day now."

The girl who would be Claude spread her cards and said something sharp, in French. The hard case groaned and the Arab slapped down his hand.

"How do you know this?" I asked.

"The fag from Bermuda talked to her. She'll blow you for five euros."

I watched the girl shuffle. She, or he, had the fingers of a female, but something about her eyes—the pupils, I think—made me wonder. "How do you know she's a girl?"

"She said so."

"But she says she lied to the cop out front. Maybe she didn't. Maybe she lied to the Bermuda homosexual instead. Maybe she's a guy who likes to suck tool but he's afraid to admit he's a guy for fear some homophobic prick like you will pound him." I did the Columbo thing where you pretend you just thought of something whereas, in truth, you thought it a long way back. "You didn't let him suck you off, did you?"

Jesse's face gave the answer.

"That means you're a homo now. For the rest of your life, you can't go back," I said.

Jesse's pink face went pinker. Neon. He licked his chapped lips and his eyes skittered. "Hold it. I'm no queer."

"You are if you've been sucked by a guy. That's natural law."

The effeminate whatever it was glanced across the room at us. He or she knew we were talking about him or her.

Jesse the little fart whined. "It's the sucker who's queer. Not the one sucked. Weren't you ever in Boy Scouts?"

"It's both. You can ask anyone." I called over to the cardplayers. "If a guy sucks off a guy, they're both gay, right?"

The Arab stared blankly, but the others nodded the way people will.

I looked back at Jesse. "See."

Jesse's jaw clench was so tight he was in danger of breaking teeth. Sweat trickled beneath his fire red earlobes. The knuckle popping took on a machine gun staccato.

I went for the kill. "Don't tell me you got sucked in Boy Scouts, too."

He was about to cry. "Hell, everyone gets sucked in Boy Scouts."

"Not me." I called over to the cardplayers. "You guys get sucked in Boy Scouts?"

This time they ignored me.

Jesse's voice cracked. "I'm no fag. I do girls all the time."

A jailer type came in the outer door. He had on a blue uniform and matching cap, and he carried a hoop full of keys.

I said, "Now I understand why you can say that word without offending Claude."

The jailer said, "Rowdy Talbot?"

"Yo."

The jailer tried two keys before getting it right. As the cell door swung open, he said, *"Sortez,"* which I took as, "Let's go."

I said, "You better check Claude out. I wouldn't want to be you."

Jesse wept.

22.

The jailer led me back through the fluorescence to the booking room, where the happy sergeant had my personal possessions box open on his desk. He was squinting into my right boot, as if I'd hidden contraband in the pointy toe.

He pushed the belt and hat my way and said, *"Allez."*

The hat felt pretty good, back where it belonged. "What did I do to get turned loose?" I asked.

"Allez, et bonne journée."

"Don't take any wooden nickels."

Outside the clouds had darkened and a mist kind of sat in the air, not falling so much as taking up space. Pinto Whiteside stood next to the Citroën, which was parked with the right tires on the sidewalk and the left tires in the gutter. Pinto was wearing slacks and a polyester shirt with the top three buttons unbuttoned, showing white fuzz on his chest.

He said, "Happy trails, cowboy."

"Did you bail me out?"

"Bail is not the precise word." He opened the passenger-side door. "Get in."

I looked in at the seat, knowing sitting in front was an honor but also wary of dog hair. "How much will it cost me?"

"Much less than it would have if I hadn't made some calls."

I've never worn *slacks* in my life. In fact, for the thirty years of life that I remember, I've worn denim blue jeans every day. Nothing else. Ever. Although, I must confess they weren't always Wranglers. Back in my formative years, Mom bought Levi's and Lee's, even some weird Pamida cut-rate brand back in grade school. The Wrangler exclusivity didn't start till I turned pro.

"Did you think that if you beat up every person in Paris, eventually somebody would cough up the buckle?" Pinto asked.

"It's a thought."

"It's a stupid thought."

I fumed while he fought the gears into first and lurched us back onto the street. Why is it whenever someone gets you out of jail they inevitably feel it gives them the right to criticize? "Where's the dog?"

"Thank you for asking. Monty is at the hairdresser." Pinto felt for his cigar. "It's Wednesday. He has a wash and fluff every Wednesday."

He lit up at a red light as a guy in a cowboy costume crossed in front of us. Even through smoke and Pinto's badly streaking wipers, I could see the hat was cheap plastic. The chaps were fake sheepskin. He looked dressed for Halloween.

"What I can't understand is why Giselle was so bent on keeping my buckle. It can't mean anything to her, compared to the nastiness I'm bound to raise getting it back."

Pinto hit the steering wheel with his flat hand. "Not one soul in France is buying the buckle story. It's absurd. Even if it's true, think of a lie that's more believable. Tell them you work for Microsoft. Armand is so paranoid he'll believe you."

"Armand told his gang I'm a CIA agent loaned out to Starbucks."

Pinto gunned the Citroën into a street not much wider than his

car. The second floors, or whatever they are in France, stuck out
from the buildings and partially covered the street, causing a tunnel
sensation. I don't care for tunnel sensations.

"How do you think he got that idea?" I asked.

"I told him."

I looked across at Pinto, who was bent forward with both hands
on the wheel. His pale eyes skittered, with his focus bouncing from
the car in front of us to up the block a ways to the rearview mirror.
He wasn't looking at me on purpose. What I wondered was why
men with excessive chest hair think it's worth showing off.

"Or, to be completely frank, I told a fare last night," he said. "I
wanted to see how long it took getting back to Armand."

"Why?"

"Why what?"

"Why would you tell anyone I'm CIA, working for Starbucks."

"Because I am."

Two men in business suits rolled by on these pogo stick–looking
things with wheels. I'd never seen anything like it.

Pinto said, "Segways. They're popping up all over Paris. Guides
take out group tours on them." We watched as the machines jumped
a curb. One man about fell, but he uprighted himself and continued
on down the sidewalk, forcing pedestrians into the street.

"There's a faction of taxi drivers who reward each other with
Italian chocolates for hitting a Segway," Pinto said.

I said, "I have to kill you now."

Pinto pretended I was joking. "We must focus on my wife."

"Let's stick to Starbucks."

He gunned a hard right and we took off up a hill. It was the first
hill I'd seen in town. "I did you a favor back there. The American
ambassador himself telephoned the chief of police."

"I don't believe you."

"Okay. You're right. But I did cash in IOUs from people you
can't even conceive of. I saved you from deportation and now you
owe me."

"If Armand's bunch had known the truth, they might have given up the buckle and be over it. Instead, you told them I'm their worst enemy. That's not a favor."

"Armand will never voluntarily hand you that buckle. I need your help with Mrs. Whiteside."

"Starbucks, Pinto. Tell me about Starbucks."

It took several blocks. Pinto kept trying to bring the conversation back to Mrs. Whiteside, the high-end hooker, but eventually he came to the point, which was that Starbucks was poised to invade France and the company wished to be welcomed with love as opposed to pipe bombs. Pinto had been sent in—he said, "inserted"—with the CIA's blessing to clear out the more radical cells of opposition.

"It would only take a few dead cats and broken windows to drive Starbucks out. They aren't nearly as geared for hatred as the burger chains. Basically they're a bunch of Seattle hippies who found a great way to make money."

"Personally," I said, "I don't give a hoot."

"You of all people should want a coffee option in Paris."

That was true. I could have died for a Breakfast Blend venti right about then. French mud was growing on me, but it wasn't coffee.

"When you so rashly confronted Armand, did you see evidence of insurrection?" Pinto said.

"They had McDonald's uniforms."

Pinto glanced at me, then back at the narrow street. "Something's going on with McDonald's. Something bigger than bricks and bats."

"There was a map of Paris on the table, with a sticky star at a six-way intersection next to a river."

"That's nothing. A T.G.I. Friday's they're planning an action against today."

"You going to stop it?"

"I can't blow my cover over diarrhea dumped in a salad bar. The McDonald's attack is the battle I can use to wipe out these jack-asses once and for all. Is that clear?"

"Not a bit."

"Win the war on McDonald's and we'll make Paris safe for Starbucks. I need you to find out what they're planning."

I let that *I need you* comment slide right on by. "And how do you know about T.G.I. Friday's?

"Not all those old drunks sitting near Armand's table at the Pléiade are deaf."

Near the top of the hill, there was a fancy church and a cluster of tourist traps on the right, what we call rubber tomahawk stores back home. Lord knows what they're called in Paris. Tinfoil Eiffel Tower ashtray traps, maybe. Pinto turned left, into a semi-posh neighborhood.

"If you're such a hotshot CIA agent, why are you desperate for cash? Why sell turquoise and drive a taxi?"

Pinto ran a stringy hand over his face. His hands with the blue tube veins made me revise my estimate of his age, upward. "I'm on loan to Starbucks, like I told you." His right eyebrow rode his fore-head like a black millipede. "In the switchover, the agency lost my paperwork. Have you ever tried to find lost secret paperwork? I can't even admit what I'm looking for exists."

The road snaked down a hill, then he hit a right and we snaked back up. The turns weren't switchbacks, but they were tighter than you would want to try in a Dodge Dakota. A full-size American pickup truck would be nothing but trouble in Paris.

"Do you keep track of all Armand's people?" I asked.

He snickered. "Down to the freckles on their behinds."

"So you knew where Odette lived yesterday, before you took me to the post office."

"Of course I knew."

"And you being in Crepes a Go Go wasn't random."

"The file clerk called me the moment you walked into the philosophy department. We are quite interested in your girlfriends' trip to Colorado."

"That means you know where Giselle lives."

"She's not home."

Pinto pulled up in front of a white house with a long front porch and Greek-looking pillars. The downstairs windows had security bars, the upstairs windows, yellow curtains.

Pinto said, "First, I must know if Mrs. Whiteside is having sex."

"She's a whore, Pinto. She's having sex."

He turned off the engine and sat, staring at his thumbs on the steering wheel. "The man I suspect her of being emotionally intimate with is in her room now. You are to go in and discover their true actions."

"Forget it."

His face flushed, angry. "How can you be so ungrateful?"

"I was raised to it. I can't believe you expect me to kick in your wife's door to make sure she's humping. That's nuts."

You could see Pinto fighting to control his voice. "Kicking in is not necessary. When a client turns violent the prostitute may need help quickly, therefore doors are never locked in a bordello. I can't believe you are so naive that you didn't know that."

I didn't say anything. I'd told him *Forget it* the once, there didn't seem much point to repeat myself. An urban squirrel ran between birch-looking trees in the front yard. A FedEx truck stopped next door and a woman got out. Pinto's fingers tapped a rhythm on the steering wheel. I recognized it—drum solo from "Wipe Out" by the Ventures. More his generation than mine.

"Have it your way," he said. "I'll take you to Giselle's afterward."

One of the last things I wanted to do, if not the very last, was get involved in the personal life of a turquoise-dealing cabdriver CIA agent with a whore for a wife. There were almost bound to be complications. But then, the alternative was to physically force him to give me Giselle's address, and, if he actually was CIA, he'd no doubt been combat trained.

I nodded at the big house. "This is it?"

"If you walk right in like you own the place and quickly go up the steps, no one will stop you, not this time of day anyway. At the top of the stairs, turn left. Mrs. Whiteside's suite is the last door on the right."

"In Juarez, they're called cribs."

"My wife works out of a suite."

The building looked like the place a senator might live, or maybe a private hospital for wealthy coke heads. It didn't strike me as a house of ill repute, but what did I know?

"I've never actually been inside a whorehouse before."

This struck Pinto as humorous. "A cowboy like you?"

"I've seen hookers in Vegas and Rock Springs. There's always a few strays hanging around poetry gatherings, but, as a rule, bull riders don't pay. It's the only perk we get."

"It'll be good for you to see how other people live."

I opened my door. "I don't care how other people live."

No blind piano player. No madam encased in rouge and diamonds with a breast of iron and a heart of melted Velveeta. Once again, my preconceptions went down the tubes. Maybe it was too early in the day. Maybe the piano player and madam came out after dark. The only people in sight were two women in nightgowns playing backgammon at a coffee table in the parlor. I guess you'd call it a parlor. It had chairs and couches and cabinets with glass shelves that I figured were named after Louis the some-number-or-other. At least, they are in books. But then books have blind piano players and crusty madams, so maybe the whole mythology is based on a fiction writer's imagination.

One of the women looked up at me and said something French.

I pointed to the staircase and said, "FedEx delivery for Mrs. Whiteside," then took off up the steps before they could comment on my lack of uniform or package. I don't think they knew English. I could have said anything.

The stairs were wide and marble with a marble banister on the outside drop-off. The wall had paintings, mostly of naked women and clothed men. More rape as art. Charlie Russell never painted rape as art, even in his Indian series. One painting looked like they were having a picnic, only the men were overdressed in suits and vests and the woman was underdressed in nothing. She held her hand over her snatch.

The hallway was hardwood. It had laminated siding to about hip level, then jaundice pee-colored paint on up. The lightbulb was forty-watt, at the most. The whole time I was in France, I never saw a lightbulb over forty watt. Bad lighting must be a cultural thing. I kind of felt my way to the end of the hall, located what I took to be the proper door, and walked on in.

Nobody was getting nailed. A man and woman were sitting at a little iron table like my mom has on her patio. They were drinking tea, I would assume. Steam rose from delicate cups with a matching delicate pot. An equally delicate plate held cookies. Girl Scout cookies, maybe, the shortbread kind.

The woman didn't seem fazed to see me at the door. She said, *"Pardon?"*

She was one of those fifty-year-old beautiful women you run into on rare occasions. Widow's peak hairline, strong forehead, posture of a ballerina, wearing a flowing dress with a turtleneck collar that seemed to be made from doily material. Heaps of dignity. Her only visible jewelry was a turquoise ring.

The man was dressed in white, in drastic contrast to everyone else in Paris. He looked like the rich uncle who leaves you seventy-five dollars in Monopoly. The fat entrepreneur. He sat forward in his chair, leaning toward Mrs. Whiteside. I got the idea I'd interrupted him in the midst of making an important point.

I said, "Oops."

Mrs. Whiteside said, *"Vous désirez?"*

"I'm here to pick up your FedEx shipment."

Mrs. Whiteside looked at the gentleman and said, *"FedEx?"*

He went off in French. After a bit, she looked back at me and said, *"Non, merci."*

Embarrassed no end, I got out of there.

I more or less ran down the staircase and out the door. Pinto saw me coming and turned on the engine, I suppose thinking we might need a quick getaway. When no one chased me out the door, he turned the engine back off.

He twisted in the driver's seat to face me. "Well?"

"Well, what?"

"Did you catch them unawares?"

"I caught them all right."

"What were they doing?"

"Pumping like elk in a rut."

Pinto's face broke into a smile. The tension flew from his forehead and his eyebrows stopped twitching for the first time since we met. "I knew it," he said, which was a blatant lie. "Who was on top? Alene or the client?"

"They were doing the dog."

"All the better. No eye contact."

"It was pure animal," I said. "She looked bored."

That almost got me caught. "Alene never looks bored. She is the consummate professional."

"The guy couldn't see her face."

Pinto nodded, building a mental picture of his wife and her client. "What about the mirror?"

I didn't remember a mirror. Hell, I didn't remember a bed, I'd been so caught up in the beautiful woman and the courtly gentleman. "They were facing the window."

Pinto nodded again, turning his mental picture ninety degrees. "Did Alene see you?"

"I was only in the door a few seconds. Neither one had any idea I'd been in the room."

"All the better," Pinto said.

"Now, take me to Giselle's place."

"She's not home."

"All the better."

23.

Cowboys, as a rule, read more than any other profession, although what they read couldn't be considered Oprah literature. Whether it's the loneliness of the campfire or the boredom of the bunkhouse, the majority of your cowboys who actually punch cows own and have read the complete works of Louis L'Amour, including all seventeen Sackett novels, and that's where they learned how to behave. Personally, my code came from Will James, although I'm not the only one. Ian Tyson — the musician we named Tyson after — has a song where he says when you're in trouble it helps to figure out what Will James would have done.

Back in the olden days of twenty years past, many a bunkhouse had one wire-thin, bowlegged geezer with a face like a topo map of the land he'd spent his life on who knew his Ovid and Homer back to front. I dare you to find another profession where there's men can simultaneously quote Thoreau and castrate. The satellite dish and a suicide rate thirty times the national average wiped out those old cranks, but their memory hasn't quite gone the way of the Indian scout.

Which is all relevant to understanding why, as a real cowboy, I had to get my buckle back or die trying, but in the meantime I was about set to stuff Pinto's cigar down his throat. Imagine the ego it takes to put your oral gratification above the misery of others. I am floored by the mind-set of the public cigar smoker.

"Giselle lives with a roommate." He blew a column of blue smoke. "Studi. She's Belgian, works for Air France."

"Does Studi speak English?"

Pinto did one of those this-and-that waves with his cigar hand. "When she wants to. We don't think she's any more anti-American than your average flight attendant. She's not out to destroy capitalism anyway. Studi and Giselle can barely tolerate one another, so I doubt if she knows any inside information."

"Like where my buckle is."

Pinto's temper flashed. "Your buckle means *nothing*. You hear me?"

"It does to me."

"How can you compare a belt buckle to protecting innocent lives and property?"

"I thought you were making France safe for Starbucks."

"It's the same thing." He puffed like dry ice in a washtub. Maybe someday American smokers will all move to France and French non-smokers will move to America and we'll have world peace. "If Studi says anything about McDonald's, you let me know."

I said, "You betcha," but what I meant was "In your dreams."

The water-head hit me for thirty euros. I couldn't believe it. He practically kidnaps me, then charges for the ride. We drove back over the river and up past this temple thing into another neighborhood without grass. He pulled up in front of a building held together by graffiti.

Pinto said, "Thirty euros."

I said, "That only counts when I sit in back."

"I'm not getting you out of jail anymore."

"I'm not spying on your wife anymore."

We left it at that.

Studi herself had platinum hair and eyebrows. I found her sitting at the kitchen table, reading a glossy fashion magazine and using a cigarette to cauterize her split ends. She was very thorough, but the burnt hair smell made me queasy.

"I'm supposed to meet Giselle here," I said.

She kept her head down, toward her hair ends, so when she looked at me her eyes were way up in the whites, the way Lauren Bacall used to look at Humphrey Bogart. "Giselle hasn't been home in three days."

"She said I should wait in her bedroom until she arrived."

Any roommate who liked Giselle would have said to wait in the kitchen or living room or someplace, but I was counting on subconscious animosity. Studi's animosity wasn't all that subconscious.

She said, "I do not understand what you men see in her."

"She's cruel. Some men get off on cruelty."

She hit her cigarette and blew smoke sideways out of the corner of her mouth, the way girls do sometimes. "And you?"

"I ride bulls. It's not much of a leap from bulls to Giselle."

She chuckled in Belgian. Or French, or whatever language was her usual. It didn't come off much like an American chuckle. "So, you're a masochist."

"You're not the first to call me that word."

Studi burned another split end. The magazine was open to a page showing women dressed for a costume dance, I think, walking down a raised sidewalk with photographers so close on each side they could look up the girls' skirts.

"She never brought home a cowboy before." Studi raised her face to look at me straight on. Her eyes were platinum, too. "You're American."

"Wyoming."

"Giselle hates Americans. How do I know you are a lover and not some freak out to steal her computer?"

"She has a mushroom tattoo here." I pointed out the place above Giselle's pubic Upper Peninsula.

"That is more than I care to know." Studi licked her index finger and turned the page to what looked like a douche ad. It was in French. She said, "Not that I care. If you want to steal her computer, I won't stop you."

"I'll keep that in mind."

Giselle collected dolls. Isn't that interesting? She had them lined up on shelves along one wall of her room. Must have been 150 dolls from raggedy to wooden to china faces with cloth bodies. Naked baby dolls and dolls whose eyes flipped open and shut. One doll sat on a toadstool. They were grouped by nationality and race, moving from Swedish milkmaids top left to a little Eskimo in a blue parka bottom right. The entire bottom shelf was black, Asian, or Indian. The only dolls she didn't collect were marketed series like Barbie and Cabbage Patch. Nothing there smelled of Toys "R" Us.

The rest of Giselle's room was more like Giselle. An autographed poster of Valerie Solanas slicing the tool off a cartoon redneck hung over the bed. I don't know who Valerie Solanas was or is, but she was or is pissed off. Giselle had been reading *The Ballad of Dead Ladies* by Dante Rossetti in English. The other books—and there were lots of them—were foreign. Hardly any had pictures on the cover. I found a dildo the size of a meat hook in her closet under a pile of spike-heeled boots, and a camouflage party dress. Even bunnies don't wear camouflage party dresses. Between the mattress and box springs, I found a pistol, some off-brand I'm not familiar with. German, maybe. It had a bolt action and a full clip. I put it back.

One of her jewelry boxes contained a glass cylinder coated on the bottom by a powdery residue. No doubt drugs. The stuff was peach-colored, like Mica's face powder, not white or crystal like any of the drugs I'm familiar with. I opened the top and sniffed, but that's just something you do when you find a strange powder. I have no idea how dope smells.

There was a *Victoria's Secret* catalogue sealed in plastic in her ceiling-high toilet tank. I took that as her most embarrassing possession.

I turned on her computer and flipped through her mail while it warmed up. The mail was all French, but it seemed to be bills and offers for beauty products. Two euros off on a thin-crust pizza. Nothing came addressed to *Terrorist*.

Next to the gear in his war bag, a rodeo cowboy's most important tool is his computer. Without the Internet, long-distance phone bills would be horrendous. You've got to check a rodeo, enter it, pay your fees, go back later and see if the animal you drew is worth the drive. If you haven't heard of the animal, you research it. And then there's pharmaceuticals from Canada.

Giselle's computer opened right up on the 'net. I recognized the Yahoo logo even though the words were French. I went under the *ALLEZ* icon at the top and backtracked through her recent visits to see what she'd been looking up lately. The top page was an eBay auction of a Frozen Charlotte doll—stone bisque, unjointed, molded hair, $75 minimum bid—which proved the collection wasn't left over from her innocent childhood. She was still at it. The next page was photos of Finnish lesbians having sex on an ice floe. I scrolled through the pictures, trying to figure out what went where. I've never understood lesbianism. I mean, I understand women who prefer each other to men, I don't much like men myself. What I don't understand are the technical aspects of positioning and penetration, or lack of it. Why would a person who can't stand males purchase a dildo? Maybe it's only the bisexuals, like Giselle, who use meat hooks, and the real lesbians stick to fingers and tongues. And without a limp tool, how do they know when they're finished?

The page below was the McDonald's crew handbook in French. Cleanliness was a big deal, and uniform maintenance. Photographs showed the proper way to mop. Below that, stretching back a week and a half, all her visits had to do with McDonald's. There were sample menus and mini-biographies of Dick and Mac McDonald. She'd rooted out a database of the eight hundred and whatever franchises in France, with little MapQuest boxes so you could find one wherever you traveled.

Next down the line came a map of Boulder, Colorado, and below that a chat room where they discussed how spiritual American Indian drugs are. The room was subdivided into cactus-derived, mushroom-derived, and toad sweat. I didn't get any farther below that because Odette walked in.

24.

"I thought I would find you here," Odette said. "I am adept at judging character. I knew the moment you were released, you would begin the tracking of Giselle."

She came up behind me and looked over my shoulder as I retreated back to Yahoo. Odette didn't touch me like I thought she would. She held a hand over my shoulder as close as you can come to touching without touching. The warmth of her hand penetrated my shirt. Made my skin prickle. Somehow, almost but not quite touching felt more personal than if she'd grabbed me. Everybody hugs everybody these days. It's the ones you expect to touch but don't who have feelings too complicated to express.

I gave Odette Self-evident Truth #8: *The only thing worse than finding out you were wrong when you prejudged a person's character is to find out you were right.*

"I'll think about that." I couldn't see Odette there behind me, but I could feel her, the way she took up air, and she smelled okay. There's a place in Joshua Tree National Park that smells like Odette. Maybe it's the Joshua tree, itself. I think I could smell Odette anywhere under any conditions and know it was her.

"Why are you no longer imprisoned?" she asked.

"I was innocent."

She snort-laughed. "That must have been difficult to prove."

"The police knew your apache friends attacked me without cause." I typed and talked. "They just didn't want a riot to break out there in the bar. Some of those folks didn't like Americans."

"All of those folks didn't like Americans, except maybe me. What I don't understand is why you are on Giselle's computer."

A list came up on the screen. Lots of Codys, Dustys, Hunters, and men with letter names—J.D. and K.W. "I'm looking up bull-rider standings. See." I pointed to my name on the list. "Winning Crockett County jumped me from one hundred and three to sixty-two. If I win every rodeo I enter from now to Thanksgiving, I'll have a shot at making top fifteen."

She didn't ask when Thanksgiving came. "That would reach your goal, no?"

"The top fifteen qualify for National Finals. I wouldn't need my buckle back if I could ride at National Finals."

Her hand finally dropped onto my shoulder. It was like completing an electrical circuit. "Is that possible? For you to win every rodeo?"

I scanned up the list to see who was ahead of me. It was a bunch of unknowns till you got into the high thirties. Not so much unknown to me, but Odette probably hadn't heard of them. The top ten were household names, in Wyoming, anyway. Ty would love me if I became a household name.

"I've won one in a row, so far. No reason to think I can't keep the streak alive."

Odette's body rustled. It's funny how with some people you can tell what they're looking at without looking at them. She was looking to see where else I'd been in Giselle's room.

"Did you find the buckle?"

"Nope." I shut off the computer. "Is Studi albino?"

"Who?"

"The roommate. I was wondering if she's albino."

"She's blond."

"She looks like a pretty version of Edgar Winter."

Odette came around to the side of the chair where she could see my face. She'd changed clothes since this morning. Now she was wearing this gingham jumper thing, with a T-shirt. In her super-clean glasses, she looked about twelve years old. "I do not know of Edgar Winter, but Studi dyes her hair to please the men she works with. Her dream is to marry a pilot."

"Back home, any girl whose dream is to get married keeps her mouth shut about it. Women in the West look at marriage as a form of giving up."

Odette's eyes darted here and there around the room, as if searching. I wondered what she was looking for—the gun, the dope, the dildo? Frozen Charlotte? She must have come to Giselle's for a reason.

I've found if you want to know something, the thing to do is ask. "So, why are you here?"

"I was looking for you," Odette said.

"Why?"

She shrugged. Bunnies could never get away with that French shrug. If a bunny tried it, she'd come off as an airhead, and Odette did not come off as an airhead. "I don't ask myself why."

"There's a difference between thinking you might find me here and coming here to find me. You had no reason to believe I was out of jail."

Odette touched her fingertips to my cheekbone and looked down at me. I couldn't tell if it was a look of affection or thinking I was pathetic. "That is true only if you are a cowboy in Paris for your belt buckle. If you are CIA or Interpol or others even more sinister, I knew you would be out."

"I'm not CIA, Interpol, or anything else sinister."

"Then why are you not still in custody?"

. . .

There's a word for thinking your species or country or football team is the center of everything. I forget the word, but plenty of people have it. I know rodeo cowboys who can't conceive of walking into a bar in Paris, France, and saying, "I was a close personal friend of Freckles Brown," and no one in that smoky-as-a-tar-pit hole knowing who it was you're talking about. If you finally convinced this cowboy that there actually is a place where thirty or more men gather to drink where no one has heard of Freckles Brown, he would spit and say, "Them frogs are the most ignorant bastards on earth." I imagine there're names a Frenchman could drop and if I didn't know them, he'd say the same thing about me — soccer players or bicycle riders, that sort of thing. Folks from New York City are the worst at this word, whatever it is. Their song is, "If it didn't happen here, it didn't happen anywhere."

Paris proved a comeuppance in my own view of reality. What I mean is, I travel a good bit, probably a hundred thousand miles a year, and it had been a long time since I'd gone to a place and not run into people I knew. It'd been so long I'd fooled myself into thinking I knew people everywhere, but that isn't true. What is true is I know people everywhere I go when I'm likely to be there.

So, even if I wind up somewhere weird like Camden, Connecticut, I'll be there when a rodeo is in town, so people I know will be there, too. Professional rodeo is a migratory city.

As Odette and I walked down the wet sidewalk, dodging dogs and dog dip, circling randomly parked scooters, and, on my part, doing my best to stay out of the way of locals with umbrellas, I kept expecting to see someone familiar. A waitress, maybe. I hadn't been anywhere since high school that I didn't know a waitress. Or maybe a stoved-in has-been. My world is peppered by old men with bad legs and lip cancer, but here in Paris, everyone I saw that afternoon walked fast and sported a full mouth. Anyone I had anything in common with was on their way to Dalhart.

"Who are you planning to strike next?" Odette said. She didn't seem to mind the mist. She walked straight up, breasts forward, as if rain and sunshine affected her the same.

"I thought I'd start with Armand."

"You've already fought him. Why not pummel someone new?" I think she was being satirical or sardonic or one of those other words that slide over my head.

"Giselle will give the buckle up if Armand tells her to, and Armand will tell her to when he sees not giving me the buckle is more trouble than giving it to me."

She moved closer to me as we stepped around a crate of rotten cabbage. Don't ask me why they had a crate of bad cabbage in the middle of the sidewalk. Our arms bumped.

"You have the problem worked out," Odette said. "Men in Paris rarely have problems worked out. Their sensitivity forces them to be indecisive."

"No one accuses me of sensitivity." She might have smiled. I don't know. Women often miss it when I kid around. "First thing you're going to show me is where Armand lives."

Some women can walk down the street with a man and some can't. Mica would rub me off on a stop sign, or blow the timing at a curb. Odette had the spontaneity of a shadow.

"No one knows where Armand lives," she said. "Even I don't know."

"No one at all? That's hard to believe."

"None except his inner circle, like Leon or Remi. Giselle might since she is his woman, but I'm not certain Armand would let a lover know where he sleeps."

I asked the uppermost question. "Have you had sex with Armand?"

"Maybe, once."

"Maybe?"

"A long time ago. When I was a girl and easily influenced by angry charisma. Armand can get any first-year student he wants."

I figured Odette at twenty-three, maybe twenty-four, so her "long time ago" was not the same as mine. To her, it could mean last spring.

"I'll bet I know someone could tell us where Armand lives," I said.

"How is that possible? Armand's movements are secret. He is political."

"Politicians in France keep their addresses secret?" That seemed odd, but, when I thought about it, I realized American politicians don't list home addresses in the phone book, either.

"Armand is not a politician. He is a French purist. He fights for the cause of our national culture. Often he works outside legalities."

We came to a babbling schizophrenic with visible nose dribble and his hand out. I stopped to dig for spare change. I've had to ask for spare change before, when I was young and not operating under the disadvantage of mental illness. I wasn't about to pass him by.

"I haven't figured out Armand's cause yet, except he doesn't like fast food."

Odette waited while I finished the transaction. The schizophrenic mumbled something that could have been translated as "Thank you" or "Fuck you." Either way.

"Armand is *rebelle du monde.* Anti-globalization. We are all anti-globalization. American companies like your McDonald's and Wendy's are destroying our culture."

The street beggar took the money and went into a burger joint called Quick that appeared to be a low-rent McDonald's, or maybe a high-rent Jack in the Box. "They destroyed our culture a long time ago. You're better off without it," I said.

"McDonald's has hundreds and hundreds of franchises in France today. They don't even call them restaurants. You Americans invented eating in a franchise."

We started walking again. Odette seemed to have a destination in mind. She didn't hesitate at intersections, anyway. I didn't ask where we were going. We passed several restaurants named Brassiere, which I thought was weird. Must be a chain. A tall, sleek woman decked out in black spandex glided past. Her shopping bag said SEPHORA. She reeked of sophistication. I couldn't help but check her out, wondering what she thought of bulls. Women either go for cowboys, or they don't. You don't meet many middle-of-the-roaders.

Odette saw the checkout and punched me hard on the shoulder. "We must drive the invaders away. I admire Armand for his battle."

I kneaded my shoulder—the right one held in place by a pin—and wondered if she'd hit that hard because I was an American out to ruin her country or a man looking at a tall woman. Girls are so complicated, they hit for one reason but there's always a second reason buried underneath, like toads in a dried-up bog. Hell, it's not just hitting. Everything girls do they do for a reason other than what would appear obvious.

"Only way to drive them out is if nobody eats there. Then, they go away. That's how it works in the States."

"But the chains are hugely successful. If we leave it to the common man, there will soon be no French culture. We will all behave as if we live in Los Angeles."

"You make that sound like a drawback."

"The French people have sold their civilization for a cheap piece of badly cooked beef." She studied my face. "You are flush. Are you ill?"

I was feeling strange. Nothing out of hand, mind you, but my jaws were grinding and my forehead felt stretched. It came to me that whatever I sniffed back in Giselle's room might have had some kick after all.

"I need to sit down."

"This is where we are going." Odette pointed to a heavy wooden door with French writing on a plaque beside the entrance. "You can cool off here."

"Where are you taking me?"

"It's a place you need to see if you wish to understand who I am."

My recoil was unintentional. "Why in God's name would I want that?"

"Come in with me and together we shall find out."

The room was darkly institutional with people clustered together looking at French exhibits on the walls. The exhibits seemed to be historical explanations and maps of what, to my alarm, appeared to be tunnels. A man in a black suit and skinny tie — imagine a high-school shop teacher gone to seed — sat in a booth behind a glass window with a half circle cut in the bottom, the kind of window you see at movie theaters in Nebraska.

Odette proceeded to buy two tickets.

"Where are you taking me?" I asked.

"Somewhere you need to go."

"I hate it when people think they know what I need."

Odette laughed, as if I meant to be funny. Then she fished in her beaded purse and came out with two D-battery flashlights. "You'll want this," she said, giving me a flashlight.

"Oh, no."

"It's more interesting if you can see."

"There's rules I live by and one of them says I can't go anyplace or do anything where I'll need a flashlight."

"For a cowboy, you are certainly a bit of a weenie."

That hurt. I wondered where she'd learned the word. I'll bet it wasn't in school. Probably that American husband of hers had taught her derogatory slang. Tallywhacker. Weenie. There should be a separate prison wing for people who think it's funny to teach foreigners dirty words.

Odette led me through a floor-to-ceiling iron gate not unlike my jail cage and into a room where steps spiraled into the very bowels of Paris. She smiled at me. I tried to smile back and failed. Down she went.

I said, "Hellfire," and down I went after her. Up went the heart rate, pumping whatever weird drug I'd ingested at Giselle's through my system. My saliva tasted like rusted shingling nails.

Your bull rider will insist there is a constant scale of bravery, say a one to ten, with those who panic at a bee in the car as a one and those willing to climb on 1,600 pounds of pissed-off Brahma at ten, and everybody else spread in the middle. But the truth is, there's more than one scale. For instance, I would chainsaw my legs at the knee and go on disability before I'd take a job in a mine. Guys who face live burial as a career choice are either incredibly stupid or incredibly brave, which is the same thing non–bull riders often say about bull riders. That brings up the eternal question of when does stupidity become courage and vice versa. I have chosen not to go there.

The steps went down ten or twelve tight corkscrews straight into the earth. I'd thought going to the bathroom at Crepes a Go Go was like dropping into a well, but that was a squat compared to this place. That thing in your inner ear that keeps you from pitching forward onto your face went blooey on me. A chattering covey of little boys filled the steps above. I risked a look to see who could be making so much racket and they were dressed in uniforms, like Cub Scouts, although I don't suppose France has Cub Scouts. Much of the noise was complaints about the speed of my descent, I think. What they did that mattered was to block my chance of turning around and getting the hell out.

The steps dropped into a cave that was someone's idea of a room. There were more historical photos stuck on the walls that were made of bricks I'd guess came from the fifteenth century. The pictures were that orangey-brown and silver kind they made before black-and-white photography was invented. More maps. Catholic symbols. Some stuff about dead people and Nazis. While I was looking at the pictures, the Cub Scouts or whatever they were filed off through a door that led to a tunnel where I didn't want to go. As rambunctious as the boys were, they'd only been gone ten seconds when the tunnel swallowed up their sound. It was as if they marched into the bedrock and vanished.

"I wanted the children to go ahead," Odette said. She took my hand. "It's nicer when it feels like no one is nearby."

The walls were breathing. I'd gone from hyperventilating on the steps to not breathing at all in the room, so it was as if the walls breathed for me.

"Come on," Odette said.

I didn't say anything. I don't think I was capable.

Odette said, "You will be fine. I will stay with you."

And I let her pull me into the tunnel.

25.

In the past I have said I don't do well in mines when what I meant was highway tunnels or kindling boxes or amusement park rides that simulate mine shafts. The truth is I'd never been in a real mine where the earth might crash down and bury me alive under a thousand tons of dirt and rocks or trap me in an airless, black pocket of space where all I have left is waiting to die knowing no one will ever see my body again.

Odette's tunnel did have a string of lightbulbs, twenty-five-watt, tops, and the walls were brick, but the ceiling was damp clay or something. It was low — five-ten, maybe — and in places it got lower and the sides narrowed to where we had to walk single file. The floor was wet gravel. I was fighting fibrillation when the tunnel went into a rolling contraction, like a throat swallowing.

I said, "Jesus, what was that?"

"Pardon?"

"What happens if we're down here and there's an earthquake?"

She stopped and turned her head to the side, as if the wall held the answer. "I imagine we die."

"That's not a comfort."

We walked a half mile or so. It's hard to judge distance when your sphincter's puckered. One of the great things about being on a bull is what it does to time. When eight seconds stretches out to hundreds of thoughts and actions and counter-actions, a lifetime feels like it has the potential of going on forever. *Time stops* is no exaggeration when you're clamped to the spine of a raging Brahma. I'm thinking distance does something similar when you're underground.

"We're almost there," Odette said.

I said, "Where?" and we came around a corner to what in a sane world would have been a hallucination.

The walls were dead people. Hundreds of thousands of dead people. Femurs and tibias, joint-forward, stacked five feet high with skulls, face-out, lined up on top. More skulls were placed in the tibia walls, like a bricklayer will set a darker brick here and there to make a pattern. Odette played her flashlight beam behind the tibia berm to show a pasture of piled-together bones as far as her light would reach.

"It is spiritual, no?"

The cowboy code says I should have repeated *"spiritual"* with a degree of sarcasm, but I couldn't get it out. There were too many dead people for me to maintain distance.

"I come here for perspective," Odette said.

"Do they know how many are here?"

"Some guidebooks say five million individuals. Some, six. It does not matter."

She started walking on up the tunnel, flicking her light from side to side, casting bone shadows. There was nothing for me to do but follow. The bones were terrible and overwhelming and grand, all at the same time. I'd never been anywhere with this many people and here they were all piled up dead. Whoever brought them down hadn't bothered with keeping each person together. They used the legs and arms to build and the skulls to decorate and dumped the rest out back. It was as if the only reason for being born was to create bricks in a wall.

Odette paused at a side tunnel that went off without the string of lights. "No one alive knows the names of these men and women, or what they were like or who they loved, whether they died old or young or had talent or murdered each other. Every human here is insignificant. Does it not make you happy?"

Happy wasn't the word I had been thinking of, but the bones did do something for my fear of mines. Not that I was suddenly comfortable, I wouldn't go that far, but I was no longer terrified.

We walked a long ways, past scads of skulls. In one stretch, they'd been placed in the wall to make hearts. In another, diamonds. None of the skulls had teeth or lower jaws. That seemed odd. Every now and then we passed clots of tourists who were peering over the piles, as if trying to see the limits of the bone yards. I heard people talking English, saying what you would expect of cool Americans. *"This one looks like your mother,"* and *"I swear to God, June, that bone way back in there is moving."*

The Cub Scouts were clustered around an altar thing, next to a plaque.

"What's it say?" I asked.

"It says, 'Man, like a flower of the field, flourishes while the breath is in him, and does not remain nor know longer his own place.' More or less."

Odette led me into a tunnel where fewer people went in and out. Her hand was dewy-warm in mine. Her face was flushed.

She said, "Two hundred years from now, we will not even be a memory."

"What was that about Nazis on the sign out front?"

"During the occupation the Germans were afraid to come into this part of the tunnels, so it's where members of the Paris underground lived. That's why they were called underground."

"People lived with this?"

"Through the war."

Odette stopped to shine her flashlight on a random skull. "I create stories about them," she said. "This was a woman. She wrote poetry and had a lover who went to sea and perished at the hands of buccaneers. In her grief, she drank poison and died in agony."

"From the cranium there, it was more likely a guy got kicked in the head by a horse."

"That is exactly what I mean. It does not matter if she was a man or woman, or rich or poor. Do you not see? Not one moment matters, except this one. Right now. Here."

"And how is that supposed to help me understand you?"

"We must recall that these are actual people. Not Euro Disney plastic, or computer generated for a Hollywood tent pole. These humans ate food and drank wine and had babies. They loved and were loved. This is truth and it is where you and I are going to be."

A real cowboy would have said, "Take it to Oprah." Treating her seriously went against my raising, but, somehow, I could not stay casual. Maybe I'm not the man I thought I was.

We came to a side tunnel blocked by a knee-high chain. Odette stepped over the chain and looked back at me with her hand out.

"Come."

"I don't think they want us down there."

"They don't."

"Maybe we should stay here, near the light."

"We won't go far."

I flipped on my flashlight and stepped over the chain, on the theory that it's better to regret the things you did rather than the things you didn't do. It is better to regret saying yes than it is to regret saying no.

We went fifteen steps or so before Odette turned and pressed herself up close to my chest. She breathed into my Adam's apple.

"William James said death is the strongest of aphrodisiacs."

"That's why bunnies are so set on sleeping with bull riders, 'cause we flirt with death."

She brushed her nose up against my unshaven chin. "In this place, death is more than flirtation. Death is life."

Odette kissed me. This kiss was unlike others I'd had with her, less foreplay and more something that counted in itself. Her lips mixed want with need and I started kissing back and in no time at all we were desperate. Odette was kissing and I was kissing and we were forcing our way into each other's skin, as if here where people had no skin or flesh we could connect as no one had connected before, or at least as I'd never connected before.

Her breath came fast and in me. I touched her face and breasts and everywhere at once. At first, it was passion, not sex. It went beyond sex and into a place I'd never been or known possible with a woman. It was more the oneness I feel on a bull when it kicks out of the gate and goes into its spin. I've had sex before, but I don't guess I'd had passion, not with a person.

She mumbled in French as her fingers tugged at my zipper. I looked across her shoulder to where my flashlight threw a spot on a tibia with a spiral fracture. I've had a spiral fracture and it was a mother. That bone in my light could not have been broken knee-to-ankle in a curl after death. Somebody, hundreds of years ago, had been in a world of pain.

Odette had my dick out and her panties down on one foot and she pushed me hard into the wall. I'd hoped to get out without touching the bones, but now it didn't matter. Nothing mattered except us and what we were doing. The past disappeared, taking the future with it. The battle was to touch, as if we might kill death and each other and glue shut the spaces between us. I never in my life thought a woman could be a bull.

I held her butt in both hands while she balanced her feet on skulls. She threw her head back. A line of sweat ran down her neck over a pulsing vein. Her eyes were animal, like a gut-shot elk running for the trees. She went into a French moan with syllables in it, the eye sockets of a hundred skulls strobed in the flashlight light, then Odette came like a banshee scream. A moment later, everything inside me let go. Thirty years of ache and shame, sadness over Tyson, rage at Dad, helplessness at the cheat life is flowed out of me and into Odette. I was no longer outside myself.

Odette fell off me onto the floor, where she knelt on her knees, balanced by a hand on somebody's dead face, sucking air. From out past our side tunnel, I heard an American say, "Let's go. We haven't checked the Eiffel Tower off our list yet." Far away, the Cub Scouts took up Odette's howl, causing it to echo up and down the tunnels.

Bent over, hands on my thighs, I said, "Jesus Christ."

Odette said, "Yes."

"What was that?"

She picked herself up and stepped back into her panties. "That was not the worst fuck you've ever been involved in."

I held myself up by leaning my forehead against the forehead of a dead person and repeated what I'd said before. "Jesus Christ."

26.

Odette and I wound back up and out into Paris, blinking against the light like moviegoers coming out of a matinee. I can't talk for Odette, but personally, I was shell-shocked. Rocket sex when you least expect it in a foreign country is a lot like getting gored. Directions were scrambled. Nothing seemed to be where I expected it to be and it was hard to see how people going by didn't know I was twisted up inside.

Odette adjusted various under and outer garments. "In France, one of our words for the climax is *la petite mort*. Little death. But of course we have many ways to describe the climax."

"Like Eskimos and snow," I said.

"Pardon?"

"Eskimos have thirty words for snow."

"You only have two terms in English—*come* and *get off*. And only men are permitted to use them." She made her voice low and gruff, a European take on the Dixie cracker. "Did you get off, babe?" She went back to her regular voice. "If you have to ask, the answer is *no*."

"You forgot *squirt* and *shoot the wad*."

"Those are male words and males do not have actual climaxes. They have squirts."

"That last one felt fairly actual."

"Yours are but a pale imitation." Odette looked to both ends of the street. "The exit is two kilometers from the entrance. No matter how often I go down, it takes a moment to orient."

I said, "I'm hungry. Let's go eat."

She smiled at me. Her smile was different now, more a secret between the two of us and less like I was a sideshow. "Death intensifies the appetite — hunger the same as passion."

She put her hand under my arm and over my biceps and guided me up the street. No woman has walked with me that way since junior year, when Mica and I went to the prom. We didn't go senior year because I had a rodeo in Dillon, Montana. Mica still throws that one in my face.

"What would you enjoy?" Odette asked. "In Paris, food is religion. We are home to the finest restaurants anywhere in the world."

"That's a strong statement."

"I think our cuisine will inspire you as much as our loving."

By *loving,* she meant sex, which is a leap of language you won't hear back in the Rocky Mountains. "I saw a T.G.I. Friday's yesterday, down by a river. Let's eat there."

She tucked her chin and looked up at me. "You are making the joke."

"It would be a change. Mostly I run with a Pizza Hut lunch buffet gang."

Odette leaned into a moving hip bump. "If that is what the cowboy wants."

"You'll like it. They have fried mozzarella."

There's a saying on the rodeo circuit that goes — Self-evident Truth #9 — *If you sleep with enough people, sooner or later, you'll fall for one of them.* Usually, it's repeated by wives and girlfriends whose husbands and boyfriends claim that banging bunnies doesn't matter. Males say outside humping is only a release of tension, no more emotional than a shot and a beer, but women rarely buy the logic. For one, shots and beers don't get preggers.

But what I'm wondering is why Odette Clavel became so important to me so quickly. Why now? We were both sexually active with backgrounds steeped in copulation without consequences. I had the background anyway, and I'm assuming she did, too. It's like with a movie star or a bouncer in a cowboy bar, let's say Warren Beatty. He gets laid by a new woman every couple of days for decades, and then one time, on the surface a time like hundreds of others, his emotions kick his ass and he's suddenly half of a couple. How does that work? It can't be all timing, and I know it's not the quality of the lay. I've had white-hot sex with girls I didn't like one bit. Could hardly stand being in the same room with them if we weren't in bed, and they felt the same about me. Then along comes Odette and eight seconds later I can't think of tomorrow without her in it.

We stepped over a double-sized pile of dog doo, new-on-old. I said, "That thing we did down there, in that place —"

"The catacombs."

"You do that often?"

"I go to the bones whenever I have a break in my studies. They give me peace."

That wasn't what I was fishing for. "Do you have relations down there, on a regular basis?" For some reason, I couldn't say *fuck* all of a sudden. Don't ask me why.

Odette laughed. "Only when I dream."

"You haven't done what we did with guys in the bone pile before?"

We crossed a street and separated to walk around this outdoor john that looked like a spaceship and cost forty-five cents exact change to use. There was a sign in English that said children under ten might drown if they were inside the john when it flushed. Figuring how that worked was way beyond my ability to picture concepts. When we came back together, Odette took my arm again. "Once. I found a Danish marine standing in the Gilbert's Tomb section, weeping. I thought he understood what I felt there. I gave him oral gratification."

Why is it men ask women these questions when they hate hearing the answer? We want women to be honest, except for when they are. I didn't need to know the details of her blowing a sailor. That's what a marine is, right? Why would she say marine when she meant sailor?

Odette sighed. "He didn't understand me at all. I found out afterward he had been crying over a rugby score."

"So it was a wasted blow job." I must have been in love. I was already saying mean things to her.

Odette didn't catch my tacky tone. "No, not at all. I would not say that. He had an enormous member."

I acted the way any American male would. I sulked until someone gave me food.

We got a window table, which was nice because outside was more interesting to look at than inside. Inside had all the uniqueness of a T.G.I. Friday's in Colorado Springs. Same uniforms on the waitresses, same dessert specials on laminated cards next to the ketchup-mustard holster. The mustard was French's, which means it wasn't French. We were surrounded by girls who read *Harper's Bazaar* and eat 1,200-calorie Cobb salads, guys who read *Maxim* for the pictures and exercise indoors. Junior executives lying to one another in English about the vitality of their existence, except in Colorado Springs there'd be less smoke.

Outside the window was your ongoing Paris scene. Drippy rain. Six multilane avenues converged in an intersection big as a basketball court where old men with curvature of the spine carried unwrapped loaves of bread and women layered in scarves walked dogs the size of the old men's bread. Another Segway shot by. A green machine looked like a Zamboni swept feces off the sidewalk. Motor scooters putt-putted in and out of traffic. In Wyoming we call fat women Vespas on account of they're both fun to ride but it's embarrassing as hell if your friends catch you on one.

I ordered buffalo wings because the menu said they came with bleu cheese dressing and I wanted to try something local. While they were good, I'd have to say they didn't use spices as hot as back in Buffalo.

As we ate, I explained the uniqueness of the American cowboy. "Being a cowboy is the only profession with its own art forms. You got your cowboy painting and sculpture, cowboy music, cowboy dance, and cowboy poetry."

Odette paused, a spoonful of hot fudge poised at her lips. A dark drop hung off her lower lip, lickable as hell. "I always saw cowboys as a mythological construct of the redneck. Like pirates and motorcycle gangs."

Her tongue flicked over the fudge drop and brought it in before I got the chance. For the best, I suppose. I was caught up in buffalo wings and a bit too greasy for public romanticism. I've never been adept at licking loose food off women anyway. I come across more cocker spaniel than hot lover.

"Cowboys spend so much time alone outdoors, it leads to deep thought and contemplation. Rednecks are too busy proving their manhood to contemplate. Cowboys are secure in their gender, so they don't have anything to prove. They can write poetry." I sucked oil off my fingers and washed it down with a house red they sold by the glass and wondered how I got started on this "cowboys are better than you think" junk. If my point was that I had nothing to prove, why was I proving it? "You think it would be bad manners to sweeten this a tad?" I popped two of those sugar cube things in my wine and stirred till they dissolved.

Odette's eyes widened in wonder as she watched the sugar swirl away. Still, she didn't criticize. I liked that. Mica was quick with the criticism when my eating and drinking habits went against her version of normal.

I stripped chicken meat off the bone. "I'm going to be a poet when I grow up."

Her eyes went from my wine to me. "Grow up? What do you call yourself now?"

"Rodeo riders don't grow up until they break so many bones they can't compete anymore. I'm fairly near the edge of that one."

"If cowboy poetry is so magnificent, why do we not study it in university?"

"I never said it was good. Not in the intellectual feel-with-your-head-instead-of-your-body literature. For one thing, it's mostly written on a horse, so the rhythm is *clip clop, clip clop*."

"We call that iambic."

"Yeah, well, in French it's iambic. In American, it's clip clop, and since a cowboy on a horse can't write things down, the lines and rhymes have to be easy to memorize. That way he can remember the poem later in the bunkhouse."

"It sounds like doggerel to me."

"Is that a put-down?"

"It's a term for poetry." Odette licked her spoon dry, then dropped it with a tinkle into the sundae glass. "Here is what I want to know." Her eyes bored into mine. I was beginning to look forward to the electric jolt that came with sudden eye contact. "How does one feel, on the bull?"

"Seriously?"

"We are not having a trivial conversation."

"I could have sworn we were."

She stole a wing. "No metaphors. No comparisons. What is the bull like? Why is it worth the risk when obviously you will not be a champion?"

"Who told you that?"

"You did. Rowdy, you are thirty years old and you have won only one competition. If you were a champion, the buckle would not be an obsession."

"I can't stand perceptive women."

When she laughed, I saw fudge between the incisor and canine teeth. "That is a lie. You love me, yes?"

"Yes, I love you," which struck me as a bizarre thing for me to have said. The only way to deal with saying it was to pretend I hadn't.

"What is the bull like?" I swished sweet wine around my mouth and tried to think of an answer that wasn't smart-ass. "For eight seconds, life is pure."

If Odette treated my inner exposure as lovable but silly the romance would go right back to straight sex. But her eyes weren't ironic or superior or anything women use when men speak with enthusiasm. She was interested, so far as I could tell. I took a chance and went on.

"There's no ego. No self. Busted marriages don't exist. Disappointed mothers. Dead dads who were never alive in the first place. Sons growing up thinking Daddy is a deadbeat. Child support. It's not that those things don't matter, they don't even exist. And no man is bigger than me when I climb on a bull, because those who think they are would not be able to do it."

"Is that the reason many of the bull riders we observed in Colorado were short?"

I let that comment sail right on over my head. The French invented the Napoleon complex, for God's sake. And, besides, how should I know what short men think?

"Knowing sooner or later you'll get hurt doesn't mean squat once the chute blows open. It's the only time between starting out and ending up where I'm completely alive, and you damn well can't tell me the female orgasm is the same."

"Why not?"

"*Little death* as a term for orgasm sounds good, but with a bull, it's more than a figure of speech. It's a possible outcome."

Odette slid her empty sundae glass to the side and cupped her wine with both hands. She stared into the wine the way I stare into coffee, as if it held the answers.

"It can be real. I can forget the past and future and everything outside myself, which is what happens when you are completely alive. Or dead." Odette's eyes drifted into a glaze of memory. "Not the five seconds leading up to the climax, of course, and definitely not the sparkly time after. Having had sex comes with too many strings for it to be pure."

"Such as?"

"Pregnancy. Disease. Do I want the partner long-term? Will he become a nuisance? What am I going to wear later? Afterglow is complicated no matter how glorious it feels, but right there, when I am in the climactic heat, I understand the part about nothing outside matters."

I couldn't help but stick in a needle. "Was it like that with Giselle the other night?"

Odette reached across the table and thumped me on the chest. "I faked that one."

"No."

"I was sleepy. She would have been at me all night if I hadn't falsified the orgasm."

That was the best thing I'd heard since the Klaxon Sunday. "I can't wait to tell her." A green bus with what looked like an accordion bellows in its midsection pulled up across the street and Remi stepped out. He walked toward us. "Isn't that one of your urban army pals there?"

Remi walked fast, directly toward us. He had something oval in his hand, like one of those bottles of wine that comes in its own basket.

Odette said, "Remi."

"What's he carrying?"

Odette yelled, *"Rowdy! Attention!"* She jumped from her seat and grabbed me by the shoulders, pulling me from my chair. I fell on the floor, but she yanked me up, away from the window. I looked back to see Remi haul off and hurl whatever he was carrying through the glass. The window imploded. The bottle slid across the floor, then it blew up, in a huge puff of smoke.

Repercussions were about what you would expect. People

screaming, running into each other in their rush to get out of the way. Tables going over. Chairs cracking. A kid who must have been fourteen jumped across the bar and started stealing booze.

"Come on!" Odette shouted.

"That's one of the bastards has my buckle."

I tore her hand off my arm and ran back into the smoke to get my hat.

Behind me, Odette shouted, *"Rowdy."*

I jumped through the hole where the glass had been.

27.

If anything, outside T.G.I. Friday's was more chaotic than inside. Inside, at least, the stampede went one direction. Outside, as many people were flooding toward the trouble as away. The air was filled with a goddamn cacophony of those double-tone European sirens that are so much more irritating than ours. *Eeee-Oooo. Eeee-Oooo.* The whole deal was a lot of commotion for a smoke bomb. I set one off in the GroVont Middle School cafeteria once and they didn't even cancel lunch. The world is so skittish these days, what used to be a childhood prank is now terrorism.

Remi the snake had crossed the avenue there and was quick-limping toward a park gate, the limp caused, no doubt, from where I bit a chunk out of his ankle this morning. When he glanced back I saw a blue-green bruise under his left eye. For an instant, the sight of me puzzled him, then I made him nervous, especially when he realized I wasn't done.

I hit the street as the light changed and four lanes of rabid French drivers stomped their foot to the floor. The fella in the first lane swung left behind me but the motorcycle in the second lane knocked me down. I bounced and kept at it. The driver cursed. Every damn Frenchman out there leaned on his horn. Most, but not all, swerved to miss me. A couple would have happily killed me dead if I hadn't dodged. The only one to hit his brakes got rear-ended.

I made the sidewalk, turned left, and ran. A policeman blew his whistle but I couldn't say if it was at me or the fuss in front of T.G.I. Friday's. Whichever didn't matter. I wasn't about to stop for a damn whistle. When I first cut into the park, Remi was nowhere in sight. Didn't take long to spot him. He was the only one running, except me. Tourists with strollers and toddlers riding on their shoulders stopped to watch as we blew by, as if we were in the guidebook listed under *local color.* A boy wearing a Knott's Berry Farm sweatshirt pretended to shoot me. A black man in a skullcap held out a set of accordion-style postcards.

I said, "No, thanks."

If this had been any of six movies I could name featuring cow-boys in Central Park in New York City I would now have con-veniently found an unguarded traffic control horse, performed a spectacular rear vault mount, and galloped away, jumping over benches and bassinets. I never understood how a horse could be a broke-back nag in one shot and a steeplechaser the next. Or, more to the point, how the movie guys thought they could get away with a flying plow horse. Did the director think the audience were idiots? Heck, McCloud did it almost every week on TV. Not once did Dennis Weaver steal a horse that balked at hurdling a motorcycle.

This is immaterial because there wasn't a horse in sight and I wouldn't have stolen one if there had been. They shoot people for stealing horses. Rightly so.

Instead, I raced around a hedge and into a man wearing a three-piece suit and carrying a white dog. Those guys are as common in Paris as ski boots in Aspen. By the time I got him picked up and dusted off—with him chewing me out like it was my fault—Remi was way off down the park.

Shit-for-brains stole a Segway. A guide and a covey of tourists had gathered at a statue of a general on a Clydesdale. They'd dismounted and leaned their machines against a fence that encircled a tree. Must have been a special tree to get its own fence. And Remi ran up, grabbed one, and rode away.

When I huffed up, the tourists were yelling at each other in what I think was German. They looked German—burr haircuts, thick quadriceps, suspenders. The guide plopped himself down on a bench and held his hands up in an I'm-sick-of-this-job gesture.

I took one of the Segways by the handlebars and tried to figure out how to mount up. The youngest German made as if to stop me.

"Don't try it, Jack," I growled. It was a bluff, but he bought it. The hat gets them every time.

I stepped up on the foot platform dealies and waited. "How do you make this go?"

The guide said, "I'm not going to help you steal my machine."

I leaned forward, searching for an ignition, and the damn thing took off.

Behind me, the guide said, "Hell, take it."

Segways are weird. There's no gears, accelerator, brake, steering wheel, or anything. You lean forward and it goes forward, lean back and it stops. Turns the same way. They're like a two-wheeled horse. At first, I was all over heck and back. The thing required better posture than mine, but luckily Remi didn't appear any more Segway experienced than me. It took fifty yards to get it going where I wanted it to go at top speed, which I figure was maybe ten. At least I wasn't on foot. Any transportation beats running in cowboy boots.

The snake caught on to his machine about the time I got the hang of mine and soon we were weaving in and out of alarmed pedestrians. He liked to slalom benches. I almost caught the bastard by shortcutting around a fountain, but he took a hard right into a single-lane, one-way street going the wrong way. We both stayed up on the sidewalk, which was an adventure. It was kind of fun, in an urban way. I decided to get me one of these and throw it in the back of my truck. Use it for beer runs.

Remi came to a pedestrian who wouldn't back down. She looked like a fashion model, but I don't know. I don't know what fashion models look like in Paris or anyplace else. Only one I ever spoke to in person worked in a semitruck wash and twenty-four-hour massage parlor in Casper and she was wearing coveralls.

Whatever this one was, she didn't give an inch, so Remi jumped the curb into the street. I said, "Sorry," and jumped after him and fell. The woman laughed at me.

I said, "You try it."

By the time I made it back upright, Remi had turned a corner onto another six-way intersection. I came around the point to see him stop, step off, and hustle into a city bus. I bailed without stopping and my Segway hit the bus stop sign. The bus driver saw me, the prick. He could have let me in. It gave him great joy to shut the doors in my face.

I yelled, "Cocksucker!" and slapped the door. The driver pulled into traffic without so much as looking back, like he owned the road. Remi sat at the window, staring out at me. I flipped him the bird. He didn't care.

I felt like a failure. I hate feeling like a failure. It's a feeling I get often, whenever a bull throws me, but I have never gotten used to it. It's as if I'm not good enough to be a real cowboy.

A tall girl on a bicycle was looking down at my Segway. She had blond hair and legs so long she could sit on the bike seat with both feet on the sidewalk.

She said, *"Bravo. C'était pas mal."*

"You want to swap?" I nodded at the Segway. "Straight across. It's a dynamite machine, but I'll never be natural on it. You know cowboys, we can't handle anything invented after the pickup truck."

She said, *"Ce n'est pas mon vélo."*

"You won't regret the trade. I guarantee."

Fifteen seconds later, I was back on the road, chasing me a bus.

. . .

The only thing to be said for the bike as a mode of transportation is that it doesn't eat. I hadn't been on one since grade school, except for the time I tried to teach Tyson how to ride. I was too big for his Kmart Huffy and I broke a training wheel when my boot-cut jeans hung up in the spokes. Tyson cried and Mica blamed me, of course. That is our family pattern. I try, Ty cries, Mica blames.

The bus carrying Remi turned right into this incredibly active street with waves of traffic going both ways. There was a huge arch big as the famous one in Utah down at the end there, and that's where the bus headed. I almost caught him at a stop in front of Eddie Bauer. Fact is, I could have caught him if the driver had shown consideration, but I knew better than to think he would, so I didn't repeat the door-in-the-face routine again.

Pedaling was hard work. I couldn't figure out the gears. Maybe French bikes use a different gear system than the Monkey Ward model Dad picked up secondhand at a yard sale. As I recall, I never got that bike's gears down, either. My first lesson, I crashed into the side of the garage and Dad walked away without saying a word.

It started looking as if I would eventually catch the sucker. What then? I didn't want to land back in jail with the speed freak from Chillicothe, and jail seemed likely if I simply jumped on the bus and pounded the snot out of Remi. I knew I could take him, but could I take him off the bus? The more subtle plan—and God knows I'm subtle—would be to follow him in hopes he was headed toward Armand and the buckle. That made sense. He would want to report the success of his smoke bomb attack on T.G.I. Friday's. Even if he didn't lead me to Armand, he might go somewhere more private where pounding snot was an option.

Right before the big archway, the bus came to a God Almighty traffic circle. Cars met from every direction possible, like spokes on my bicycle, and merged together with no stoplights or signs, not even a Yield, into a six-lane racetrack. It was bizarre. They slid into the circle from the right, then jumped lane to lane as they sped around the arch until they finally spit themselves back out on the right into another street. The bus dived in. I watched, waiting for a gap that never came. Finally, I said, "Hell," and rode out into the thick of the mess.

The feeling was akin to diving into whitewater rapids. Cars zipped at me from both sides. They sped up, slowed down with no warning. Lane changes were made without a clue. Traffic flow was based on bluffing and it's tough to pull a bluff from the back of a bike when everyone else is in a car. The bike negated the hat.

Up ahead, the bus muscled its way around the circle, past five or six exits, then it took one.

Those French have an unnatural attachment to horns. The cursing and honking and fist shaking was even worse than back at the street where I jaywalked against the light. Imagine it's 1840 and you're stuck in a buffalo stampede. Riding a three-legged horse. Blind. A three-legged blind horse, with rickets.

Soon as I could, I parked myself in the exit lane and rode, nice and slow—to hell with the honkers—keeping my eye on the slot where the bus had gone. When the turn came, I pointed out my direction of travel and cut into the proper street, in time to see my bus tipping a rise.

I stopped, right boot on the curb, to catch my breath. Then I clamped my hat on tight, and pedaled.

Remi left the bus at a wide avenue that ran along the base of a ridge, and since I'd only seen the one hill in Paris, I figured this was the same one Mrs. Whiteside lived at the top of. The street sign, which they put on bricks in the wall there instead of signposts like any normal town would, said the street was named Pigalle. Near as I can tell, Pigalle is the French word for filthy perversion. You never saw a street like this, at least not in the Rocky Mountains. Every store sold something smutty. Arousal gear, mostly. Also paintings, photography, books, statues, and movies. Video games. A sign at one place said LIVE SEX. This was the only part of town where they had English on all the signs.

A street beggar with horrid teeth and a Janet Jackson T-shirt offered to help me find what I was looking for if I would give him five euros. What I was looking for was Remi, who had crossed the street and was hurrying by a cafe that advertised nude lesbian bartenders, so I had no need of the beggar's services. Instead, I gave him the bicycle. He seemed to appreciate the gift.

I crossed the street—with the light, for once—and followed Remi. I couldn't help stopping at the nude lesbian bartender cafe to see if the bartender was really nude. I don't know how you're supposed to tell a woman is lesbian if she's not wearing clothes. They all look the same naked. I couldn't see her snatch area because she stood behind the bar, staring at me with all the expression of a Gila monster, but the woman was topless. I can verify that much. Her hair was wet mop–colored and she stood with the posture of a redneck with knockers. She was about as sexy as a urinal cake.

She said, "Clint Eastwood."

I said, "Granny Clampett."

Remi was moving right along, not looking into the stripper bars or peep shows. He knew where he was going and I had to hustle to keep up. We passed a dance hall called Moulin Rouge. I suppose they named it after the movie. Almost everyone we walked by was carrying a camera, and that led me to believe the street was aimed at tourists, not locals. Well-dressed Asians and poorly dressed Americans. The Arabic community was well represented. No black people. Black people don't waste their time on spectator porn.

Another half block of dirty stuff later, Remi turned into the Sacré Coeur Sex Shoppe. I loitered at the door, interested in the window display. They had Grand Marnier–flavored panties, fur-lined handcuffs, a farmer sodomizing a Holstein milk cow, and a leather halter thing that might have gone on below the waist, I wasn't sure. These silver balls hung on a cord, like a miniature double ball and chain. I didn't know how they were used. My imagination failed me.

I gave it five minutes and, when Remi didn't come out, I went in.

28.

A bell tinkled over the door as I entered, which, because it was so low-tech, I took as cool. A woman sat behind a glass display case on the right, talking French on the telephone. She reminded me of Miss Crump from *The Andy Griffith Show* reruns. Nice dimples.

The woman put her hand over the phone mouthpiece and said, *"Bonjour, monsieur."*

"Bonjour, mademoiselle." I got it out fairly well.

"Is there any item you search for in particular?"

"I'm browsing—travel presents for the family. You know how it is, you can't come home without a present."

She smiled. "Simply ask if you have a question," then she returned to her phone conversation.

The shop was a high-ceilinged room set up with inflatable girls on the left and dirty videos on the right. A middle aisle was covered by sick toys like I'd seen in the window and a remarkable display of dildos. The dildos were what caught my attention. I'd seen plenty of inflatable girls in my life. These in Paris had names like Pepette and Rosanna. Their boobs were more realistic than the bazoombas you find on American blowups. Other than that, they were your standard, off-the-shelf babes.

But the dildos! The dildos were amazingly creative, coming in a wide variety of shapes, colors, and levels of firmness, from a smallish — by dildo standards — circumcised number with a slight arcing curve to the huge meat hook I'd seen back in Giselle's bedroom. Snakes the size of a python. Insertable fence posts. A bunch had double heads, for going in both sides at once, I suppose. The concept must be uniquely French. Many of the dildos were the strap-on kind, and a couple of the inflatables had been rigged to show how the straps attached. One looked like Giselle, same Ping-Pong-ball tint to the skin, same Rottweiler eyes. I'd bet the ranch she was the model for whoever designed the doll. Her attached dildo could have poleaxed a wolf.

What I didn't see was the classic truck stop condom machine French tickler. I blew seventy-five cents on one once in Arizona, to see what it was, and discovered a latex ring deal meant to fit over your pecker, with plastic fringe along the top that theoretically brushes up against the clit as you move in and out. I was too embarrassed to pull it out in real life, afraid the girl would either scream or laugh. Maybe French ticklers are like French toast. There's no such thing as French toast in France.

A blue beaded curtain hung across a door at the back of the shop, beside what looked like a medieval rack. Barring secret passages or cubbyholes, Remi must have gone into whatever was behind the curtain. I looked back at the nice lady who had her head down and was speaking earnestly into her phone. I imagine it was a domestic situation. With her head down, I seized the opportunity and went through the curtain.

Three Japanese businessmen were sitting on folding chairs, looking through a glass panel at a man and woman who were performing live sex. The viewing room had ultraviolet tube lighting so the businessmen glowed a faint shade of purple. I think it's called mauve.

The man and woman behind the panel were in a room decked out like an artist's studio, the kind you find in an attic. They were facing each other on a desk chair with wheels. The man looked

early fifties, and the woman late thirties. Neither one had an ounce
of fat. You could count their ribs. Her breasts dangled a bit, bouncing up and down not quite in sync with her hip action. Screwing
in a chair is an overrated art, so far as I'm concerned. I've tried it
now and again, only to prove how open I am to new experience.
After a few minutes jiggling while my feet go dead from lack of
blood, I've managed to channel the exercise back to a more Chris-
tian position.

For a while I thought the businessmen were looking through a
one-way mirror, until the man in the desk chair shot me with his
thumb and index finger pistol, same way the guy had back at the
money-changing booth in the airport. He leaned down to whisper
in the woman's ear and she looked back at me and laughed.

I've never understood the lure of watching other people have
sex. It's like watching people eat. If you can't do it yourself, I don't
see the thrill. I've shared motel rooms with rodeo cowboys, saddle
bronc riders, as a rule, who watched pay-per-view soft porn all
night. I can take about five minutes before cracking open a book.

To me, the Japanese guys were more interesting than the couple
behind the glass. One was a generation older than the other two.
They all three had on earphones and the old one wore wraparound
sunglasses. I decided to write a poem about a rich man in Japan
who wants to teach his sons the finer points of love, so he flies them
to Paris, where they end up watching a man and woman screw on a
desk chair.

Maybe they weren't even Japanese. I have no experience telling
Japanese from Chinese or Korean. You throw a bunch of Navajos
and Cheyenne in a room, I could sort them out, but I know nothing
about Asians. It's probably a cultural bias to say the men watching
the sex show were Japanese.

"You guys see a runt with pointy sideburns come through
here?" I asked.

They ignored me. No doubt they didn't know English, or maybe the headphones were cranked up high. I can't help but wonder what they were listening to.

I said, "Don't mind me," and went looking for an alternative way out. The wall on each side of the glass panel was covered by a velvet curtain over a door. The door on the left led to the filthiest bathroom in Europe. Which is saying a lot. The toilet was a hole in the floor with shoe prints painted yellow on each side to show you where to stand. The sink looked like men in the viewing area had used it for relief. I'd go on the sidewalk before I'd go in there.

The curtain on the right covered a staircase leading up. I chose door number two.

Two landings later I walked through a door into a bare room that I would call cheerless. Pine floor, plywood walls, one window, it reminded me of a stock grower's office. A computer sat on a card table connected to a printer on the floor. Papers lay scattered about, as if placed by the wind. Bailed tracts were stacked next to one wall and sabotage supplies along the lines of wine bottles, rags, and red gasoline cans lay next to the other wall, all the makings of trouble. From a door on the far side of the room, I heard the murmur of people talking French. Remi's was the only voice I recognized.

I crossed to the computer and glanced down to see what they were up to, but it was all gobbledygook. There wasn't time to dick around on it like I had Giselle's. All I had time for right now was counting *one, two, three* then busting through the door and kicking French ass, which suddenly felt easier to do in theory than practice. Before I reached *two*, a cell phone over there played one of those little tunes that make cell phones even more irritating than they are naturally.

Armand grunted, *"C'est qui?"* I remembered his voice from before—oily slick—like a singer who fronts for a band but doesn't play an instrument himself. I've never had any use for those guys. They think highly of themselves.

Armand exclaimed something I translated as *Jesus Christ,* then he came charging into the room where I waited.

He said, *"C'est ce foutu cowboy."*

I nodded to the gas cans. "You planning a revolution here, Armand?"

Remi, Leon, and two tough guys I hadn't seen before followed Armand into the room. The tough guys had broken-nosed sneers, like Jack Palance in *Shane.* I think they were brothers. A woman I hadn't seen before either slinked out after them—anorexic, multi-pierced, shaved head with an amoeba tattoo over the crown— followed by Giselle herself. Giselle wore a McDonald's uniform shirt with the top three buttons open, revealing the top edge of a demi-cup bra.

Armand looked over at Remi and snarled something I didn't catch. I imagine he wasn't happy Remi had led me to the hideout. Remi whined his excuse, Lord knows what it was. He had no excuse.

Armand turned his attention back to me. "Starbucks must be desperate to rely on someone so stupid as you."

"You're the one relying on Remi here. Who you calling stupid?"

Armand made everyone wait while he lit a cigarette. I hate that. Smoking's bad enough without forcing others to go on your schedule. "Remi was a fool to lead you to me." Armand blew smoke my way. "You are a bigger fool to invade my offices without a weapon."

"Who says I don't have a weapon?"

That stumped him for like three seconds. "Produce it."

I shrugged. There wasn't much I could say that wasn't flippant or foolish. This didn't seem the time or place to fall back on either of those.

Armand said, "I thought so."

Remi smirked. I hate smirkers. He and Leon were drifting up opposite sides of the room, as if I wouldn't notice if they stayed casual. The other two guys flanked Armand. They were all obviously expecting to rush me soon, and were only awaiting the signal. I figured the longer I put off the signal, the better.

"I'm here for the buckle. Give it to me and there will be no trouble."

"You cannot possibly expect me to believe you came all the way from America to retrieve a belt buckle."

"It has sentimental value."

Armand frowned. I don't think he knew the word *sentimental.* Giselle leaned against the door frame and glared at me with the kind of hatred you can only have for someone you've slept with. The bald girl was more aggressively snotty. Those were the two I had to watch out for. The guys might beat me to a pulp, but those two women would happily cut off my balls.

"Armand," I said. "Bud. You've got an impressive operation going here." I swept my arm to show the tracts, computer, gas cans. The works. "You don't want to risk losing the ranch for a belt buckle." He smoked, listening. I needed to keep him listening. If Armand stopped listening, I had a problem.

"Let's say this turns out terrible for me and you have old Leon there break my neck. The Paris police aren't going to sit still for killing an American tourist. It's bad public relations."

He held the cigarette between his finger and thumb like a joint instead of a cigarette, showing off how cool he was for the girls. "That might be true if you are a simple American tourist, but we know you are not."

I made a mental note to strangle Pinto Whiteside. "Whoever told you that CIA and Starbucks baloney was pulling your chain." *Baloney* and *pulling your chain* may have been too much slang to expect a French purist to catch in a single sentence. I went on anyway. "They wanted to see if you would buy it. They lied."

"The information came from a trusted comrade."

"Yeah, but the man who told him lied. Your trusted comrade passed on bad information."

Armand flicked ashes on the floor. What a slob. "Why would I believe you over an ally in the battle against American tyranny?"

"Because I don't give a damn. You can throw all the smoke bombs you want, it doesn't affect me one way or another. What you do to McDonald's is your business."

At the word *McDonald's* Armand stiffened. The whole bunch stiffened, even the ones who didn't know English. You'd think I just peed in the vino.

"What do you know about McDonald's?"

I was walking on the egg carton here. Time to think about what I said before I said it. "I'm not an idiot. You have all these McDonald's shirts around." I gestured at Giselle, who hadn't blinked in two minutes. "I assume you're up to more than looking for after-school work. The thing is, I don't give a flying hoot for or against your cause. Be an outlaw if it gets your rocks off. All I want to know is, where's my buckle?"

Giselle reached into her cleavage and pulled out my Crockett County Bull Riding Champion belt buckle. Even though I'd only seen it for ten seconds or less, I would have recognized it anywhere.

She said, "Throw the cowboy out the window."

That was the signal.

Repercussions were about what you would expect, especially if you expect to get the crap beat out of yourself. Remi was a sadistic prick and Leon knew how to hurt people. The two might-be brothers fought like they were the political theorists of the cell and not the muscle. Mostly they waited till I was down and then kicked my head.

Leon was a pro. He led by slapping me, open-handed, in the ear hole. That would have been enough. I would have gladly jumped out the window right then, and I headed that way, but he grabbed my left arm and twisted it up, popping the shoulder ball from the socket. Remi bit my other ear. I could hardly believe it. The bastard thought he could inflict pain by biting my ear off when my shoulder was already popped. Next to a popped joint, all the torn flesh in creation is diddly.

Then I was on the floor and the poli sci majors were kicking my head, until they got in each other's way and the one decided my crotch and kidneys were handier targets. I made it to my knees and crawled for the window. Remi stomped the fingers of my left hand. Leon gave one last rib kick and stepped back to give the others a turn. I looked over at Armand and the girls. They were watching with all the detached interest that the Japanese had shown watching the couple nail downstairs.

After a short but intense spell of pounding, Leon grabbed a handful of hair and lifted me clear off the floor. That's how strong he was. Remi tried for my feet but I kicked him away, which was probably not the thing to do with all my weight pulling on my hair roots. It felt as if the hair had to rip out soon, or the scalp had to rip off. Something had to rip.

Leon turned my body and held it like a baby. The relief was so great, I wanted to thank him. The look in his eyes was not unlike kindness, dare I say love, as he carried me to the window and threw me out.

29.

No two cracked skulls are quite the same. Sometimes you're knocked senseless and wake up to a brutal headache they skip over when the hero gets coldcocked in Western movies. Other times, you keep going on about like normal, only later you look back and there's this gap in your life. A day will be gone. The opposite of time standing still, it's more like time skips. I've seen cowboys come out of a two-month coma thinking they were still in the arena.

I came to after an unknown period of time in a skinny alley with garbage cans and outhouse-looking toilets. Barrels leaking oil-slick rainbows. Walls tagged in French with bars on the windows you couldn't see through for the grime. Directly beneath my head a nice-sized puddle of blood had coagulated, so I'd been out that long anyway, long enough for coagulation. What I could see of the sky through the mist was darker than it had been last time I looked. Night had fallen while I was out.

Up against the wall by a wooden door, a street alcoholic squatted on his heels on a collapsed cardboard box, a bottle in his hand, watching me.

I said, *"Christ."*

He didn't say much of anything.

I pulled up my knees and tried pushing off the ground. Incredible pain shot through my shoulder. The ball was out of its spot. I could see it over my pecs, inside my chest. The bit-off ear and bleeding head and whatever was wrong with my ribs could have been fought through to the other side, but the shoulder had to be taken care of. Now.

As I made it to my feet, I managed to pull what was left of my shirt off. Lucky for me cowboy fashion demands the button-up. I could never have done it with a pullover. I held the shirt to my temple where most of the blood seemed to be situated.

"I can do this. I make my living on hard falls."

The alcoholic didn't react. If anything, he was in worse shape than me. His nose ran badly, and he drooled a touch. His eyes had pinprick pupils with mismatched directional orientation. One eye stared my way while the other eye drifted off to the sky. His clothes looked like he'd done his laundry with Kleenex in the pockets. The bottle had no label. The liquid in it was green.

"Only difference is out here, nobody's likely to gore a man while he's down," I said.

I stumbled over and held out my left hand. The fingers were fairly mangled. "Hold on here." I pointed to the wrist.

His head nodded up and down just a bit, and he commenced to hum.

I took his hand and showed him how to hold my wrist. He had a fairly good grip, for a wino. My bet would be syphilitic, too. You get a case and don't take care of it, in no time flat you'll be urinating in a bag.

"Hold tight," I said, then I lurched back and yanked the arm straight. I hit the joint with the flat of my right hand and popped her back in the hole there. The relief was dramatic. One moment, you're on fire, and the next, you're not. It's sore as hell, I grant, but sore beats the daylights out of excruciating. The thing is, I'd blown both shoulders three or four times in the past—even carried metal clips in the right one—and, while the hurt never improves, the more times you do it the easier it comes out but also the easier it goes back in. I've heard Houdini the magician could pop his shoulder in and out like opening a drawer.

"Much obliged," I said.

The humming turned to a bit of a song, only I didn't recognize the words or tune.

I said, "I appreciate you not rolling me while I was out cold over there."

He held out the bottle, offering me a swig. The drool and scabby mouth were off-putting, but I've never in my life wiped the lip of a bottle before drinking after a man. I wasn't about to start with a guy who had delivered me from pain.

"Thanks, bub." I drank enough so's he wouldn't be insulted yet not so much to where I was taking alcohol he might need. It's a narrow line.

"Is this absinthe?"

He shrugged.

I held the bottle up like I was selling it on TV. "Absinthe?"

He grinned, mostly toothless. "NyQuil."

I gave the guy what money I had on me. It wasn't but seventy euros or so. Most of what I had was back in Odette's dirty clothes pile. It's a good thing I carry cash in my right front pocket. I'm not sure I could have gotten into my left.

"Go buy yourself some proper whiskey," I said.

He stared at the euros that had appeared in his hand as if they were magic beans and I was a wizard. I suppose having a man fall out of the sky and then get up and give you money must be disconcerting. I looked up at the window I thought was the one I came out of. It wasn't but twenty feet or so up there. I'd have been okay if I hadn't landed on my head.

"Now they've got my hat and my belt buckle."

The drunk grabbed my right wrist. I guess he figured if grabbing the left earned him seventy, grabbing the right might get him more.

"No, thanks," I said. "I've got to be somewhere."

. . .

The bum fella was hunched by a doorway, only from outside I couldn't see if it led to the Sacré Coeur place or not. I hadn't found a door going out when I was in the live showroom, so rather than take a chance, I abandoned my Good Samaritan and went around the block onto the street. A rat was playing in swill there on the corner. I stopped to watch. We don't have rats in Wyoming, at least, not that I know about. We have chiseler ground squirrels that look like rats. It's funny the difference in how people see squirrels and rats. Squirrels are cute, rats are ugly, yet they look basically the same. There's a lesson in life for you.

The tinkling bell still tinkled. The woman still sat behind the glass case full of toys, but she wasn't talking on the phone anymore. She was reading a French paperback and when she saw me something akin to horror leaped to her eyes. I liked that. I crossed the floor between us quickly and she drew back, afraid I was going to strike her. I wouldn't strike her. I can hardly believe she thought I might. Instead, I ripped the phone from the wall.

Of course, phones don't rip from walls the way they did when I was young. Now, all she had to do was wait till I'd gone upstairs, plug back in, and call Armand again, so I yanked the other end of the cord from the phone itself and stuffed the wire wad into my back pocket. I'd be come and gone before she found another lead-in.

I said, "Stay put."

She didn't seem likely to go anywhere. I must have looked like roadkill itself. My left arm was semi-useless and I hadn't felt to see what remained of my ear. I handed her the blood-soaked shirt.

"Here."

She took it. I don't know why I gave it to her or why she took it. I'd had a crush on her earlier, but that was over. The woman watched in silence as I worked my way down the dildo display, hefting the big ones, testing for weight and thickness. I almost went with the meat hook model I'd first seen at Giselle's. It had a circumcision ridge would have looked nice on Leon's forehead, but I settled on this twenty-inch enamel number, looked like a black adder. I whacked it once on the countertop — *Whack* — solid and satisfying.

I looked back at the woman. "Put this on Armand's tab."

She didn't move a muscle.

The Japanese businessmen were long gone, replaced by a teen tour from Lewisville, Texas. I know because two of the boys and one girl had on Lewisville Fighting Farmers letter jackets. The boys' said TRACK on the back, the girl's said CHEERLEADING. In GroVont we didn't give letters for cheerleading.

The man and woman on the other side of the glass were still going at it. They'd left the chair and were performing a modified beast-with-two-backs against the bureau.

One of the girls — not the one in the letter sweater — said, "That must be heck on the lumbar."

A boy said, "Mrs. McConaughy's going to be P.O.ed we didn't go to the Picasso Museum." The others laughed at him and I knew how he felt.

The man saw me through the window. He mouthed some kind of exclamation and pointed me out to the woman, who had to twist her neck to see what he was exclaiming about.

One of the Fighting Farmers said, "Holy cow, what happened to you?"

"I was ruined by Internet porn," I said.

The others turned to stare at me.

"Don't let it happen to you."

The door was open upstairs. I went across the front room as fast as possible without making a lot of noise and walked on into the back room where people were gathered around a wood table, eating bread, lunch meat, and olives from a bowl, and drinking wine — same bunch as before, except they'd been joined by Bernard, wearing a McDonald's shirt buttoned clear up to the Adam's apple. There was only the one chair and Armand had it, so the others ate standing up or sitting on licey-looking mattresses against the wall.

The trick is don't waste time. Go to it. I walked up to Leon and hit him hard as I could, dildo to medial collateral ligament. He went down like a sack of cement falling off a truck. The bald-headed girl screamed and Remi dug for his knife. I tapped him upside the head and that was all she wrote for Remi.

I whirled and whacked, whirled and whacked, the avenging angel dealing God's justice on my terms. Samson had his jawbone of an ass, Rowdy Talbot had his dildo. One poli sci guy yelled and ran from the room while the other went fetal and blubbered. Bernard didn't fight back but I popped him anyway, for sleeping with Odette. Leon was the only one man enough to need more than one whack. He took three, including shots to the trachea and the base of his spine, before he gave it up.

Armand didn't move, the dumb cluck. I think he thought he was observing life and not part of it. The bald-headed girl kept screaming till I faked a backhand at her amoeba. That shut her up. Giselle backed against the wall and glared at me with that trapped-animal look of hers.

Soon as everyone who was willing to put up a fight was done with, I walked over and stood close up in front of Giselle.

"My buckle."

"You wouldn't hit a woman. It's against the cowboy code."

"Who told you about the code?"

"I heard you and Odette, while I was in the toilette. You cannot cheat a friend or hit a woman."

I poked her between the legs with my dildo. "Read the rules, honey. There's exceptions for bull riders."

Armand spit. *"Donne-la lui."*

She looked over at Armand, her eyes flashing almost as much hatred at him as she'd laid on me. Her fingers dipped into the demi-cup cleavage and came out with my buckle. She'd had it hooked over the strap between her cups. Couldn't have been all that comfortable.

"That's the spirit," I said. I took the buckle with my left hand, which wasn't easy, but I was afraid to set down the dildo to use my right. Leon might get a second wind. I glanced at the buckle, noticing again how the cowboy's riding arm was out of position. Whoever made it had stressed Western romance more than accuracy.

I said, "Let that be a lesson to you."

My Stetson was on the floor, under the lunch spread table. When I bent to pick it up, the room spun.

Armand said, "Go back to the States. Do not let me see you in Paris again."

"Crap," I said. "I forgot about you."

I went back and sapped Armand, right across the bridge of his French nose. On a one-hundred-point scoring scale, the satisfaction level was in the high nineties.

30.

The teen tour kids had gone off to wherever American teen tour kids go at night in Paris, back to the hotel to practice lessons they'd learned on their field trip, I suppose. The man and woman behind the glass were still going at it, in bed, now. Woman on top. Their eyes lit up with expressions of perfect delight. I stopped to watch their faces but not their bodies. It's not that often I see happy people and, when it happens, I try to take notice. It came to me that those two must be in love. Why else would they keep the show up after the audience had departed?

I gave the woman behind the toy counter her dildo and phone wire. She seemed grateful.

"You should find a job working somewhere else," I said.

She said, "I will."

Back out on the street, the weather had stopped fooling with that mist-hanging-in-the-air stuff and gone on to serious rain. I was shirtless, blood-spattered, worn out, and lost. To tell the truth, chasing down the buckle had been an emotional drain. I didn't know how much of a drain until after I got the buckle back. I'd been operating on adrenaline since Colorado, and now it all came crashing down, even though this wasn't a convenient location for a crash. Part of me wished I hadn't given the NyQuil man all my money. I could have held back some for a bus ticket or a cup of French coffee.

I was staring at a thirty-weight slick in the gutter, wondering whether to turn right or left, when the mustard and metallic blue Citroën appeared at the curb. Pinto Whiteside rolled down the window and said, "Need a lift?"

He had the dog back — Monty, washed and fluffed — and now that it was nighttime, Pinto had gone to wearing sunglasses. I've never met a silver-ponytailed guy wearing sunglasses at night yet who can be trusted.

"Not from you," I said.

He said, "Get in the automobile."

I hesitated, weighing the odds of making it till daylight without him. They weren't that good.

"Do you require help with the door?" he asked.

"I can open the damn door."

And I could, and did, but that was about the limit of my abilities. I sat in the front seat with the heater blowing on my legs and I closed my eyes. The dog licked my chewed-on ear.

"I don't have any money," I said.

"We'll extend credit, this once."

Pinto slid her into gear and we lurched into the wet street. Close as I was to unconscious, I could still tell his clutch was doomed.

"Did you get your buckle back?" he asked.

"Yep."

"Was it much trouble?"

"Not much."

Pinto let out a low chuckle devoid of humor. "You cowboys are so macho. I used to hate that in New Mexico. It's as if the worst thing you tough guys can possibly do is admit you have a problem."

I talked with my eyes closed. "Macho's got nothing to do with tough. Those are two separate items. Toughest rodeo cowboys I ever met were the gay bull riders."

"Are there a number of those?"

"Enough they have their own circuit. Gay bull riders catch it from both sides — bulls and rednecks who wear hats. You don't want to cross a gay bull rider."

"I'll keep that in mind."

The tires *whish*ed as we sped up the hill. I like the sound of tires on wet pavement. It reminds me of driving into Jackson with Dad in his old Willys truck with the split windshield. He didn't have air-conditioning so we rode with the windows down. You don't see people driving with their windows down anymore, except kids, who love the sensation of wind lifting their arm like a bird. Mica completely freaks out now when Tyson sticks his hand out the window. She tells him the story of a little boy from her youth who lost his arm from the elbow down on a speed limit sign. Dad didn't care if I rode with my arm out or not. I should probably resent him for that, but I don't. There's too much else on the list.

"Where we going?" I asked.

"To get you patched up?"

"I don't need patching. I need a ride to the place where my passport is."

"Why can't you lift your left arm?"

"I can. I'd just rather not."

"That cut on your head needs stitches."

"I can't afford the hospital."

"In my line, we don't use hospitals. We'll take you to a safe house and put you back together. After that, we need to talk."

I groaned. "Nobody, ever, anywhere, *needs* to talk."

"We do."

"That means you want to talk and you expect me to listen."

Without warning, Pinto whipped into a narrow street climbing up the hill. He was humming a Johnny Cash song called "Ring of Fire." Monty put a paw on my thigh, whining. He wanted to be petted but he was on my left side there and I didn't feel up to the effort. It's terrible when you've come to a place in your life where you can't pet a dog. The thought should have sent me spinning into a reevaluation of what matters but I was too tired to dwell on it. What I needed was a nap.

Pinto pointed to a building coming up on our right. "Van Gogh lived on the fourth floor of that house." He downshifted for a hard turn up the hill. "His ear was a mess, too, same as yours."

31.

The safe place Pinto took me to get patched was his wife's bordello. As there wasn't any street parking left, he drove up the sidewalk and parked in front of the gate so people coming in and going out had to walk around his rear bumper. He and Monty got out. I stayed where I felt comfortable and dry.

"Your wife's in there," I said.

"Mrs. Whiteside is a trained nurse technician. She only prostitutes for money."

"What other reason is there?"

"Most of the women in quality houses are here for the prestige. Or they're bored at home. Did you ever see *Belle de Jour*?"

"No."

Monty whined in Pinto's arms, wanting in out of the rain.

"Come, Rowdy, the damp will frizz Monty's do."

I said, "She'll recognize me. She'll know I was spying for you."

"You told me she didn't see you this afternoon." Pinto stooped down to look in the window. "Am I correct in assuming she did not look at you? You wouldn't lie about something that important."

I opened the door and swung my legs out. "I don't lie. I'm from Wyoming."

Inside after dark was more along the lines of what a fancy house of ill repute ought to be. Before, it'd been like the waiting room in a day spa. Now, there actually was a piano player. He wasn't blind, but he was black, which is almost as good. He was playing "Bridge Over Troubled Waters," leaning to the side and smiling during the intense parts. The women ignored him. There were five of them, mostly reading thick magazines and smoking cigarettes. They glanced up when the door opened, saw it was Pinto, and went about their business. Not a one in there was under thirty-five. They could have passed for a secretarial pool. No wonder it was a slow night for fleshpots.

An older woman in a shiny red slacks suit came charging across the room, chattering French all the way. Her hair was legal pad yellow and teased into a wasps' nest. Regal rouge. Solid jewelry. She looked surprisingly close to Yancy Hollister's grandmother, known in Texarkana as the Queen of the All-You-Can-Eat Buffet.

The woman I took as the madam jabbed a finger at me. Maybe it was because I was dribbling on her nice hardwood floor, or maybe they had a "no shirt, no service" rule. Something about me set her off. She didn't think I was good enough to be in her whorehouse.

Pinto's French was impressive, I have to admit that. She gave him what for and he gave it right back. I kept an eye on the prostitutes. None of them seemed interested. If I lived in a foreign country and a bleeding, bare-chested cowboy came into my parlor, I'd at least look at him. I guess, at their age, those women had seen it all.

Finally, Pinto grunted, *"Oui."* He dug in his front pocket and came out with a chunk of turquoise. It was more veined than the one he sold me, a darker blue. The madam lady snatched the turquoise from Pinto's hand and threw me a look of scorn.

As we mounted the staircase, Pinto said, "You owe me, buster."

We waited in the hallway, outside Mrs. Whiteside's room. Pinto smoked a cigar. I admired the paintings. He said, "La Pastille has been an establishment on this location for over two hundred years." He nodded toward the geezer I was looking at—bent nose, white hair, effeminate jacket. "Dumas himself got his ashes hauled in this building."

I nodded as if I knew who Dumas was. I'll bet I would have known if I'd seen it spelled out. French names are hardly ever pronounced the way they read on paper, and I only know the famous ones from reading.

"Weren't those women downstairs kind of elderly to be hooking?"

Pinto coughed, politely, not a real cough so much as making noise in hopes someone will hear you. "The women here do not consider themselves hookers. They are legitimate courtesans."

"Legitimate courtesans. Isn't there a word for that?"

"You're thinking of oxymoron."

"No, that's not what I'm thinking."

The door swung open and a man in a military uniform I'm sure wasn't American came out of Mrs. Whiteside's room. He was a spiffy general or admiral or some other high-rank fella with a mustache and stick-up-his-ass posture. The man didn't look at us and Pinto didn't look at him. It must be awkward. I've stood in line at Home Depot behind guys I knew had Mica. There's a natural urge to stove in their rib cage.

We found Pinto's wife sitting at the iron patio table, smoking a brown cigarette. She was wearing a pearl gray lounging robe and writing in a notebook. I suppose she kept trick records. She said something sharp to Pinto, I figure something like, "Close the damn door," because that's what he did. Then she said something else that made him take his sunglasses off.

He waved the glasses in my direction. "Rowdy Talbot, meet my wife, Alene Whiteside."

I was embarrassed, not so much from my condition as I was at seeing this stately woman so soon after she'd done whatever disgusting thing she did for money. Mrs. Whiteside still came off as dignified. Her hair was clean without looking overbred. Her robe was casually modest. She wasn't ruffled like a woman who'd just had sex with a stranger. I don't think Mica or any other American girl I've met would come off as dignified in her position.

"I'm sorry, ma'am," I said.

Mrs. Whiteside recognized me right off. I could see it from her face and I'm not sure how Pinto couldn't. When it comes to wives, men see what they want to see. She knew who I was and where she'd seen me, and it only took her two seconds to put together why I'd barged in earlier. I guess it was no more to her advantage to blow my cover than it was mine to blow hers.

"Vous êtes blessé." She glided over to me, the way I picture an angel gliding. Her fingers went to the cut on my forehead. She murmured words that sounded like comfort.

"Sit on the bed," Pinto said.

"I'll soil the sheets."

"The sheets are already soiled. She has to change them anyway."

Pinto threw a spread over the mussy stuff and I sat on the end of the bed while Mrs. Whiteside moved into her toilette there. I heard drawers opening and closing. She spoke softly to Monty, who went under what I would call a makeup table. He circled three times, clockwise, and settled.

I said, "Don't bother yourself on my account. All I need's codeine and bag balm, and there's some of each back in my saddlebag."

She came out carrying water in a blue basin, fancy soap, butterfly bandages, and some spray stuff. Bactine or the French equivalent.

"Mrs. Whiteside was a nurse when we lived in the Middle East," Pinto said. "She took up her new profession after we moved to Paris. She needs something to do while I travel."

"That's interesting."

Her fingers pressed on my chest, lowering me to the bed. The touch was wonderful. You know how sometimes you go to the emergency room and a nurse touches you and you know right off this woman is here to take care of you. You are no longer the sole person holding yourself together. You can let go. That's how Mrs.

Whiteside's fingers felt, like I was a child and she was the mom other people have.

Pinto paced like a man feeling his nerves. "The time has come to answer questions."

"Not me."

"You must, anyway. We have no room for error after tonight."

Questions were the last thing I wanted. What I wanted was to float under Mrs. Whiteside's hands. She washed the cut on my head first. Even though it was visually speaking the most gruesome of my aches and pains, it didn't cause that much discomfort. Head wounds tend to bleed more than hurt.

"How many of Armand's people were in the building when you left?"

I didn't answer. She sprayed Bactine or whatever it was on my cut. It stung like hell, but in a good way. Absence of pain means you're dead, so sometimes a good sting is what it takes to prove you're alive.

"How many?"

"Eight, except one ran out. Another one or two might be dead. I don't think so, but you never can tell."

"Did you see signs of McDonald's paraphernalia?"

"Can a shirt be paraphernalia? Two of them had on McDonald's shirts."

Mrs. Whiteside's hands moved over to my left ear, the one Remi bit. The ear Leon slapped hurt more. He'd jangled something inside, past the wax. Remi just chewed cartilage.

"Which two were wearing McDonald's uniforms?"

"Giselle, the snuff queen I met in Colorado, and Odette's boyfriend, although he might be an ex-boyfriend by now. Bernard."

The bed shifted when Pinto sat on it. My extreme wish was that he would go away so I could sleep under his wife's hands. She struck me as one classy woman. "Were there computers? Printouts? That sort of thing."

"One computer. And piles of pamphlets. They had the makings for Arapaho bombs—gasoline, rags, wine bottles."

"That's called a Molotov cocktail."

"Back home they're Arapaho bombs. I'm fixing to pass out now, so I'll answer any more questions later."

Mrs. Whiteside moved off and came back with what looked like a jade jewelry case but was in fact a mobile hospital. I think. It was one heck of a well-stocked first aid kit. She swabbed my ear with a deadening agent that not only killed the pain but made my eardrum vibrate like there was that sound of a landline computer connecting to the Internet in my brain. She murmured soft words I couldn't catch as she pulled a curved needle I would have thought was used to sew canvas out of the box. Pinto said something French and her answer wasn't near as soft as whatever she'd been saying to me. I watched her thread the needle with this brown wire about as thick as dental floss, then I closed my eyes and let her go to it. There wasn't any pain to speak of. More of a sensation of a foreign object passing back and forth through my flesh. I enjoyed her fingers on my skin a lot, at least as much as I usually enjoy nailing.

If I ever pay for sex, here's what I'll do. I'll go to a woman in her fifties, like Mrs. Whiteside. She was kind. Instinct tells me whores my age or younger are not kind. They haven't been around long enough to forgive. I don't see the point in paying for a bang, but I can see paying a woman to stroke my face and murmur, "Poor boy, you're going to be okay."

Pinto said, "You must go back in."

I said the first thing that popped in my head. "Fat chance, hoss."

"Lives are at stake."

I opened my eyes. Mrs. Whiteside smiled at me. Her eyes were dun with tobiano flecks. Behind her, Pinto's skin glistened, as if he'd been spritzed with 7UP. Behind him, the mirror reflected the back of his ponytail and the back of Mrs. Whiteside's frosted brown hair. I was too low on the bed to see myself, which was for the best. Way across on the far wall, Jesus hung spread-eagled on a cross.

Pinto kept at it. "Giselle bought poison in the mountains outside of Boulder. She smuggled it back here in her tampon tube. Armand and whomever paid for her trip are conspiring to kill McDonald's customers. They will destroy the business and put thousands of people out of work, and I can't stop them unless I know which stores he's going to hit and which employees are plants. I need you to find out."

I concentrated on not moving my head while she sewed. The *whomever* bothered me. I never have gotten that one figured out. "So shut down all the McDonald'ses in France. That wouldn't be a great loss. People can switch to Wendy's."

"There's eight hundred franchises in France, nine within the Paris *périphérique* itself. I can't close all of them."

"Your buddies at CIA could."

Pinto stood up and walked to the window. I could see his back in the mirror as he looked out on the street. He spoke facing away from me, so he was hard to hear. "My superiors in the agency are not taking the McDonald's threat seriously."

"If your boss doesn't believe you, I don't either. I'm not even sure you know anybody at the CIA. I think you're a turquoise-dealing taxi driver."

"How did you get out of jail this morning?"

"Got me."

"Think about it."

Mrs. Whiteside finished my head and put away her needle. She pulled out a bottle of stuff that smelled like Vicks VapoRub and moved down to my chest. I closed my eyes again, drifting toward sleep. When I was a kid and dragged home scraped up, I got out my own Mercurochrome and Band-Aids. Mom claimed messiness made her woozy. Dad said a little bleeding never hurt anyone. It only seemed natural years later when Ty came along for me to be the one who cleaned him up when he got hurt. Mica would smoke her Salem Light and tell me not to baby the boy while I washed and wrapped. Even at two, Ty knew kissing a hurt place didn't make it better.

I slept on and off for a couple hours until the Georgia Tech basketball team showed up downstairs and Mrs. Whiteside told Pinto she needed her room professionally. I thanked her for taking care of me. She gave me a T-shirt with the second amendment printed on the back, left by a gun nut from Alaska. As we were leaving, Pinto, Monty, and I passed the team coming upstairs. The kid in front was about seven feet tall. I started to explain to him how rodeo athletes must train and work to master our sport whereas all he had to do was be tall. He pretended he couldn't see me.

In the taxi, Pinto gave me the silent treatment. He was angry and wanted me to know it, but silence was my best friend, right then. Anger isn't that bad if whoever's feeling it keeps their mouth shut.

The silence was too good to last. "The poison is manufactured in Gold Hill, Colorado, from a toadstool called *plueus villosus*. One flyspeck will kill a customer before he gets out the door. Giselle brought in enough to murder five thousand innocent people."

"I'm tired," I said. "I want to go home."

"No one will patronize McDonald's for months."

We came to a stone bridge over the river. A boat lit up like a Christmas tree was passing under the bridge as we went over. It was pretty, in a tame way. I wish I knew the name of the river.

"Why don't you do it?" I asked. "Kick in the door, bust everyone in sight, and save McDonald's. You'd be a hero. They'd put your picture on a Happy Meal."

He took the sunglasses off, I suppose in hopes I would think he was telling the truth. "That would expose a cover I've spent twenty years building. You think I enjoy drinking all day and boring strangers in bars? You think I'm content, married to a whore?"

"You wife seems sweet to me. Better than mine."

There was a gigantic statue on the far side of the bridge, Neptune or Pluto, one of those gods. People milled around, not going anywhere. I wondered what there could be to do outdoors in the middle of the night.

"I cannot believe you would cross the world for a belt buckle but you won't lift a finger to save an American company in need. Where's your patriotism?"

"I left it in my other pants," which is a cocky thing to say, but he was pissing me off. If I thought actual human beings were at risk of dying, I would have gone back and done whatever had to be done, but I'd taken a sniff of Giselle's tampon-shaped powder and I didn't die, assuming it was the same stuff and I ingested a flyspeck and Pinto wasn't exaggerating about the amount it took to kill you dead. I felt weird, but there's a big difference between feeling weird and death. If she wanted to send McDonald's customers into psycho wonderland, that was her business.

"How'd you find out about the poison in the tampon tube anyway? You didn't mention it this afternoon."

"A client told Mrs. Whiteside."

"That's awfully convenient."

"We funnel men with secrets to her room. You'd be surprised the things they will confess in the arms of an artful courtesan." He pulled up in front of Odette's apartment. "Alene has always supported my career. Most agents don't even tell their wives what they do."

"My wife thinks my career is a farce."

We sat awhile, looking at the rain. The Chinese takeout place had a pink neon sign with Chinese writing. Neon looks best in the rain, and we don't get much rain in Wyoming, so we don't have a load of neon. It's not cowboy, but I think the stuff looks kind of neat. Monty whined, wondering why he wasn't going.

Pinto's spirits took a dive. He fell into that deep funk I'd seen him fall into when we first met, only this funk was even deeper. "In point of fact, I am not in good graces with the CIA, at the moment." He looked across Monty, his eyes old and doleful. "I was a vital agent, ten years ago. In the loop at every step of an operation. The old CIA respected me."

I was just beat up enough to sympathize. "It's like riding bulls. You give everything to your dream and, unless you are a champion, no one cares."

"How true. No one cares. I could handle hatred, but this treating me like I don't matter is worse." A choke came to his voice. "My handler says I am *quaint.*"

If he'd been a girl, I would have held his hand. If he was a cowboy, I would buy him a drink. Since he was old, I didn't know what to do.

He said, "If I squash the McDonald's plot, they might realize I am still vital."

I didn't say anything. The truth was, all I wanted was to lie down and rest. I was too worn out to separate the good guys from the bad guys. In France, they overlap. Maybe Pinto was telling the truth and McDonald's customers would die, but how was I to know? He was a skinny-legged old man in a ponytail. He wore sunglasses at night. He made me apologize to a dog. This was not a man to risk violent death for.

Finally, for lack of anything better, I said, "Good luck." He could take that however he wanted.

Pinto rolled down his window and sucked in night air. He nodded at Odette's door. "Twenty-two, twenty-five."

"What's that?"

"The code to get inside. Twenty-two, twenty-five."

"I wondered if there was something I didn't know about."

"I'm sharing the information because this is the appropriate point for you to bring me one hundred forty euros. A hundred for the taxi and forty for the cabochon. I won't charge you for Mrs. Whiteside's time."

I said, "Hire a collection agency."

"Surely you aren't planning to stiff your guardian angel."

"If it wasn't for you, I wouldn't have needed any angel." I got out and leaned down with my hands on his windowsill. "Don't bother coming back to take me to the airport. I'll find my own way."

I couldn't tell if he was fixing to cry or get out and hit me. "Are all cowboys rude, ungrateful, and selfish?"

"Hell, I'm better than most."

Pinto drove away in a cloud of hard feelings, leaving me on the foreign sidewalk. I went over and punched numbers. At first, it didn't work. He hadn't told me you hit the numbers, then the tic-tac-toe key. I had to figure it out through experimentation.

Frankly, my ass was dragging in the dirt. It wasn't all from getting beat to smithereens and chucked out a window, either. There was an emotional exhaustion. Ever since the phone call with Tyson, I'd been jerked up and down and around like a rider hung up on a bad bull. I don't recall ever suffering this level of exhaustion before. Dad's funeral, where they kept the casket open, maybe. Or when Ty was born. Maybe exhaustion this deep in your bones is one of those things that are so awful you forget them.

And it wasn't over yet. I had my buckle but I still hadn't figured out Odette Clavel. It appeared we were in love, as if either of us knew what the word meant. I sure as hell was in something I'd never been in with Mica or any other woman. Odette had gone from an anonymous lay to someone important I'd just as soon not be without. What was I supposed to do about that?

I hoped she was home and not off gallivanting at three or four in the morning, or whatever time it was. I couldn't face the thought of threatening the old lady downstairs again, to get into the apartment. I was burnt out on threatening people. Being hated takes more energy than you would believe.

I traipsed up the dark stairwell to the third floor that was really the fourth. In Paris, they don't light stairs and hallways with nobody in them. There was no doubt a timer switch on the wall somewhere, for the situation, but I'd be damned if I was going to grope around like a boy scared of the dark.

I stepped off the third-floor landing and started down the hall toward Odette's door. It's hard to figure what happened then. I saw a lightning bolt and incredible pain cracked the top of my spine. Then my head caved in.

32.

Odette's voice brought me back. "Wake up, my cowboy. Please awaken and be with me now."

My eyes fluttered, involuntarily, and I could see her although the focus was still out. Odette shimmered, like looking at her through someone else's bifocals.

She smiled. *"Bonsoir."*

"Why am I here?" Here was her couch. My boots had been taken off, and the top button of my Wranglers undone. Robert the cat sat on the far arm of the couch, looking down at me. Odette held a damp cloth to my forehead.

"I heard a sound in the hallway, and when I looked out, I found you."

Odette's hair and eyes were the exact same shade of loam brown. If we ever got married, I would ask her to pull the iron out of her eyebrow and nose. Maybe even her lower lip. I had enough metal in my body for the family.

She murmured. "You will be well now. I will take care of you." Those brown eyes shone with a devotion I'd never run into on the circuit.

"I always wanted to hear someone say that."

"It is true. You are safe with me."

Safe? It took a few moments to recall why I hadn't been safe on my own, without Odette. Frequent knocks on the head scramble time sequencing, but, lying there with a woman holding a wet washrag on my head for the second time in one night, my short-term memory came back with a fury.

"Holy *Christ.*" I arched my back and clawed for my back pocket. "It's gone."

"What?"

"My buckle. The asshole-prick-shitheads took my buckle."

That was it. Last straw. Or brick might be the better word. For the first time since Uncle Ed shut me in the kindling box, my chest shivered like I was cold even though I wasn't and the tears came flowing. I cried like a baby. All through the annulment, divorce, separation, second divorce, and enough bull wrecks to kill most folks, I hadn't broken down the once. But there on Odette's couch, I lost control. Life was nothing but a gyp. Every time I got hold of something that could help me be the way I wanted to be — Dad, a wife who was on my side, Tyson — fate or some jerk acting as fate snatched it away. For no reason. My whole basis for going on was the belief that if you fight hard and never give up, sooner or later, good things will happen. That's the American way. The cowboy way. Only it isn't true. Cheaters win. A lot.

Odette didn't bat an eye at me crying. I've never had any use for men who cry in front of women, or women who cry in front of men, either. Tears should be private, shed in the loneliness of a truck. I didn't know if Odette would have anything to do with me after this or not. At the moment, it didn't matter. I was beat.

"Ça va aller, mon chéri," she said.

I said, "It's not fair."

The tear part didn't last fifteen seconds, but it was enough. Then, I cussed — *shit, crap, cocksucker* — only not pissed-off cussing, more in the lines of no hope. End of the trail. Odette bathed my brow and waited while I gathered myself.

"Why?" I looked at her with some fierceness. After all, the bastards were her friends. "You tell me, why? That buckle doesn't mean a damn thing to anyone in the world except me, and maybe my kid. Why would anyone want it so much?"

She was gentle around my sewed-together ear and the forehead bandage. "Some people will not rest if their enemy has what he wants, even if they do not want it themselves."

I blinked teardrops. "That is incredibly fucked."

"But true."

Odette kicked off her Keds and lay down beside me on the couch. I had my right arm across her shoulder with her face cradled against my collarbone. The cat jumped off the couch arm and snuggled in between our knees.

I ran my fingers through Odette's hair and listened to her breathe. She was the one good thing to happen since Ty was born over seven years ago, and I'd messed up with him. What I wanted now was to lie here with her on the couch as long as I could because I knew this was okay and as soon as I went on to the next thing it might be another seven years before I was okay again.

"Tell me why you want this buckle," Odette said.

I stared up at the ceiling. Whoever put on the plaster had tried to make fan patterns. He pulled it off, mostly, except around the light fixture.

"Dad died in the avalanche. My mare had to be put down. Mica left and took my son with her. He'll hate me soon, if he doesn't now."

Her breath was soft on the collar of my borrowed T-shirt. She seemed like the first person I could tell the truth to. Mica would never have put up with soul-searching, even at the peak of our time together.

"I never had a thing in my life that didn't get yanked away. This once, with the buckle, I decided not to stand for it anymore. This was the test—winner or loser. I had to find out what I am." I stroked Odette's hair. "I guess I found out."

She inched up my body, nibbling on my neck, then chin. She skipped the mouth and kissed each eyelid. "You will go after the buckle again, no?"

"No."

She stopped, mid-kiss. "But you are the rider of bulls. You do not stop."

"Odette, honey, I'm a terrible rider of bulls."

That said, it was time to go on to the next part of my life's story, the part where I wasn't indestructible.

"Hell," I said, "if Giselle or Armand have it, they'll throw the buckle in the river. If it's anyone else, I've got no way to track it." I eased Odette off of me and sat up. "Could you bring my saddlebag over here. There's codeine in the bottom."

Odette padded into her bedroom. I sat up and rubbed the goose egg on the back of my skull. Self-evident Truth #10: *You only get a certain number of knockouts in life, before you go away and don't make it all the way back.* Consequences become permanent. I'd had two in one night, which is pushing your luck, even for a bull rider. Maybe it was time I quit the bulls and went into poetry full time. If I stopped now, I could say I won the last rodeo I entered. I could talk like a winner even though inside I would know better. Why would a person feel so much passion for doing something they weren't good at anyway? For every champion who says he would ride bulls even if he didn't get paid, there are twenty cowboys who do. Suddenly, I could not see the point.

Odette came back in, my saddlebag across her arm. "You are quitting?"

I flipped the flap and dug for pills. "I am quitting."

"Is not that against the code of the cowboy?"

"I guess I'm not cut out to be a real cowboy."

She slapped the holy shit out of me. "I did not waste my years looking for a man to have him not be a man."

I felt my face. One more blow to the head and I might be looking into street beggar as a career.

"Jesus, Odette, I don't know what to do."

"If you cannot fight for the buckle, fight for me."

I hate it when women are right. Maybe I wasn't worth a damn as a cowboy, but I was still a person. Even if I was lousy at sitting on a bull, I could still drink coffee and watch the creek go by. Write a poem. I wasn't gone yet, and so long as you're not gone, you've got a fight on your hands. People who whine are whiners. Surely there's something between cowboy and whiner. Most men spend their lives in that gap, but those were men I didn't have much use for. I didn't want to join the vast, dull-eyed middle ground.

Odette's lip pouted. "What would Will James do?"

I stood and waited for the wave of whirlies to settle. It was touch and go as to whether I would fall on my face or walk upright.

Odette didn't offer to steady me. "You said when you don't know what to do, you think about Will James, you consider what he would do."

"But those are stories."

I walked over to the sink to wash down the codeine. To hell with the high risk of Paris water, I drank from the tap. The water tasted like tinfoil.

"You do not believe the stories?" Odette asked. "You were an *imposteur* all along?"

"*Imposteur?*"

"Fake."

"I'm not a fake."

"What are you?"

Her keys were on the countertop, beside her glasses and the beaded purse. I picked up the Disney World key chain and bounced it in my palm. What was I? I'd spent an awful lot of my life climbing onto bulls, even if I wasn't good enough to stay put. I couldn't see how it was possible to be a fake and a bull rider at the same time.

So, what would Will James do, in Paris? "Did your American husband give you this key chain?"

She looked at the key chain there in my hand, as if trying to recall what it was. When you carry something every day, you tend to forget what it looks like. "We visited both there and Epcot Center on our honeymoon. It is the only time I have been in the States, before my trip to Boulder."

"Why Disney World? Why not Yellowstone Park?"

"His mother lived nearby."

Something inside me clicked. "I don't know what Will James would do, but what he wouldn't do is sell the ranch."

Odette came over to the kitchen counter, looking at me, as if expecting more.

"Your friend Giselle is fixing to kill people."

"Giselle is angry, but she would not kill anyone. I know her."

"Why was she in Boulder?"

Odette gave me a look, but not an answer.

"Your philosophy department never heard of Giselle. Why did she go to Colorado?"

Odette gave the French shrug. "She said it was to view the Rocky Mountains. I suspect she came on the trip in hope of seducing me. Giselle likes women the same as men."

"Did you and Giselle ever drive up into the mountains? A place called Gold Hill?"

"I did not have sufficient time for drives. She may have, the day I presented my paper."

I crossed back to my saddlebag and pulled out my second best cowboy shirt. Best after tonight. It was white cotton with a blue flannel yoke and artificial pearl buttons. The gun nut T-shirt was beginning to feel like it belonged on someone else.

"Our three-way started with you in front and my dick in Giselle. Do you remember her pulling out a tampon?"

"What kind of question is that?"

"A girl about to get nailed in her period has to stop and pull the plug. Unless she did it in the can earlier, but then it wouldn't wind up on my floor. You weren't having your period, were you?"

"I do not enjoy relations during the time of bleeding. It is difficult to achieve climax."

Now I was on to something. Will James would like this. "You
know much about French literature?"

Odette nodded, suspicious of where this was going. "I studied it
in lycée, before Santayana and James."

"Help me." I bent over with my arms outstretched and she
pulled the T-shirt off over my head. I couldn't do it the normal way.
"Would a person write a paper on 'Gide as Proto-Heroic Parisian
Male'?"

Odette laughed.

I said, "What?"

"André Gide was a renowned homosexual. He was to France
what"—she paused to come up with an example—"Liberace is in
America."

I opened my billfold and flipped through various receipts, credit
cards, and photos of Tyson until I found the card I was looking for.

"Telephone this number and tell whoever answers that we need
a taxi."

Odette's face lit up. I'd made her day. "You will stay in Paris
now and fight for the buckle?"

I pulled on my cowboy shirt, leading with the right arm. "The
buckle's gone. I'm going to save McDonald's."

She held the card between the fingers of both hands, somewhat
dubious. "You can do that?"

"While I'm at it, I'll make the world safe for Starbucks."

33.

Forty minutes later, Odette and I emerged from her building, arm in arm. To the casual observer, the arm-in-arm stuff would have appeared as pure affection, which was mostly but not all the way truth. There was an element of holding me upright. We came out soon after daybreak to a rainy street that was empty except for the Chinese guy unlocking the retractable fence that covered his shop across the street, and Pinto, sitting in his taxi, in a bad mood. He leaned over and rolled down the passenger-side window and stared at me from behind his sunglasses, without talk. His silver hair hung down, loose. He looked like he hadn't had much sleep. Monty'd stayed home.

Odette picked up on the less-than-friendly vibration. "We should take the metro. It goes wherever you wish and it is cheaper."

"We'll do it my way this time." I leaned low for a better angle on Pinto. "The fare you told I was Starbucks by way of CIA, you happen to catch a name?"

"He was your pal from Crepes a Go Go, the blond American you spilled your guts to before I could get there."

"The kid from Orlando, right there next door to Disney World."

I held the back door open for Odette. As she ducked in, I said, "It's time we paid a visit to your husband."

She didn't speak until she'd settled on her side of the backseat and I'd gotten in behind her. Then she said, "Surely you are not jealous."

"Michael, right?"

Odette's cheeks paled a shade. "I do not think he would approve if I were to reveal his address."

"We already know it." I looked forward to Pinto. "Don't we?"

"I can take you to the apartment on rue Cler where I dropped him yesterday."

Back to Odette. "Is it on rue Cler?"

She nodded.

Up to Pinto. "Let's go."

The street where Michael lived and, I guessed, where Odette used to live, was considerably more trendsetting than any other part of Paris I'd seen so far. It was clean. The pavement was old bricks and the buildings were glaringly white with curved-arc edges and balconies crammed full of potted bushes. A gun barrel–gray Rolls-Royce slid by, going the other way. A couple girls pushed babies in carriages along the sidewalk. I got the idea the babies in the carriages did not belong to the girls pushing them. It was the Hollywood view of Paris you see in movies, which made me think the neighborhood was full of Americans.

"This is a pretty hot-stuff block for a graduate student," I said.

"Michael's family owns the company that invented puffed cheese. You have heard of them, no?"

"Not me."

"Michael blames his parents and their group for the cultural genocide of France. His dream is to rekindle the French tradition of pride in eating."

I watched a woman I took as a hired hand struggle with seven yippee dogs on leashes. She got them across the street all right, but then they split ranks around the stoplight pole. "He could donate a couple million to a museum. I don't see any call for forcing people to eat decent food if they don't want it."

"Armand says Michael suffers from class guilt."

I thought about the blond stallion who'd offered me a girl to have sex with. That kid had reeked of entitlement. "It's hard to picture the Michael I met feeling guilt over anything."

"You would be surprised. Michael Gunner is more complex than he appears."

"Assholes usually are, but that doesn't change the smell."

Pinto pulled up in front of an apartment house with the entrance set at an angle to the street corner. The double doors were flanked by these seven-foot-high vases looked like they'd come from the pyramids.

Pinto pulled off his sunglasses. His eyes looked worn out. "That's forty-three euros."

I dug for my replenished billfold as Odette got out on her side and moved over by the building. I said, "How'd you know telling this Michael character would get back to Armand?"

"I went fishing." Pinto took my three twenties and didn't offer me change. "I knew he was connected to Armand through her." He nodded toward Odette. "I wanted to see how connected."

"So you knew the girl I was looking for and the guy I was talking to were married to each other."

Pinto pocketed my money. "Have you chosen to behave like a patriotic American now?"

I got out, shut the door, and leaned into the open front window. "Somebody has to do your job."

Odette punched a code and walked in like she owned the place, which, I suppose, at one time was more or less true. The lobby was plush carpeted with more vases. A couple even held flowers. The walls were tile and the chairs modernly uncomfortable. A little nervous man rubbing his palms together came from a closet-sized room to greet us. He had a napkin tucked into the top of his shirt.

He said, *"Madame Gunner."*

Odette said, *"Bonjour, Paul. Monsieur Gunner est à la maison?"*

The man took on an extra level of nervousness. He rubbed his palms like a Comanche starting a fire. *"Oui, mais —"*

"Ce n'est pas la peine de l'appeler, allons-y."

Odette led me across the lobby rug to an elevator with stone pink-pearl framing, the shade of your higher-priced grave marker.

When the elevator came I was surprised to see it was full-sized, like a regular American elevator. Odette stepped in. I stepped in. Grim-faced, she punched the four button, which meant five. Her fingertips brushed against mine. She said, "The taxi driver was with you yesterday, at the university."

"He's my interpreter."

"You lied when you said you are working for no one but yourself."

What could I say? It hadn't been a lie when I said it, but she had no call to believe that. We left the elevator and walked down a hallway you'd have to describe as swank. Odette dug into her purse and I discovered what door one of the other keys on her Disney World key chain went to.

"How long since you and your husband split up?"

"Thirty-nine days." She slid her key into the lock. "But I prefer not to count."

Showing up at your ex's soon after the crack of dawn is a fine way to look for heartache, even finer if your ex is a known chow hound. I only did it the once with Mica, coming off an all-night blizzard drive from Scottsbluff. I wound up wishing I'd slept in the truck, snow or no snow. I have no idea who was in the house. She blocked the door with her body so I couldn't look around her and told me I'd lost my dropping-by privileges. She was wearing the Trashy Lingerie teddy I'd bought her for Christmas. I didn't see Tyson.

I can't blame Odette for being tense, and, for a moment, I regretted bringing her along. I could have left her behind, I guess, although it would have been complicated getting from the street into the apartment.

The thing about Michael Gunner's apartment was in my wildest imagination I couldn't picture Odette living there, not after seeing where she lived now. It wasn't so much that every surface was clean, which it was, but pretty much every surface was reflective. Furniture came in white, silver, and black. There were more vases without flowers and little foot-and-a-half-high statues of naked women on pedestals. Cowboys put women on pedestals, metaphorically speaking, but we don't make them stand there naked. He had art all over but no books to speak of, which seemed odd for a student. Maybe they were tucked off in a library or conservatory or some other room with a pretentious name.

He had a crystal chandelier, a tabletop made from a slab of black marble, and a mirror with a frame big as a hayloft door. Fish of exotic colors and shapes swam around a big tank.

"Did you buy this furniture?" I asked Odette.

She dropped her beaded purse on the marble table. "Michael hired an interior decorator. I chose none of it."

"That's a relief."

Michael came from what I assumed was the kitchen, wearing a maroon silk robe that said *MG* on the breast in fancy script, carrying a black enamel tray with two steaming mugs of coffee, two pastries, and a glass bowl full of assorted berries.

He said, "Slick."

"What'd I say I would do if you called me that word again?"

"You walk into my home uninvited, I'm allowed to call you any name I want."

He and Odette studied each other. There's always this competition when two people break up where each one wants to go to pieces less than the other. For most couples it comes down to the together one gets re-involved the soonest. I have no doubt that was most, if not all, of Bernard's appeal. It's hard to see anything else he had going. For people who split up frequently and for whom re-involvement is not a challenge, it's who moves up or down the social pecking order. So, right off, Odette sees the two mugs of coffee and knows whoever comes out of the bedroom will be measured against me.

Michael gave Odette a thick-lipped smile. I don't know diddly when it comes to elective surgery, but those lips looked professionally poofed.

"Come see who has dropped in for a visit," he said.

Giselle slouched from the bedroom in a white terry-cloth robe more than likely stolen from a hotel.

Odette flew off the handle. You never heard such a French tirade. She charged Giselle and, for an instant, I thought she might batter the bitch. So did Giselle. Soon as Giselle realized the attack was vocal as opposed to physical, she attacked back.

Michael and I stood amazed. Men are mystified by fights between women. Pride goes out the window. Carefully constructed walls of personality crash down. It's the exact opposite of fights between two men or a man and a woman. There's no bullshit.

"You want her coffee?" Michael offered the tray. "It's American."

I could have kissed him.

Thank God he didn't know that. "I mean, it's Tanzanian peaberry," he said. "But it's dripped through a filter, the American way."

I held the mug with two hands and closed my eyes for the first sip of real coffee since Starbucks in the Denver airport. I tried counting back the days to see how long ago that was, but the flight across the Atlantic had thrown off my inner calendar. The rodeo was Sunday, I hit Paris Tuesday, I'd slept twice, which left today at Thursday and I had a plane to catch tonight. That meant three days without decent coffee, which was the longest I'd gone since eighth grade. I figure I don't chew and only drink after sunset, so I have coffee coming. Man with no addictions at all strikes me as suspect.

Michael was idly watching the girls yell at each other. Far as I could see, he didn't have a care in the world.

"When we were in Philosophy, looking for these two, why didn't you tell me you already knew them?"

I'm not absolutely certain what sardonic means, but I can come close, and, in my mind, Michael was sardonic. "You didn't ask."

"That's the sort of answer gets people punched out."

Michael bit the tip off a strawberry. I imagine Giselle had told him what happened with Armand and the gang, so he knew I was capable of violence, but he still came off as casual. You have to give him that. "I knew you could find the twats without my help. What I wanted was to see how long you would take."

"And that bull malarkey about Gide as proto-male?"

"I was pulling your leg," which is the Southern way to put it. We don't pull legs in Wyoming. "Graduate school humor, like out in your country when you tell tourists about jackalopes. Having an outsider believe your lies makes you feel intellectually superior."

I drank more coffee, considering how everyone who knows something thinks they're better than those who don't. "Do you have my buckle?"

Michael looked over at me in surprise. "God, no."

"Do you know who does?"

"Giselle said you have it. Don't tell me you lost your precious belt buckle again?"

By then the noisy part of Odette and Giselle's argument had wound down and they'd gone into the silent stare-down section. Giselle was so much taller than Odette that she had an advantage. I knew how Odette felt, which is why I generally skip over the stare-down as quick as I can and go straight to hitting.

I held out my mug. "Got a refill?"

Michael hesitated, then took my mug and went to the kitchen. I walked over to Odette.

"Why're you upset?"

She blinked a couple times, not wanting to shift her focus off hating Giselle. "Because this one is supposed to be my friend."

"But you and Michael broke up."

"He is despicable. I hate the air he exhales."

"Then what difference does it make if Giselle humps the bum?"

Odette's hand went to my upper arm. "Sisters of the battle do not betray one another."

Giselle spit on the carpet—a wet noogie next to my boot.

I gave Odette an unpleasant truth, which isn't quite the same as self-evident. "Friends always sleep with each other's exes. The best you can hope for is they wait till you're actually split up."

"Just now Giselle boasted that she did not wait."

"That's different, then."

Michael came back and handed me a fresh cup. "You've porked them both. Which is better, in your mind?"

Odette's grip tightened on my arm to the point of feeling more claw than hand—the signal that I'd better answer the question to her satisfaction.

"I have trouble relaxing with a woman who might slit my throat in the afterglow," I said.

Giselle said, "I would not be too confident as to which of us that is," which is something I'd already thought about. Odette and I might be in love, but that still didn't mean I knew her well enough to turn my back.

Michael went off to the bedroom, leaving the three of us in an awkward silence. He kept the door open in case we wanted to watch him throw off the robe and dress. No one did.

"So give up the truth for once," he called back. "Who are you?"

I'd been considering that question all morning and the answer didn't seem the same as yesterday. But then Michael probably wasn't looking for navel gazing. "Name's Rowdy, same as it was the first time you asked."

He came to the door, shirtless and barefoot, wearing dress slacks. My guess would be Hagar but they could have been Armani for all I knew. He had the body you see on guys who exercise incessantly but have never worked an honest day in their lives. He said, "I'm guessing Disney. You're too slick for CIA."

"There's that word again."

"You could be American Mafia. They send feelers into Paris every few years."

I chugged down the second cup, fast as I could. Once I started pissing him off, there might not be a chance to finish. Michael slipped on a dress shirt and came back in the front room, still barefoot. "The only thing I know for certain is you didn't barge in here looking for a belt buckle."

Time to kick open the gate. "I first came to Paris for the buckle, but now I'm more interested in stopping you from killing folks."

34.

Giselle's face turned to wax—which was odd because I'd thought it was wax already, during the argument with Odette. Her face at the word *killing* made the old Giselle look positively perky.

I said, "I don't give a rat's hairy ass what you do to McDonald's its own self, but I can't let you murder folks whose only sin is to eat a chicken nugget."

Giselle said, "Murder?"

Michael said, "It would be best if you shut up, Giselle."

Michael was dreaming if he thought he had the power to shush Giselle. "Psilocybin does not murder. It makes the eater sick. The vomit, then the hallucination."

"Maybe so, but they tell me that stuff in your tampon tube causes sudden, painful death."

"That is absurd."

Odette had gone hyperalert. You could practically see her tingling nerve ends. By contrast, Michael went the other way. He was one of those rare snakes who appear to relax as they coil. When he spoke, his Southern accent was thicker than it had been. "I'm interested in who *they* is."

"Hell, half Paris knows you're planning to poison McDonald's."

"I didn't know," Odette said.

"You're the wife. Wives never know when their husband's fixing to slaughter innocents."

"Whatever person told you this lied," Giselle said.

I finished my coffee, down to the last drop. "That is possible, I'll give you. It's also possible you were lied to. I'd put the odds at about even."

Giselle said, "Michael would not lie."

"What?" Odette had the look of the flummoxed. Of course Michael would lie. He lied continuously, and both girls knew it. The fact sank in on Giselle without me having to point out the obvious.

Her voice wasn't quite so certain as before. "I myself am to take the powder, in order to become ill and deflect suspicion to others. All the embedded employees are to take it."

Michael walked to the fish tank and shook in this stuff looked like Parmesan cheese. The fish went nuts, what we call a feeding frenzy.

"If Michael is willing to kill random strangers, what would stop him from killing you?" I asked.

"But we made love."

Odette said, "And?" leaving the rest unsaid. Giselle got the point.

Michael studied the fancy fish, as if they were more interesting than anything else in the room. "When customers simultaneously get sick at several McDonald's, it will shut down the franchises."

"For a week, maybe. Only death will close them long-term." I concentrated on Giselle. "Think with your head instead of your snatch for once. He's not going to risk this"—my arm took in the vases and naked statues, the marble-topped table, the huge mirror, the stupid fish—"to make people vomit."

Giselle's eyes focused on the mid-range, thinking, adding up reality. Odette stared at Michael. Giselle was wavering, but separated wives are more than happy to believe the worst. Odette said the meanest insult she could come up with on the spot. "Michael, you are nothing but an American."

"I'm an American who has done more for Paris than any of your ridiculous Frenchmen. You think Armand and his band of stooges could have put together this operation without me? Until I came along, their idea of revolution was a brick through the window."

"A ridiculous Frenchman is superior to an American with good intentions," Odette said, which I thought was pretty good, worthy of a foreign self-evident truth. Personally, I'd about decided France would be better off without help from Michael, Pinto, or McDonald's.

Giselle walked into the bedroom and came back carrying a stressed-leather handbag. I thought she was leaving.

So did Michael. "Giselle, honey, don't go. Think about all I've done for the movement while this clown still says he came here looking for a buckle. Who are you going to trust?"

Giselle's hand dipped into her bag and came out with a pistol. I wasn't certain, but I thought it was the gun I'd seen under her mattress earlier.

She said, "Let us discover who is lying."

It always floors me how a handgun commands attention. I haven't been around them as much as you would think, what with being a cowboy and all. I mean, every pickup truck in Wyoming has a gun rack sporting a couple rifles, maybe an over/under shotgun, but those aren't the same as a pistol brandished indoors. When a pistol comes out in a room, all eyes stay on it for the duration. Real people aren't near as cool about having weapons pointed at them as movie people.

Giselle kept the barrel aimed more or less midway between me and Michael. "We shall feed the cowboy a dose of the powder and if he dies, we know he is telling the truth. If he only becomes ill, it is you."

I had to speak up. "What a terrible idea."

Michael turned away from his fish. "Do you have any powder on you?"

"You know I do not. It is hidden at my workplace."

"The doses are spread all over the city by now. How are you planning to lay your hands on a sample?"

Giselle reached into her leather bag again. This time, she came out with a cell phone. "We shall have what you call a dress rehearsal."

After Giselle made her phone call she herded us into the bedroom so she could dress without risk, and I got to see her naked again. Giselle did have a statuesque body. Strong. Ripe. Anti-gravity on parade. I mean, Odette's body was warm and inviting, only with her it was primarily attitude. You could tell Odette was at home in her skin. Giselle was more *holy cow, look at that!* I had to remind myself that this woman collected dolls. What I wondered was whether or not bisexuals are by nature tougher than heteros or homos. Does the lack of boundaries make them less tolerant? I thought about it awhile and decided I didn't have enough evidence to say.

Giselle slid into a black skirt and V-necked shirt. She and Michael argued, moving from French to English and back, slaloming languages. Michael's point was they had a plan and they should stick with it. Giselle's point was if the plan involved her death, she was going to make a modification.

"We must hit every store the same day or it will not cause the right amount of panic," Michael said.

"One restaurant won't ruin it for the others," Giselle said. "People vomit in McDonald's every day."

Odette caught me checking out Giselle's breasts and snapped a backhand into my bad shoulder. She said, "You are monogamous, now."

"Since when?"

"Since today."

It's not fair that women are always the ones to decide that commitment folderol. The guy never chooses at what point going steady commences. All three times I married Mica I didn't know we were doing it until she told me. The breakups took place in her head well before I knew about them, too.

Giselle slid on her black boots with heels that looked like fancy cafe pepper mills. She waggled the pistol my direction. "Time to move."

Michael said, "This is a mistake."

"Where we going?" I asked.

"What difference does it make to you?" Odette said, which was true.

Giselle had us take the stairs instead of the elevator so she could keep everyone in front of her. In the lobby, she draped one of Michael's sweaters over her arm to hide the pistol. I think it was cashmere, but what do I know about sweaters. It could have been mohair. The getup looked blatant to me, but the nervous man didn't seem to notice. I doubt if he'd say anything even if he did see the gun. One thing you have to say for the French is they respect people's privacy.

Out on the street, Giselle nodded at Pinto's Citroën. "We'll take a taxi."

Odette started to speak up about Pinto, but I gave her a look and she didn't. While Giselle kept her cover on me and Michael, mostly, there was no doubt Odette was also on the captives list. Giselle didn't trust anyone at this point. She motioned Michael into the front seat and me and Odette in back with her. Odette in the middle.

Pinto said, *"Où allez-vous?"*

Michael looked at him closely and said, "I rode with you yesterday."

"Lots of people rode with me yesterday."

"But I know you," Michael said.

"No talking," Giselle said to Michael. To Pinto, she said, *"Conduis."*

"Where?"

"*Champs-Elysées. Je vous dirai quand vous arrêter.*"

As Pinto pulled into traffic Giselle flipped open her cell phone, punched numbers, and started rattling on.

Odette and I held hands. "Who's she calling now?"

"Armand," Odette said. "She wants him to meet us at McDonald's on the Champs-Elysées."

"Great, that peckerhead is all I need."

Pinto's sunglasses tilted up as he checked us out in the rearview mirror. "Any of you folks interested in turquoise? I have some exquisite pieces."

Pinto drove us back over to the street where I'd chased the bus on a bicycle. It was odd to have been in Paris long enough to recognize streets. If I stayed another day or two I would no doubt establish hangouts and start keeping up with the private traumas of waitresses. Being on the road so much, I'd developed the ability to infiltrate scenes. All that's needed is to ask a couple of questions.

Although there wasn't street parking and I couldn't see how the people on the crowded sidewalk had gotten there, Pinto pulled up and stopped. The guy in the car behind him threw the usual Paris driver hissy fit.

Pinto put his arm on the back of the seat. He said, "Twenty-two euros."

Giselle looked at me. "Pay the man."

"Are you nuts? Hostages don't pay cab fares."

"Jesus Christ." Michael pulled out a wad of cash. "I'll pay."

Pinto coughed us up on the sidewalk and drove away. We stood next to one of those urban beech trees they have that grows out of grates on the concrete. We were between an outside dining area and the buildings, and I couldn't tell which cafe the dining area went with. There were several choices.

A woman not in black moved from table to table, spare changing. She was wearing an orange wraparound skirt and had a green scarf over her head.

"What's that?" I asked Odette.

"She's a gypsy."

"Oh, yeah?" I watched the woman, wishing she would come and hit me for cash. I would have gone over and offered, but I did that once in Santa Monica and the panhandler turned me down. He said, "No, thanks. You need it more than I do." Since then, I've been afraid to risk rejection from beggars.

"I never saw a real gypsy before," I said.

Odette stared at me. "I cannot tell when you are kidding."

"The only place I've seen gypsies is at county fairs and those weren't real. They were girls in costumes."

Michael shot his arm out and looked at his watch.

I said, "You in a hurry?"

"I have a full schedule today."

"I figure the person holding the gun gets to decide what we do next."

That's when Armand and Leon came wandering up the street. Armand had two black eyes. Leon's head was bandaged like a man with an impacted molar. They both pretended not to see us.

Giselle shifted the possibly cashmere sweater into position over her arm. "We will go indoors now."

35.

McDonald's was inside this mall thing and downstairs in the basement. You don't see basement McDonald'ses in the Rockies. The walls were baby poop yellow brick. Water pipes lay exposed across the ceiling. Even though it was fairly early in the day, the place was packed. Each of the five cash register stations had a line must have been fifteen customers long. Bernard worked the line on the far left. He still hadn't shaved.

Giselle motioned with the sweater. "Over there."

We stood in Bernard's line behind a covey of schoolgirls in pigtails and uniforms. The one good thing I'd found about Paris so far was most of the people are short. Being able to look across the crowd was a new deal for me.

Nerves make me talkative. "People in Wyoming would never put up with a line this long. How can you stand living here? I've seen Garth Brooks concerts with less wait than it takes to get a Quarter Pounder in this town."

Giselle said, "Be quiet or I shall shoot you and find another guinea pig."

Michael said, "I'll get us a table."

She poked the sweater into his armpit. "Stay put."

Odette held my right hand with both of hers and chewed on the hoop in her lower lip. She was taking the death possibility seriously, and, as we shuffled closer to Bernard, I figured I'd better do the same. I'm just not hard wired for heavy anxiety. With bulls, there are two choices: get on or don't get on. Taking the danger seriously does not help if what you want is to get on.

But Paris isn't a bull ride. This time, I wasn't in danger because it gave life meaning. This was the opposite—danger that proved life is meaningless. I didn't want to die here and leave Tyson without a father. What would Mica tell him if I died in France? They wouldn't know I had come here for him. Far as they could tell, I'd called from Crockett County on Sunday and shown up dead in Paris Thursday. Mica would think I was here for fun.

"Do you love me," Odette asked.

"Yes, I love you." She squeezed my hand and we moved up another spot.

Armand and Leon slinked over by the bathrooms, which were beside the exit, and leaned against the wall, somewhat cutting off my run-like-hell option. Remi was nowhere in sight. My fondest wish was I'd put the bastard down for good.

Michael turned to face back, behind us, away from Bernard. He spoke quietly. "We have worked two years setting this up, Giselle. You are putting the operation at risk."

Giselle said, "Do not speak to me of risk."

Odette leaned close. I could feel her lips against my ear. "I apologize for the behavior of my husband and friend. They are idealistic, but I disagree with their methods. If I live through this day and you do not, I shall publicly renounce them."

"That's a fucking comfort."

Odette blinked three times and looked like she might cry. I'd hurt her feelings, but Jeez Louise, *publicly renounce them*. Whatever happened to *cut off their genitals*?

"You are bitter toward me?" she said.

"*Love is more important than saving your culture.*" That's Self-evident Truth #11.

"I am not so certain as you are."

"Tell you what, Odette. You've got about two minutes to figure out which side you're on."

"But what can I do?"

"You'll think of something."

Pinto appeared at the door. He looked around, took off his sunglasses, and slid over to stand across the entryway from Armand. I couldn't tell if he knew Armand was there or not. So far as I could tell, Pinto hadn't even seen me. As I watched his futile attempt to blend in with the wall, it came to me that one of them — Pinto or Michael — had to be lying through his teeth, and if it wasn't Pinto I was in big trouble. So, I had to hope the good guy who was supposed to be on my side and there to save my ass was lying when he said the powder would kill me, and the bad-guy leader of the terrorists was telling the truth when he said it wouldn't. What were the odds?

"When we reach the front, order medium fries and a Coke," Giselle said.

"I'd rather have a beer."

"Medium fries and a Coke."

"Okay, but you're wasting your money on the Coke."

"Do it."

Bernard looked past the schoolgirls he was taking care of and saw us. He blanched, which is a good word for what he did. He blanched, his right hand tugged at his ear, and he screwed up the girls' order. I think they wanted burgers with no pickles and he gave them pickles. Or the other way around. Whichever it was, they were peeved and took it out on him in French.

Finally, my turn came. Odette stood on my right, holding my hand. Michael and Giselle were behind me where I could feel the barrel of her *pistolet* up against my tailbone.

"What am I supposed to order? I forgot."

Giselle spoke through clenched jaws. "Medium fries and a Coke."

I nodded to Bernard. "What she said."

He looked blank-faced past me to Giselle. She muttered, *"Allez."*

Bernard got my Coke first. When he brought it over, his hand shivered a touch. Then he went and filled the medium-sized red box with fries. As he turned, his right hand came from his pocket and sprinkled something on the fries. I looked quickly down the line at the other employees. There were eight or nine, not counting the cooks behind the half-wall, and none of them saw what Bernard had done. He must have practiced with salt, because he was pretty smooth about it, but still, you'd think someone would have seen.

He walked back to me and set the French fries on the counter. "Your fries, sir."

Then he picked a couple from the box and popped them into his mouth. Behind me, Giselle jerked the gun up and said, *"Non."*

Bernard said, *"Y a quoi?"*

I felt Michael dig an elbow into Giselle's arm, giving her the shut up signal. She'd forgotten to warn Bernard. Poor sap. Of all the villains I'd met in Paris, Bernard was the most pathetic. Even his own friends forgot to tell him the poison might be lethal.

He swallowed and said, *"Deux cinquante-cinq."*

"I'm sorry. I don't talk French."

"Two euros, fifty-five."

I dug in my front pocket, figuring this wasn't the time to claim proper hostage payment form. Bernard ate another of my fries. In Laramie, he would have been fired in a heartbeat.

Giselle reached around and grabbed a five from my hand and threw it on the counter. "Keep the change."

I said, "But—"

She picked up my fries. "Move."

We left the Coke sitting on the counter. I don't know why she made me buy it. Maybe ordering the Coke was code. Saying *beer* might have meant *Plan canceled.* Hell, I don't know.

We stepped away from the main traffic flow and Giselle thrust the fries into my sternum. "Eat."

I was watching Bernard. "Let's sit down first, so I won't hit my head when I fall."

"Now."

I looked over at the bathrooms, with Armand and Leon on each side of the doors, and Pinto to the other side of the exit. Armand and Leon were watching me. Pinto wasn't.

"Eat," Giselle said. "Or I shoot."

Odette squeezed my hand.

I said, "To hell with it," and stuck a handful of French fries in my mouth. They had a hint of pecan flavor that I suppose was caused by the foreign substance. Otherwise, they were the same as the fries at the airport—cooked in oil that wasn't hot enough.

"Not bad," I said.

Giselle said, "More."

I ate another handful. Bernard was still upright, waiting on a family. The kids chattered at him like chipmunks on speed and he wasn't catching any of it. If Pinto hadn't exaggerated, or outright lied, Bernard should hit the floor about now.

I turned to Giselle. "I'm not dead yet."

"Eat more."

Michael watched with a half-smile on his smug jock face. "I told you the powder is harmless."

Odette said, "Are you okay?"

"I could use some ketchup."

I sucked air and grabbed my stomach, then bent double and moaned.

Odette said, "Rowdy?"

"Jesus, help me!" I fell over a chair onto the floor. Thrashing, rolling side to side, fingers clawing my belly, *"Make it stop! God, make it stop!"* I went into spasms. Arched like a sick dog. Dry heaved. A good bit of activity broke out above me. Cries of *"Un médecin! Un*

médecin!" and *"Appelez une ambulance."* I could hear Bernard freaking out.

I howled and spazzed again, then curled on my side, fetal.

Odette was beside me, on the floor, talking fast French. She rolled me onto my back and I felt her fingers on my throat, searching for a pulse. Her fingers were soft. Pleasant. Her mouth covered mine and she blew into me.

Pinto said, "Move up."

Odette shifted to the side of my head and Pinto straddled my stomach. He punched me hard in the chest, then went into a rhythm of pushing and leaning back. Odette breathed into my lungs.

"Check him again," Pinto said.

Odette turned her head so her ear floated over my nostrils. *"Non."*

Then she went back to breathing for me while Pinto pumped at my heart. This went on for thirty seconds or so before Odette stopped. Her fingers felt for a pulse again, then she sat back on her heels. "He is dead."

Repercussions were about what you would expect. Bernard screamed. Michael shouted, "It can't be!" Giselle put two bullets into Michael. At the sudden gunfire, bodies surged away. I heard Armand shouting. Someone shoved someone who fell over me and bounced back up.

I turned my head to the side and opened my eyes. Michael was on the floor, our faces less than a foot apart. Blood trickled from his nose and the lower edge of his lips. When he coughed, a surge of pain swept through his body.

He said, "You're not dead."

I smiled. "Nope."

"Slick."

"I told you not to call me that."

Above us, Pinto had Giselle's gun arm up behind her back. Gendarmes were pouring into the room. Armand tried to break for it and they caught him. Leon roared and bowled over a cluster of offi-cers who pulled him down. As Giselle stared at me, her eyes took on a wild, cat-like hatred—the same look I'd seen on her face when we made love.

It took all Michael had left to ask the question. "Who are you?"

I stood and brushed off my jeans, certain now that I knew the answer. When I leaned down to pick up my hat, I looked Michael right in the eyes.

"I am a cowboy."

Michael died.

I walked out of there.

36.

Odette waited for me outside, next to the tree growing from the sidewalk. She gave me a hug I will remember when I'm an old cuss drooling in a wheelchair trapped in the overheated rec room of a state-run nursing home. I will look back on my life and remember that hug.

She said, "If Will James were here he would slap your cute bottom and shout *Yahoo!*"

"What about William James?"

"He would say you have had a religious experience."

"Got that right."

As Odette and I hugged, I looked across the avenue to the sidewalk where Mrs. Whiteside stood beside a phone booth, watching us. She wore a black raincoat and a floppy hat, like that woman at the end of *Casablanca*. Monty Clift was in her arms. I couldn't see her face well enough to know what she was thinking.

Odette broke off the hug and stepped back to look in my eyes. "Is my Michael dead?"

"Looks like it."

Her eyes did a drifty thing where the focus went off and came back. "If someone must die, I am grateful it is him and not you."

More and more gendarmes converged on the mall. Police cars and ambulances came wailing up the street. Unlike American emergency vehicles, the French have a volume control on their sirens, so you think the thing is going full blast and then suddenly the loudness triples. I hope cops in Wyoming never discover volume control.

Pinto fought the flow of bodies going in and down the stairs to join us on the sidewalk. He had a silk hankie wrapped around his left hand. "The bitch bit me," he said.

Odette bristled. "Who are you calling the bitch?"

"Any woman bites Pinto Whiteside is a bitch."

I had my own call to bristle. "So what's the deal, am I likely to keel over dead in the next ten minutes?"

"Not likely, but you may talk to God in an hour or two."

"You lied to me, you clown."

He tightened his handkerchief. He wasn't wrapping right, but I didn't feel like showing him a better way. "Would you have stayed in Paris to protect American interests if I'd said they planned to send McDonald's customers on a psychedelic trip?"

"No."

"Just as I thought." He held his right hand out to shake with Odette. "You came through like a Marine back there, little lady."

Odette didn't shake hands with him. She didn't even speak to him. She spoke to me. "Who is this person? Tell me the truth."

"Like he said, the name is Pinto Whiteside. Unless he's lying about that one, too."

"Is this moron the reason my husband is dead and my friends are going to prison?"

"I'm afraid that's me more than the moron. I'm the reason Michael is dead. I'm sorry."

Odette gave one of her French shrugs I love so much. Her eyes slicked up, just a tad. "The inheritance will be a comfort in my sorrow."

Odette and I had a nice moment going there until Pinto jumped in and spoiled it. "An American corporation has been saved," he said. "Collateral casualties are a small price to pay."

My first impulse was to nail him in the nose. I mean, Michael may have been an evil prick, but he wasn't collateral. The problem was, I just couldn't get up the emotion it takes to hit somebody. There'd been enough nailing for one day.

Instead — "Where's my buckle?"

He flushed, watermelon pink. "How should I know where your blasted buckle is. Last time I saw the thing it was in your back pocket."

"You were the only one wanted me to stay in town, the only one who knew I was at Odette's apartment."

"God knows, Rowdy, if I had your buckle I would give it up. You deserve a reward for making Europe safe for American business, but all I can offer is your nation's gratitude. Or would you rather have a nice piece of turquoise? "

"In one minute, I'm going to show you where you can put your turquoise."

Pinto laughed. He said to Odette, "I don't know what you see in him."

Pinto and Odette studied me, I suppose trying to figure what she saw in me. Made me self-conscious. I took off my Stetson and wiped sweat from my forehead, then set it back on again. "Don't you have somewhere to be?"

Pinto nodded. "I'd better get back inside. Make sure the Paris police arrest the right people. It would be like them to blame the tourists and let everyone who speaks French go home."

As Pinto turned to leave, I said, "Give my best to Alene."

He stopped to look back at me. He almost said something, then he thought better of it.

Pinto hadn't noticed Mrs. Whiteside standing across the avenue. Before Odette and I turned to go, I waved at her, just to make sure she knew I'd seen her there. Mrs. Whiteside and I locked eyes for a long moment in which I felt as if an entire stream of unspoken information was flying back and forth across the avenue. Then she nodded. I would have given almost anything to know what the information that went unspoken was.

"Was that man CIA?" Odette asked.

"Starbucks. But he used to be CIA. I don't think he is anymore." She nodded toward Mrs. Whiteside. "Is she CIA?"

Mrs. Whiteside turned and walked the opposite direction, away from us. Once again, I admired the way she held herself. It's not easy to carry a dog with dignity, but she pulled it off. "Maybe. It's possible. Might even be probable." She disappeared into the crowd. "The only thing I know for sure is she's not a whore."

"Whoever said she is?"

Odette and I walked with my right arm over her shoulder and her left arm across my hips, natural as water flowing downhill. We cut through a long park with trees and statues and squirrels. Tourists. Guys with carts selling postcards. Young Parisian couples staring into each other's eyes. The rain had stopped and everything had a freshly washed look.

We came to a palace like the one in *Beauty and the Beast,* the part at the end there where the Prince and Belle two-step and the dishes turn into people. Tyson loved that part. I was knee-deep in a fairyland fantasy when Odette said, "You will stay now, and search for your buckle."

She felt warm under my arm, like we were spot-welded at the hip. Mica was too tall to make arm-in-arm walking go, and with other women we mostly drank in chairs, cowboy danced on the dance floor, or had sex. I don't recall much walking-next-to.

I leaned over and sniffed Odette's hair, there behind the spikes in her ear. French shampoo smells sweeter than Head & Shoulders. "I've been here long enough. My plane leaves tonight."

Her breath caught. She stopped. "But we are in love. You cannot go away when you are in love."

When I turned to face her, Odette was staring into my eyes with a fawn-like vulnerability. She was the most beautiful vision I'd ever seen. I knew, right then, there in the Paris park, this is the best it will ever be for me. My life was at its top.

I said, "It's hard, isn't it."

"It is impossible."

I broke the eye contact. "Not quite."

Odette's face clouded over. "Do you know how many people experience real love?"

"Not many. I never have before you."

"It is immoral to throw that away."

How was I supposed to explain? I felt like a suicide, justifying the act to his family. "Come on, Odette. We have real love today, but if I stay, in a year or two we won't. I have to go now while it's still perfect."

"That is so stupid."

"Paris isn't Wyoming. If I stay, you and whatever amazing thing this is will keep me going for a while, but sooner or later I'll shrivel up and lose myself away from the Rocky Mountains. I'll turn out needy. You won't like me anymore."

Odette pouted. She was able to take the pout far deeper than I'd seen it taken before. In other women, pouting came off as self-pity. Manipulation. Odette made it the expression of universal sorrow. In her face, her eyes and lips, the soft curve of her chin, I saw the shared desolation of being human. "You said love is more important than saving your culture."

"Yeah, well, I am my culture and nothing else. How would I live in a place where peeing is a crisis and everyone dresses like Johnny Cash? Even the air here makes me feel like someone I'm not."

"None of that matters." Tears seeped from Odette's eyes, and, to tell the truth, mine, too. Her posture that had been so outstanding suddenly slumped.

"I have to go, Odette. It's time for you to give me the buckle."

Her eyes flashed. Her voice was bitter. "I do not have your asinine belt buckle."

"Yes, you do. Pinto wasn't the only one wanted me to stay in Paris."

She stared at me, tears making little rivulets on her face. I reached across and touched the back of her hand. "I'll bet it's in your purse, right there."

Odette stared at me so long people passing by started giving us glances. In Paris, you expect emotional scenes on the street. They are the lonely person's entertainment.

Odette reached into her purse and pulled out my buckle. "But you love me."

I took it from her. "Yes."

"And I love you."

"You're the first."

I put the buckle in my right back pocket and took the turquoise cabochon from my left. "Here, you can have this."

She held my turquoise in her hand, staring at it. Then she threw it way down the park. "I want you, Rowdy, not a souvenir." Odette caught my wrist, holding it tight. "Why are you leaving me? It makes no sense."

I tried to think of a reason she would understand. "There's a bull, in Dalhart."

"Your stupid rodeo is more important than the only chance either of us may have at real love." She said it as a statement, not a question.

A tear caught on the down of her cheek. I touched it away, then tasted the salt on the tip of my finger. "Odette, I'm a bull rider. I can't change that."

She sniffed and kept her eyes over on the palace. The whole handsome prince, beautiful princess, happily-ever-after thing always seemed farfetched to me. I guess it's different if you live in a town full of palaces. "You are a fool. You can't change that, either."

"I never said I wasn't."

Odette almost but not quite smiled. "Admitting you are stupid does not make you less stupid."

I felt her release, like a bull giving up. The bad part was over. "Giselle says I'll vomit soon, and hallucinate. You think we could go back to your place for a while? My stuff's there and I'm not leaving till evening."

Odette turned and we walked some more. She slid her arm around my waist again. It was okay.

I kissed the stud in the top flap of her ear. "What did you hit me with before?"

"Côtes de Duras, 1998."

"Did the bottle break?"

"Of course not. I only gave you a love tap."

"Maybe we could pop open that Côtes de whatever and practice a few more weird French positions."

"Maybe I will hit you on the head again."

It took ten minutes, but we found the turquoise.

Wyoming

37.

One thing and another held me up to the point where I didn't make it to GroVont till early May. Dalhart was a washout—bull busted my ass two seconds out of the chute. Yancy said I'd left my concentration in Odette's drawers. Then I got thrown in Mesquite, New Braunfels, and Tulsa, that last by Ripple hisownself. I finished third in Rapid City, but then in Aberdeen a bull dogger backed a horse trailer over my foot and broke four bones. They outfitted me with a walking cast and I wintered in Aberdeen, working graveyard at 7-Eleven. You might say it was a low point. I lived in Budget Suites and didn't have the money to go out.

In late February, I got an e-mail from Mrs. Whiteside, of all people. In Paris I'd assumed she didn't know English, which just goes to show you Self-evident Truth #12: *Never make assumptions about foreign women*. She said Pinto had discovered she wasn't what he'd thought she was. He and Monty left for Switzerland to take advantage of the faux cowboy need for turquoise. I looked up *faux* and, in this case, it means drugstore. "He no longer works for the company," her e-mail said, by which I figure she meant the CIA. I didn't believe her.

Mrs. Whiteside said Odette was living in Michael's place on

rue Cler. She'd thrown out the furniture and redone it, Odette-style.

Giselle was out of jail, waiting trial for killing an American. That's how Mrs. Whiteside worded it: *Killing an American,* as if they had a separate category of crime, somewhere between manslaughter and murder. Armand and Leon were also out. They'd convinced Interpol or whoever was in charge over there that Bernard was the mastermind behind the dark belly of Paris's underground. Bernard was in prison and it looked like he would be spending his life there. In my mind, he got what he deserved.

Mrs. Whiteside attached a digital photo of Pinto and Monty standing by the Citroën. Pinto was wearing white shorts tight around his crotch and a sleeveless shirt. He looked like one of those eighty-year-old weight lifters you see hanging out at public swimming pools. His eyes had the glossiness of a man on the low end of a mood swing.

By April, I got out of my cast and things started looking up. I had a two-night affair with a woman who sold real estate and collected bull riders. She had a trophy wall. Made me feel like a real cowboy again, as opposed to a clerk at 7-Eleven. Only a sicko would collect 7-Eleven clerks.

I came in second at a poetry gathering in Deadwood City. My poem was this thing I'd written over the winter called *"Quarante Cents à la Fuite."* The title came from the BabelFish Web site. It was the story of an elderly wrangler who dreams all his life of retiring to the city where he can sleep in the afternoon and weather doesn't matter. Finally, he saves enough to move to a big town—I didn't name which one—and at the bus station there he discovers it costs forty cents to piss. He reacts about the way you would expect, spends a weekend in jail with a speed freak, then he beats it back to the ranch, where he swears he'll never go to a city again.

"I'll die after one last leak in the dust," he says at the end of the poem.

They gave me two hundred dollars for that.

So I was feeling flush and optimistic as I propped my Tony Lamas on the low iron fence marking off the outdoor deck at The Roasted Bean, a boutique coffeehouse opened on Main Street there in GroVont by a couple from Santa Barbara who'd decided to ditch the rat race for the simple life in small-town Wyoming. Those people come and go faster than the flu, but they're friendly enough while they're here.

It was 3:10 P.M. and I was propped up at a table midway between GroVont Elementary and Mica's house. The house I bought Mica. The Teton Mountains sparkled over in the west. A red-tailed hawk wheeled across the cobalt sky. The weather was ideal if you like cool and the air was clear as my conscience. We don't get many days like this in GroVont in spring, where it's usually raining except for when it's snowing right through Memorial Day.

Tyson and a boy I didn't know came walking down the street, kicking a pinecone back and forth. Ty had on a blue day pack and when he turned to kick the pinecone I saw Spider-Man's web across the back. His tennis shoes were blue, too.

"Tyson."

Ty stopped and stood there in the road, looking at me. He'd grown a good inch since I last saw him, and his blond hair was cut in a burr. I couldn't tell you what the other kid looked like.

He said, "Rowdy."

"You can call me Dad if you want."

Ty didn't say anything. The other boy looked at him, then at me, then back at Ty.

I moved my feet, clearing the way to the seat next to mine. "Take a load off, son."

He looked at the other boy and mumbled words I didn't catch. Then he came across the curb, shrugging off his pack. The other boy wandered down the street, leaving the pinecone in the gutter there.

Tyson placed the day pack between us, next to my saddlebag. He pushed himself way back in the seat so his feet dangled, not quite touching the deck. He kept his hands in his lap.

"Can I get you something to drink?" I asked.

He nodded. "Hot chocolate, please."

I called the waitress over. She was a broad-shouldered girl with a ski tan and strong legs, wearing short shorts and a Guangzhou Hard Rock Cafe shirt.

"Hot chocolate for my son here."

She smiled down at Tyson. I could tell she thought better of me because I had a child. "You want whipped cream on that?"

"Yes, thank you."

She touched his head and said, "Polite young man," then she bounced inside toward the kitchen. It came to me that the waitress was closer to Ty's age than she was mine.

He nodded at my cup. "What's that you're drinking?"

"It's called espresso. I got a taste for it in Paris."

"Paris, Texas?" He asked because there's also a Paris, Idaho, but it's not very big and doesn't have a sanctioned rodeo. People outside our part of the world probably wouldn't know the town exists.

"Paris, France. I was there last fall."

The girl brought Ty's hot chocolate. When he took his first sip, the whipped cream left a thin, white mustache on his lip. I could have died right then.

"Paris is full of people who talk French," I said. "When they sell bread in the store, it doesn't come wrapped in plastic."

He wiped his face with the back of his hand. "What's it wrapped in?"

"Nothing. Just a loaf you carry home in your hand."

He glanced up at me, checking to see if I was making up a story.

"It's not sliced," I said.

"Oh."

"What's your favorite subject in school?"

"Language arts."

That stumped me. They didn't teach language arts when I went to GroVont Elementary. I didn't know what it was so I couldn't very well say, "That was my favorite, too."

"I'm learning to play piano," Tyson said. "Monroe is teaching me."

I didn't ask the obvious question but Ty told me anyway. "Monroe says if you show your face around here, there will be trouble."

"You tell this Monroe fella I'm ready whenever he is."

We let that comment lie on the table there, pretending it didn't mean much. The day was too pretty and we hadn't seen each other in so long, neither of us was in the mood for drama. Tyson swung his feet back and forth while he drank his chocolate. One of those sparrows that hangs out on outdoor decks in every country on the planet hopped on the slat next to my chair. Either of us could have kicked him to tarnation, but the sparrow seemed to know this was too civilized a coffeehouse for that to happen.

I flipped the top flap on my saddlebag and pulled out a small white box. "I brought you a present."

"What?"

I opened the box to show him the belt buckle. I'd shined it up good with Blue Magic. "It's a championship buckle. It means I rode bulls better than anybody else in Crockett County, Colorado, last year."

Tyson took the buckle in his hands. He turned it around so the writing faced him.

"Do you have a place where you put things you want to keep and not show Mom?" I asked.

He nodded.

"Put the buckle there. Whenever I'm not around and you want to remember me, you can take it out and look at it."

Ty ran his fingers over the raised gold surface on the enamel, first the bull and then the cowboy. Then he touched the words in the circle — CROCKETT COUNTY RODEO 20 BULL RIDING CHAMPION 03.

I kept my eyes on Ty's face. "Someday when you grow up, you'll be proud to own a championship buckle."

He slid off his chair into a standing position. "I have to go now."

"You didn't finish your chocolate."

"I have to go."

Ty carefully unzipped the outside pocket on his Spider-Man pack. He slid the buckle into the pack, then, just as carefully, zipped it shut.

"Can I have a hug?" I said.

He looked at me dubiously.

"A shake, then."

I held out my hand. Tyson shook hands, solemnly. After a moment, he stepped forward between my knees and hugged me around the belly. I bent over and hugged back. His hair smelled good. Little boy good. Earlier I'd thought the hug from Odette was the hug I'd remember when I got senile, but now I changed that. This was the hug that made going on worth the mess.

"No matter what your mom or anyone else says, you know that I love you, son."

Ty nodded his face against my chest. Then he stepped back and picked up his pack. As he started to walk away, I said, "What do you say, Ty?"

He stopped and looked at me. "Thank you."

Tyson walked on down the street without looking back. I watched till he turned the corner, then I signaled the waitress. "Bring another espresso if you would."

"Another double?"

"You bet."

AUTHOR'S NOTE

The first Starbucks in Paris opened its doors on Friday, January 16, 2004. By the next Monday, there were two. As of the end of the year, ten Starbucks stores were up and running in the city of light. All are successful and all opened without incident.

SELF-EVIDENT TRUTHS

1. The world over, cowboys are the envy of honest men and heart's desire of adventuresome women.

2. You can't tell a virgin by her face.

3. Foreplay changes the nature of interesting.

4. You can't hit every asshole you run into.

5. If you don't stretch regular, the falls will break you.

6. You can never knock on wood too often in a tunnel.

7. Sleeping-next-to is at least as intimate as banging.

8. The only thing worse than finding out you were wrong when you prejudged a person's character is to find out you were right.

9. If you sleep with enough people, sooner or later, you'll fall for one of them.

10. You only get a certain number of knockouts in life, before you go away and don't make it all the way back.

11. Love is more important than saving your culture.

12. Never make assumptions about foreign women.

ABOUT THE AUTHOR

Tim Sandlin is the author of several novels, including *Jimi Hendrix Turns Eighty* and *Skipped Parts*, a *New York Times* Notable Book. He lives in Jackson, Wyoming, with his family.